AUNT MARGARET'S LOVER

Mavis Cheek was born and educated in Wimbledon, and now lives in West London with her daughter. She worked for the art publishers Editions Alecto for twelve happy years before becoming a mature student at Hillcroft College for Women, where she graduated in Arts with Distinction. Her short stories and travel articles have appeared in various publications and her first book, *Pause Between Acts*, won the SHE/John Menzies First Novel Prize. She is also the author of *Parlour Games, Dog Days, Janice Gentle Gets Sexy, Sleeping Beauties, Getting Back Brahms* and *Three Men on a Plane.*

MAVIS CHEEK

Aunt Margaret's Lover

faber and faber

First published in 1994
by Hamish Hamilton Ltd
Open market paperback first published in 1996
This paperback edition first published in 1996
by Faber and Faber Limited
3 Queen Square London WCIN 3AU

Printed and bound in Great Britain by Mackays of Chatham PLC

© Mavis Cheek, 1994

A CIP record for this book is
available from the British Library

ISBN 0-571-20628-x

2 4 6 8 10 9 7 5 3 1

For Joe, EA, and the twelve happy years

This book is also respectfully dedicated to the honourable women and men of this planet who struggle and may fail but who nevertheless attempt the good.

O, thou art fairer than the evening's air,
Clad in the beauty of a thousand stars.
Brighter art thou than flaming Jupiter,
When he appear'd to hapless Semele:
More lovely than the monarch of the sky,
In wanton Arethusa's azured arms,
And none but thou shalt be my paramour.

Not tonight, Josephine.

Woman, 39, seeks lover for one year. I offer good legs, bright mind, happy disposition, in return for well-adjusted, solvent male between 35 and 40. April to April. No Expectations.

Part One

Chapter One

It is not at all surprising that Elizabeth I of England chose not to marry. Indeed, given the forces surrounding her birth and upbringing, she needed to be one neck short of an execution block to even contemplate the notion. Since her formative years were spent ducking the whizzing heads of assorted uncles, cousins, stepmothers, not to mention her own mother, and other once favoured wives were either dying of broken hearts or forced into sisterhood, her unwed state seems a peculiarly oblique debate among historians.

The comfortably scholarly notion that marriage would have made her submit to her husband as her Lord and therefore cede her sovereignty is bullshit. The uncomfortably hysterical notion that she was physically unable to receive the Noble Kingdom of the Phallus due to gynaecological malfunction is quite batty and says more for male medical hierarchy than it does for female common sense. When in doubt, commit calumny. Ben Jonson to Drummond after dinner at Hawthornden: 'She had a membrana on her which made her incapable of man, though for her delight she tried many . . .' Well, Ben, I do hope so . . .

No, no. At heart (aye, and stomach too as she affirmed) Elizabeth was a woman: a romantic woman, but not a fool. Quite simply, she had seen too much of where the other state could get you and said codpieces to it. Wise woman. She appointed a lusty and beautiful favourite or two to flatter and fawn on her (a state halfway to Paradise) and got on with it. So what if the Tudor line died with her? So what if the poncy, proselytizing James of Scotland should follow her on? She had chosen happiness in the single state and went to her death battered by no one's supreme hand but her own. She had seen what other husbands could do and she did not, fair enough, like it at all.

It is therefore not surprising that others who have witnessed filial destructions surrounding *them*, choose the same maidenly path in modern times. Others like Aunt Margaret, who stands alone, a little apart from the other spectators, on the rather chilly dockside at Portsmouth. She waves a fluttering handkerchief at the immense grandeur of P&O's cruise ship, bound for New York, as it slowly slides away. She is, herself, of the age that Elizabeth reached when her counsellors began to panic seriously about her spinsterhood. And she, too, for the first time in eighteen years, is suffering a mild panic about the issue of aloneness herself. It will pass, she counsels, as the ship hoots, the bunting flaps and the band on the quayside plays jolly rousing tunes. She waves more heartily. The handkerchief was one of her father's and she knows it will be seen. She squints and can still just make out Saskia waving back, her bright young face alight with excitement, her golden head tipped to one side as if to see better, her new pink angora sweater a fuzzy cloud among the drabness of raincoats surrounding her as she leans across the rail.

'Go with my love,' calls Aunt Margaret softly, the words lost in the roll of the sea. 'Go and good luck.'

And she means it. Surrogate motherhood is free of that umbilical dimension a blood mother might feel. She experiences only a profound relief mingling with the tears. A job well done. Now her niece is bound for a reunion with her father. Her real father, not a surrogate. The father she has not seen since she was a tottering toddler. Saskia will be away for a year. Margaret Percy thinks she will be away for a great deal longer than that, for when she returns she will be someone else. Bound to be. Little Saskia has gone, to be replaced by someone different. Little Saskia has gone for

4

ever. Inevitable. Margaret Percy is sad but has no sense of ownership. Two strands have reknit themselves. She has expected this moment to happen and endured the requirement to encourage it when it did. Mothers possess by the right of birth pain, the owings; aunts do not. Margaret Percy turns away and walks back to the car. She is alone now, as she always expected to be, and mild panic is also inevitable.

She takes one last look at the receding bows of that great floating world and then looks up at the sky. To the dense clouds above her she says, 'Take care of her if you're up there!' And she wonders what will happen in the somewhat blank year ahead. 'Look on it as an adventure,' she says as she gets back into her car.

She revs the engine. 'Thirty-nine is not *that* old.' She revs it again, perhaps a little harder than necessary. 'At any rate, it isn't, yet, forty.'

Chapter Two

On a summer's night in his MGB, in the waning days of
flower power, mysticism and universal love, Dickie Donald
was driving very fast, very dangerously and very drunkenly,
through the English countryside. He was returning from
Petworth – not the stately home of Turner fame, but the
locale. He had just sold a pair of his watercolours for a very
handsome price. It was what his young sister-in-law, Margaret Percy, afterwards referred to as his Judas money.

The small-time aristocratic couple who had bought the
pictures were pleased at the story they would have to dine
out on, both about the acquisition and about the painter.
'My dear,' they looked forward to saying over the brown
Windsor, 'he was an absolute hoot. Drank like a fish and
pinched Lucinda's bottom *twice* despite his wife being there.
Nice little thing. Pretty. Adores him of course ... Who
wouldn't with those eyes? And then he positively *roared* out
of the gates in his battered old sports car and raced away to
his Bohemian hovel somewhere.'

Dickie obliged them by putting his foot down hard and it
almost came true.

Almost.

But not quite.

He roared out of the gates, sped along the lane, and raced
straight under the wheels of a lorry. He was thrown clear
with minimal damage. His wife, pretty little thing, was
scattered all over the countryside, mercifully dead. And the
small-time aristocrats had a slightly different story to tell

over the rattling soup spoons. 'Such a tragedy. Never heard of him since. Never exhibited in London again. Work in great demand because so little of it exists. And Bertie and I made a killing – *whoops* – I mean doubled the value of our two overnight . . . Tragic of course . . .'

It was not the first time, as Margaret told the coroner. Sometimes it was drink, sometimes it was drugs, sometimes both. It was why Lorna went with him to places – to keep watch, make sure things didn't get out of hand. She left their daughter, Saskia, with me that day. She quite often did. I feel part of his betrayal. I introduced them to each other. I thought he was dashing and fine, loved him myself in a dazzled way – adored the wedding, which was wild, wanted one like that for me when the time came. Apparently he puked all night. Lorna was three years older than me and imagined herself on the shelf. Saskia came quickly. Saskia because of Rembrandt. Delusions of grandeur. He puked all night after that, too. He was a lousy husband and a lousy father. Saskia will stay with me. I am her aunt. I will bring her up. He can disappear off the face of the earth for all I care . . .

And so he did. He made no contact except through my father's solicitor, through whom he agreed to my caring for his daughter and taking on the tenancy of their crumbling hole of a house in Holland Park. I chose to live in it, with Sassy, and eventually had to buy it or get out. I chose to buy it and looked upon the mortgage as my carapace for life. Nobody, I thought, looking at all the noughts on the mortgage agreement, ever escapes from something like *that*.

I looked from the noughts to Saskia. Love. Commitment. A double bind.

My father found the whole thing too difficult to deal with. My mother had died five years before and he was still smarting from that. How could she go and leave him just when he was about to retire? If I sound cynical, I was. But not so much now. Time is more than just a healer, it is an

7

instructor. There are many worse atrocities in the world than murder by drunken driving, and there are more betrayals in the world than a father retiring to Dorset and remarrying a blue-rinse. When Dad died, Millicent didn't exactly hold on to every last farthing, but she made it clear that artefacts, memoirs, perhaps a little furniture from the old days, were acceptably mine. The rest was hers. The grieving widow.

She began to say to me a few months after the funeral, 'Your father was not quite the gentleman I thought, you know ... Our marriage was not *entirely* without its seamy side, dear ...' I told her that was enough, I did not want to know. I had done with poor marriages and bad husbands, just as Gloriana made judgement and had done. My father died when I was thirty and Sassy was nine and by that time I was settled, secure, and did not need to hear about marital iniquity. Was I not tucking up its results every night?

Chapter Three

Well, well. At least I had both a heart to love, and a job to pay for the noughts. And business in both departments became, happily, both satisfying and rewarding. I even had something of a patroness.

I had been framing Mrs Mortimer's pictures for years. Big ones, little ones, abstract and figurative ones. She was an avid and compulsive collector and, as some people left alone in the world choose to garner objects or signatures or stamps, so Mrs Mortimer chose art.

Her wheelchair only enhanced her élan. That she was sixty when I first met her and buying post-war modernist stuff increased it further. No turgid English landscapes or safely pedigreed genre stuff for her, though she did draw the line at Life Seen Through a Tampon and Conceptual Used Lavatory Paper.

Those were the days of no ramps, no concessions to the chair-bound unseen, and her visits to galleries caused interesting havoc. Sweated havoc. Mrs Mortimer bought, Mrs Mortimer bought well. Mrs Mortimer had to be accommodated somehow. And she would emphatically not do what the Queen, whom she loved, might do. She would not go separate and alone to special viewings. Oh no. Mrs Mortimer went to private viewings. And she liked to be in amongst the Rioja-swilling crowd. I think Mrs Mortimer really enjoyed getting firmly and obtrusively in the way.

She laddered my Mary Quant tights at the Blake Gallery. I was quite poor then, doing framing out of Dickie's old studio at the top of the house, with Saskia to support and no certainty of success. Framing was more or less the last account to be paid by artists or their galleries, and 'cash flow' was an over-ambitious term for the way the money came in. So a laddered pair of gentian blue and highly prized hosiery was not something to dismiss *en passant*. It had been a bad day in any case and I was *damned* if an elderly lady, wheelchair-bound or no, was going to have me apologize simply for standing still. So instead of saying, 'Oh, don't mention it,' as one who has been a Brownie should, I said, 'Oh, for God's sake now look what you've done . . .'

She said, 'Why didn't you move out of the way? Surely you saw me?' And I said, 'Because I was trying to see the Rosenquist and I *didn't* notice you.'

She looked at the picture. 'It's a good one. Not a great one, as they say. But a good one. It could, however, be better framed than that. Aluminium is boringly prevalent nowadays. And look how the shine detracts from the paper's edge. They could at least have given it a matt finish.'

Since I had been thinking much the same, I said that it would look better in a simple dull mahogany moulding, floated more generously so that the deckle edge showed. She nodded agreement and I went and found her a glass of wine. When I came back she gave me a pound note.

I said, 'Oh no. The wine is free.'

She said, 'It's for the stockings, dear.'

I said, 'Tights, actually.'

She said, 'I wonder if they are as *hygienic*?'

'I don't know,' I said. 'But at least you don't need suspenders and all that bother.'

'Yes,' she said, 'I can see that must be quite a plus. Nowadays all I have to do is hook mine over my knees and they stay there. So simple. I used to hate suspenders. Give me garters every time.' She said all this quite loudly and then lifted her skirt up a little way to prove it.

A middle-aged man with a pink cravat, yellow shirt and long curling hair gurgled embarrassedly behind us. It was hardly the conversation of the cognoscenti. I laughed. Shook her hand. Moved on. As I moved away she called me back.

'Why are you so interested in the framing of things?'

'It's important to me,' I said, and added, more pompously than I meant, 'And it's important to the picture. It's my job.'

She wheeled herself forward, looked interested. 'You do it for a living?'

'Yes,' I said. 'Though not for much of one.'

'Give me your telephone number,' she said, 'and I shall put a bit of business your way.'

'I'll bet,' I thought.

But I was wrong. I reframed the Rosenquist exactly as I had described it and it did look very good. And when I delivered it to her house in Parson's Green I understood what a genuine connoisseur of the contemporary she was. She might look like Arsenic and Old Lace but her collection, mostly drawings and prints, was unrelentingly modern.

'Why?' I asked.

'Why not?' she said briskly. 'Enough of me lives in the past already.' She raised a finger. 'Perpetual modernness is the measure of merit in every work of art. So said Emerson and I quite agree with him. He was about eighty when he died, so it kept him going.' She smiled. 'I expect it will do the same for me . . .'

From then on everything Mrs Mortimer bought came to me to be framed. And other smaller stuff that she kept in portfolios and drawers was gradually sifted through – Dubuffet to Dine, Hepworth to Pollock. Infinite variety showing catholic taste and a positive eye. She was not fond of, and did not buy, Hockney. I was surprised. He was, after all, highly sought. '*Not* a very good painter, dear,' she said. 'And not much above being a common or garden graphic artist. If you want to see a really lovely line look at Matisse or Roger Hilton . . .'

She had a small Matisse *Head of a Girl* which I coveted beyond anything. It made me feel like crying – it was so lovely, so tender and in it I could recognize Saskia's innocent childishness. Matisse had captured the melancholy beauty of transience, that feeling the owners of children seldom experience in their company unless they observe them asleep. When I looked at this, through the blurry haze of emotion, I saw exactly what she meant about the lovely line.

Through Mrs Mortimer's connection I also picked up a modest amount of other business, though I was never going to be, nor did I want to be, a contract framer. I left the hotels and restaurants to others and concentrated on galleries and private customers. Sometimes I framed pictures for the artists themselves and I dreaded this. Either they had no clue about *what* they wanted but knew, in abundance, what they did not want. Or they knew *exactly* what they wanted to the nth degree. I never worked out which was worse.

So I was busy and eventually moved the business out of the studio and into a small shop near Hammersmith. My niece grew up alongside me self-aware, self-assured, happy. She looked so like Lorna that I sometimes ached. She had her mannerisms too – a way of putting her head on one side, a half-smiling pucker of the lips when she wanted something but didn't quite know how to ask.

Its most poignant appearance came when she had a question about her mother. What kind of clothes did she wear? Did she tell jokes, eat spinach, wear her hair long or short best, like cats? Easy to answer. Easy to get out the photo album.

Its most excruciating appearance was when she wanted to know something about her father. I always felt this was a betrayal. After all, she knew he had killed her mother. How could she want to know more than that? But of course death is only a word to a child, only that, not a concept of taking-away. Since Saskia had no real concept of what had been taken away, *ergo* the deed was not especially heinous or inexpiable. Her friends had fathers, even if they did not live with them, and so must she. I could not deny her questions, but they hurt because, really, I wanted her to hate him and hate what he had done. I did.

I don't know exactly when my resolute bitterness about him faded to just plain contempt. Around the time my father died, I think. I remember hearing the name Dickie on someone's lips at the funeral. They were looking at Saskia, recognizing what I chose not to in her. And I was aware, suddenly, of it somehow being less painful. I hadn't wanted Lorna to die, she had died far, far too soon, and she was my beloved sister. But I looked at Dad's grave. At some point, I thought, we *must* set things down. Or at least bury them a long way out of sight.

Gradually it became as easy to answer those questions – Did he live here for long? What kind of pictures did he paint? Was he handsome? – as it was to talk about Lorna. Time is not only a healer, it is an instructor. It teaches you how to respond to what is important in the past, and what to set aside. Saskia had a father. It could not be ignored for ever.

Grudgingly I brought out photographs, the ones I was unable to destroy, of Lorna and Dickie together – usually laughing, certainly always looking the beautiful couple – and Saskia kept them in her room, innocently glad to have them. She had been made by two people and I had to accept it. In any case, she soon began to show a talent for drawing and painting, and not only a talent but a passion. As she studied this or that picture waiting for collection, she had such a look of her father about her that it would have been pointless to pretend. One day, I knew, she would seek him out.

Dickie was somewhere in Canada. He had been sighted, like a rare and fabulous creature – only once – by a friend of mine who was passing through Montreal.

'How does he look?' I asked, galled.

'Thinner, wiser and embarrassed to see me. He's not exhibiting so far as I know. It was all quite by chance.'

'He's still painting, then?'

'Faces and torsoes mostly. I think he sells, just doesn't show.'

I remembered how Lorna had looked after they pieced her together. 'Apposite subject matter,' I said grimly. 'Don't tell Saskia. Not yet.'

One day, I told myself, but not yet. And when the time came, around her sixteenth birthday, for her to say in sudden and illuminated wonder, 'I should like to meet my father,' I concurred. Time, the aged nurse, had more or less rocked me to patience . . . Nothing was for ever except time itself and I didn't own that, only a small piece of it. The only certainty was change.

I went on working hard and enjoying it. And being Aunt Margaret – a title coined at the beginning by friends and well-wishers in amused deference to my tender years and which, for some reason, was never dropped. I was as social as any single parent can be, took Saskia on holiday to places like Club Med where she made friends while I read and lazed and had occasional dalliances, flitted around galleries in London, went to the theatre and cinema. Generally I was quite happy. Very occasionally I had flings – but not many, and I was certainly not interested in anything deeper.

Colin, my last lover in those days of yore, was quite nice really – Saskia named her hamster after him – but the potential between us was more than I wanted and I let it go. Besides, hamster or not, Saskia at five could make any man feel he was a usurper. Colin put a bolt on my bedroom door to counter the possibility of mistaken child rape. A timely precaution since once, when we were actually at it, we suddenly found we had a threesome. Saskia had slipped under the duvet. Than which, I declare, there is nothing more designed to deflate one's sexual appetite; the guilt of the corrupting harm unleashed by one's frivolous, selfishly adult pursuits on an innocent child (or so I looked upon her apparent guilelessness then) was salutary. He went straight down to B&Q the next morning with a very determined jaw-line.

But Colin's lock, of course, did not work. She just banged on the door with her fists. And I defy anybody to deal with a small child bent on being disruptive. Yes, certainly, you can put them back to bed – but try getting smoochy with a background melody of hysterical screaming. You can get a babysitter and go to a hotel for a night – but . . . Well, the courtesan anonymity soon wears off and you find yourself wanting your own bathroom. You can get a babysitter and go to his place, and there is a certain delicious wickedness in driving back across London still steamy from your lover's embrace and paying off the babysitter while trying not to simper. You can do all these, and more, but what you cannot do is *relax*. And so, at the end of the day, I chose tranquillity. It was just easier. Besides, I was working so hard it was scarcely a choice. And if I had *really* wanted to – if I had met the combined talents of Picasso, Shostakovich and Auden, with the physical attractions of Paul Newman and a *Playgirl* centrefold – then it might have been different. But the combination never presented itself. Besides, I was aware that the kind of man who attracted me had just those elements – dash, style, danger – that had killed my sister. I was not going to risk Saskia's affections being betrayed or usurped again. The sandal-and-sockers with their patient smiles and caring dispositions left me yawning into the distance, so I stayed with friendship and company, which was a very reasonable compromise.

Marriage? A love match? I never came near. I met Roger when Saskia was sixteen. He was undemanding, pleasant company and went fishing a lot. He also loved music, Schubert and Grand Opera in particular, which is where he must have sunk all his passions. This made it easy. We buffered each other and seldom did anything of a hands-on nature. It was so dull if we did. He was in his forties, and a schoolteacher. He suited my purpose. Ovid says you should never tell a failing lover what their faults are unless you want to bind them closer, for they will try to improve them. Good advice if you wish to remain free.

Colin was still around, too, but only as a friend. He went away, after the door-locking incident, and then came back again years later and lodged with me for a while. He had married, divorced and had a son who lived with his ex-wife. He had been caught cock-naked, as he put it, humping the Spanish au pair spoonlike into the linen cupboard. Apparently she was always bending down with her legs straight and wore skirts. He assured me it was the quintessential male fantasy and irresistible. I made a vow never to do such a thing myself – which was unlikely anyway since I mostly wore jeans or leggings – and I told him that, while he stayed with me, if he ever saw me approaching a linen cupboard, he should jolly well shut his eyes.

But what he described going through in ending his marriage redoubled my resolve about serious relationships. He laughed and said that if I hadn't chucked him out, he would never have got into the mess in the first place. I thought, Oh yes you would – only you would be doing it with *my* au pair. I had to admit it was a sexy notion, though – not the au pair but the manner of it. I dallied with the fantasy of such fun for about an hour and then set it to one side. Fun could happen later, if at all, and certainly after Saskia had grown and flown . . . Anyway, fun did not necessarily mean being wedged into a small space smelling of Persil with your face down in a pile of towels.

Roger was definitely not the linen cupboard type, so that was that. I suppose the sustaining aspect of *him* was that he was fully house-trained and you could take him anywhere. And if you didn't take him, he didn't seem to mind. *He* was more amenable than amusing, more reliable than desirable, but he was kind and patient, especially with Saskia, who, though essentially good, nevertheless had her moments. And if these virtues of his did not set the world alight, they certainly oiled the turn of its axis. But it was not the bedrock of a fun-packed relationship. And nothing to do with that other activity, either, the one that makes hearts beat, blood pump, joy and despair crave equal partnership . . . No. Nothing to do with love.

Around about the time that we started preparing for

Saskia's departure a certain restlessness invaded me, which gave everything a new and disturbing edge. I put it down to the immense change about to occur in my life, the menopause of surrogacy, and thought, as I helped Saskia plan her trip, of Mrs Mortimer and how enviable she was in her tranquillity. I longed to get to that point, to being a fulfilled woman, a woman at peace, and to end my days like that. She had her collection, her home, her routines, and her daily woman. She seemed to lack for nothing.

Over the years we had become quite close. Once when I had delivered something and we were having a six o'clock sherry, I spoke my thoughts aloud: 'If I could end my days as calm and at ease as you are, I should be very pleased.'

'Ah,' she said, 'but being wheelchair-bound is rather an important ingredient in that. Don't wish your life away. You are half my age with a good pair of legs to run about on. Enjoy it. Nothing lasts for ever.' She pointed to the bottle. 'Including sherry.' She chuckled and held out her glass. 'Money helps,' she said. 'Money helps a great deal. And you must remember that since I was married I have never had to earn a living.'

'Amen to that,' I replied.

'Have you ever thought about giving up the shop? Doing something less pressured?'

I smiled. If her pictures were contemporary, her understanding of life was very old-fashioned. Saskia had a few more years of dependence ahead when this conversation took place, so the notion was quite untenable even had I the motivation. 'Impossible,' I said.

'You have missed out on fun,' she said. 'Don't you mind?'

I thought of the linen cupboard and smiled. 'Not really.'

'Well, you should,' she said thoughtfully, sipping from the little crystal glass. 'I certainly did in my youth!'

I smiled again. I doubted her notion of fun corresponded with the one I had just recalled.

I did eventually sell the shop though, but not for hedonistic motives. The economic climate – or rather the economic blanket fog – saw me struggling and when a Greek Cypriot framing chain offered to buy me out, I had no choice. From then on I simply became the manager and was surprisingly glad. For the first time I was free of accounting anxieties and it was like getting rid of a headache that you never knew you had until it went.

When Saskia decided she was going to see her father, she was very open about it and, like the sale of the shop, I was surprised at how easy it was to accept. They corresponded for a while and then one day the telephone rang. I answered it, and a hesitant voice – slightly transatlantic – said, 'Margaret?'

I knew it was Dickie, took a deep breath and answered, 'Yes, Dickie.'

He said, 'How are you?'

I said, 'I'm well. I'll go and fetch Sassy.'

He said, 'I wanted to thank you for –'

But I cut him short. 'Forget it,' I said, and called his daughter to the phone.

Saskia planned to go to New York by boat (having a romantic nature and a friend who had done it) and to effect this by working her passage. At the last moment the arrangement fell through, so I paid. It was my eighteenth-birthday gift and nothing – not even Saskia's urgent dissuasion – could deter me. It came to an interesting sum, one which meant remaining firmly in gainful employment, and one that had my friends' eyeballs whizzing like the symbols in a fruit machine.

'But you can't,' said Verity, who lived in my road and wrote sharp modern feminist stories and scripts. 'You'll need a second mortgage for this!'

'Don't forget that the house is really Saskia's. I would never have got it if Dickie hadn't –'

'How are you going to pay for it?'

'I have taken out a second mortgage.' I looked at her. 'Only a very *small* one,' I babbled. 'Really. Very small indeed.'

Verity looked at me as if I were sipping hemlock. 'The fun?' she asked.

'That'll happen,' I mumbled. After all, I still had my savings. Not a vast nest egg, but enough to cushion me if business at the shop declined, and a sum I took comfort from whenever those midnight panics about security took a hold.

'Hmm,' she said. 'You work dawn to dusk as it is.'

'I want her to have it. I want her to have New York and Canada in style. And if you say anything to her about the cost, I shall brain you.'

I knew that all I said was true, but I also knew that there was another important aspect. I did not want her to have to take one penny from Dickie when they finally met up. Nothing. Zilch.

After Verity's response, I decided to lie to my oldest and dearest friend, Jill. If Verity whom I had only known for about five years reacted like that, what would a pal of thirty years' duration say?

'It's a trust fund,' I said when I telephoned her.

Well, it sort of was.

'She'd do better to keep it and go by Virgin,' said Jill. 'Come on Aunt Margaret,' she said, in her no-wool-over-my-eyes telephone voice, 'you just don't want Dickie muscling in on the act, playing the generous father.'

'She needs to have a sensible amount of spending money,' I said, trying not to sound defensive.

'Saskia wouldn't mind working when she got there. Or taking some of what's due from her father. She would hate to think you were overstretching yourself just to make a point.'

'I want to do it,' I said firmly.

'Cut off nose, spite face,' she said.

Sometimes I am very glad that Jill lives a long way away. Her starry eyes can occasionally go quite hard.

'You should have a fling. A romance. You deserve it now.' She sighed, a long, mournful exhalation.

I changed the subject quickly.

'You sound a bit low. Are you?'

There was a pause and then another sort of musing sigh. 'Well,' she said eventually, 'I'm looking across the sitting-room. At the far end, resplendent on my flounced chintz couch lies the husband of my life, the father of my children. Those same children who smile gummily down from their photographs. The son and the daughter whom we laboured over and who are now respectively at an agricultural college in Amsterdam, and breeding my grandchildren in Wiltshire. It is to be hoped that Giles is, at least, having a few frolics among the tulip-growers. Amanda is, alas, a clone of her parental example – '

'Don't be bitter – '

'I am not,' she said peevishly. 'Let me continue. The *Sunday Times* is draped across his upper region, which has a certain rotundity not noticeable when we used to bonk all night in Brighton. This rotundity moves gently up and down. The eyes are closed, the head thrown back revealing a slightly stubbly chin – *not* designer – from the regions of which there issues the noise of an adenoidal two-part harmony. We have exchanged several interesting words this morning. Like "Pass the marmalade," "Have you got the *Review*?" At lunch it hotted up. "Pass the mint sauce." "Is this English lamb?" "I'll need two shirts on Tuesday morning – one to wear and one to pack." "Potato, please . . ." Tonight we are having one or two of his colleagues over because they can't quite get all their talking done during the week and – '

'Enough,' I said. 'You paint a pretty picture. I'll come up for a weekend soon. After Saskia sails. I won't be able to spare much more time at the moment . . .'

Jill sighed. 'Don't leave it too long,' she sighed again. 'For I believe I am turning into wallpaper. Bye-bye for now. Lo, Leviathan stirs . . .'

After Saskia sails. The phrase had a dull resonance like a hammer on a long-unpolished gong. Loneliness, that was my fear. How to turn it into freedom?

Chapter Four

Thus to Mrs Mortimer's exhortation to 'kick up my heels' for a bit, I smiled ironically. I really wasn't in a safe financial position to do anything immoderate. At least, that was my excuse. Perhaps a bit of travel would be fun, but I wouldn't have wanted to trek across the desert on a yak. She laughed when I said this.

'How different we are,' she said. 'I should love to . . .' She eyed me for a moment. She was good at this, and possessed a disconcerting perception. 'How are you feeling about life after Aunt Margaret?'

I did not mention the lacklustre resonance of the gong. Instead I changed the subject. For I am quite good at that. 'I do admire the way you live alone. I always assumed a wheelchair would make its occupant domestically dependent.'

'Not at all,' she said. 'You adapt very quickly. Though I dare say as time marches on it will be different. I shall cross that bridge when I come to it, for the very notion of paying a companion − or worse, some kind of nursing auxiliary − is most unedifying. No doubt Julius will sort something out for me eventually. The Stanna he put in is an absolute godsend. He's very good. If only he didn't like Victorian painting, we should get along very well . . .'

Julius, her son, who had done India and the Maharishi, finally settled down to a job in Post Office senior management. He married his secretary, had two children, and lived in Virginia Water. Like so many from that time, he swapped his laid-back, drop-out days for the solid bourgeois comforts of life in a rural Lutyens estate, and had nothing left to explore. He thought his mother had a screw loose – a wheelchair = low brain power, especially in elderly ladies – and she was happy to let him go on thinking so. Mr Mortimer senior, a solicitor, had been dead for some time before I first met her. She said little about him except that he had left her very comfortably off and had been a good man. Her wealth was not boundless but enough to indulge her whim of collecting, to take the occasional cruise, lose a little here and there at bridge, and generally conduct herself contentedly.

The major excitement in her life, some years previously, was the purchase of an electric wheelchair. She wanted a wheel on the wild side, and when she first took delivery was unstoppable.

I first confronted this new and dangerous phenomenon when she fairly charged into Cork Street for the opening of an exhibition of Picasso etchings. Very erotic – or should I say *explicit* – etchings, produced in photo-gravure. I was already in the gallery when she arrived and looking out for her. The car set her down, the two ramps that the hire company always used for her transportation were put in place, out she came backwards, and then, like some fairground toy, she whizzed around with a look in her eye that I can only say made me glad to be on the safe side of the glass. The chair was extremely smart – black and chrome – and had buttons on the arm. She pressed one, accelerated, ran straight into a couple who were preparing to make an entrance, and knocked them out of the way as cleanly as a skittle ball. There is a kind of horrible humour in the frustrations manifest upon those who have been severely bumped by a wheelchair. On the one hand they wish to shake their fists, to swear, to hit back, at least to protest loudly. On the other, they perceive a disadvantaged member of society. The man readjusted his hat, the woman gave her battered ankles a rub, and Mrs Mortimer, with a brief apologetic exchange, sat, completely in the way, and waited for the gallery minions to aid her through the door. Once through and spotting me, who it must be said was frozen from both suppressed laughter and a desire to remain unnoticed, she bore down Nigel Mansell-style, scattering the cognoscenti in her way like slaves before Nero.

'What do you think?' she asked, eyes bright, fingers playing with buttons that turned her hither and thither until I felt she must surely be sick.

'Very dashing,' I said. 'And potentially lethal.'

'I could probably take you for a short ride if you sat on my lap,' she said cheerfully. 'Care to try?'

'No,' I said, though a little part of me thought how wonderful it would be to ride down the length of these polished boards. By this time the art world had got very fusty and pompous and the old days of iconoclastic happenings and events had long gone. We were well and truly into gilt-edged, blue-chip, safe investment – the Picasso exhibition being a part of that.

'I'll get you a drink,' I said, 'while you look at these.'

'Oh no,' she said. 'I'll get you one. Watch.' And off she went.

I did watch. So did the owner of the gallery. So did his wife and his pinstriped helpmate. So did his assistants, customers, poseurs. We all watched. And the expression on the face of the white-jacketed barman as she did her Ironside towards him was worthy of a snapshot by Diane Arbus. She made it to the drinks table, collected two glasses, and with the touch of a button began the slightly slower journey back to me. The barman never took his eyes off her. Neither did anybody else. I doubt if Pablo would have appreciated in his dotage (as he would have in his youth) the way his works on the walls were forgotten for the more immediate interest of one old lady clutching two glasses of wine and steering herself past those hallowed exhibits like something out of Fellini.

'I think,' I said quietly, 'that we should just go slowly along looking at the work or there's likely to be a rebellion. Can you put that thing on manual and I'll push?'

'I don't want to,' she said. 'And there will not be a rebellion because they know I shall be buying.'

'Will you? You haven't even looked at them yet.'

'They are Picasso,' she said. 'And etchings. New ones. I can afford them.'

'Maybe,' I said. 'But have you looked? I don't think they are very good.'

'You seem in a very dismal mood this evening, Margaret,' she said with an uncharacteristic sniff.

'All geniuses have to fail sometimes,' I said. '"If you have genius, industry will improve it," says Reynolds. Well, I don't think in this instance he was industrious enough.'

'Reynolds was a pompous portraitist,' she said grandly. 'And I shall judge for myself.'

And off, in her chariot, she went.

It was not particularly good and there were a lot of them, a portfolio publication containing about twenty prints to a set, each print signed and numbered out of quite a large edition. A set hung on the walls, framed exquisitely (not by me, alas) in the thinnest polished brass and looking extremely important – as indeed they were given that their creator was not long for this world and, as it turned out, they were among the last things his hand gave life to. But they were self-indulgent things – the old theme of aged bull-men with thrusting pizzles and a bevy of lustful virgins (their blooming sexes so minutely detailed, so enlarged by the artist's horny stylo, that they were only good for cavorting; they could certainly never have walked anywhere with such endowments). I thought the pictures were private works – like a poet laureate's dirty doggerels – and rather bathetic. But Mrs Mortimer decided differently.

It was the wheelchair that did it. It gave her a wild lack of judgement on that initial night. She signed her cheque with a flourish and spent a considerable amount of time once this was done in manoeuvring herself about like a child – into tight corners and out of them again – her pleasure apparent by the pinkening of her cheeks and the flash of wild blue in her eyes. And I didn't mind that. Not at all. Why shouldn't she do exactly what she liked? I quite enjoyed the idea of them all being shaken up with their 'Oh, it's Picasso, then we must go to it' attitude and their principles of accountancy, the flavour of the times. I actually heard someone say of the portfolio, 'Yes, but will it make a first-class investment?' and someone else suggest they would keep theirs in the bank 'for safety'. I should like to think that Picasso, in his hey-day, would have walked through the show on hearing such things and torn everything up. A smart operator he may have been, but not so much that he would wish his pictures to sit, unseen, in the vaults of Messrs Coutts.

'How would you frame them?' Mrs Mortimer asked as, later, we waited in Cork Street for her car to come.

'Rather like they have,' I said, but without enthusiasm.

'You think I have made a mistake, don't you? You don't think I should have bought them? Well, they will be an *excellent* investment.' She gave me a very wide-eyed stare, as if to defy any further comment. And I was silent. And oddly sad. For Mrs Mortimer had never before spoken of investment in her collection. Of course she bought good stuff, but that was always secondary to the first consideration – love, desire, inspiration. Her pictures were like her lovers, really, and I felt in this case she had been a careless and fickle amourette.

'Well, Margaret?'

'Brass,' I said flatly.

'And do you think I have made a mistake?'

'I am sure they will go up and up in value.'

'That is not what I asked.'

'Brass,' I said again, this time more lightly. 'Definitely *brass* . . .'

She blinked. 'Well, I shall have a think about it before deciding. I *quite* like the brass, but perhaps . . . ah . . . here is the car. Goodbye, my dear . . .'

And off she went, up the ramps, whirr, whirr, and with a small wave once ensconced in the back. We never talked of

25

the etchings again and they never came to me for framing. I assumed that, piqued, she had gone elsewhere with them and that they perhaps hung in a part of the house to which I was not privy.

The thrill of the electric wheelchair abated and, though energized by the freedom the extra power gave to her, much needed as she grew older and frailer, she never re-created in my presence that funny fairground night in Cork Street. Nor did she ever, to my knowledge, put investment potential above her critical eye again. The next things she bought, some months later, were two portrait drawings, with mysterious, unnerving, fish-eyed heads by the prolific and rather wild John Bellany. That made me feel a great deal better, for they were good and not at all the sort of thing the Coutts cognoscenti could get their pea-brains round, no matter how many catalogue introductions they pored over. I framed those in richly carved and gilded wood, for they had an ancient quality about them, and I knew I had done well when she hung them in the drawing-room, removing a good Dubuffet to make space. I was glad it was the Dubuffet and not the small Matisse head and told her so. She smiled as we viewed the two new additions. 'Oh no,' she said. 'I would never move that. It is my favourite.'

'And mine,' I said firmly.

I felt we had put the incident of the Picasso portfolio behind us. It was only at the will reading after the funeral that I found we had not.

Chapter Five

Coincidence is the fusion of two apparently unconnected happenings which result in a synthesis. Mrs Mortimer died a few days before Saskia was due to depart these shores. The two events seemed to balance out the sadness of each other: both feared, both inevitable, both here. Even the funeral was on the same day as the farewell party. Sassy suggested we change it, but I decided not. To be surrounded by large numbers of young people, with just a sprinkling of wrinklies such as myself, struck me as a good way to confront mortality and a graveside farewell, and providing I did not get maudlin (which meant modest dips into the champagne only) I was sure it would be an unshadowed success.

The only dimmer was that Jill could not come. She and David had flu. I decided with relief that this accounted for her low spirits on the phone. She had been going down with something. When she rang to apologize, she was still in low spirits, though largely because Amanda was there looking after them. 'Do you know,' whispered Jill down the phone, 'that she thinks Canada would be a wonderful place to live. Can you imagine?' Amanda was serene and pretty, just like her mother, but unlike her mother she had been spared a romantic streak. She was absolutely David in that. At her age Jill would have been dreaming of the ochre and blue of the Adriatic, of the scent of jasmine in the velvety night air.

David, of the new-found rotundity, was now chairman of some sort of Anglo-Japanese financial group based in Newcastle. Their house was impressively Georgian. Made homely despite its size and lordliness, it looked out over the Cheviot Hills. He was another Julius, really – one day he was travelling the magic bus, the next he wore a suit. Jill, who fitted somewhere in between, had submitted to reality, kissed the dreams of fond mortals goodbye, had two children, raised them, and now ran a little market garden. Much more fun than the hard, uncertain graft of my framing business. 'You should have married someone rich like me,' she used to say. She had stopped saying it now.

I had especially wanted her around that night, not only because the party was a landmark in my and Sassy's life, but because I wanted her to stay up with me and talk into the small hours. Funerals and farewells make for restless feelings and she might have had some ideas – until I came back to the shores of routine peacefulness again. She would probably suggest a man, some idealized swain. She usually did. Besides, I had been invited to Mrs Mortimer's will reading, an event on which I wanted to conjecture with someone who would not think me callous. This was to take place – another curiosity – on the same day that the ship sailed and I was grateful. It would certainly give me something else to think about.

That there was to be a will reading, and that I should be asked to attend it, was no surprise. I expected Mrs Mortimer to leave me some token of our friendship, for she had said as much, but what it was I had no idea. Of course I fantasized, but the only thing I fantasized about was far too valuable to be left to anyone outside of the family.

Saskia and I went to the Pomme d'Amour on her last night. Just the two of us. We laughed at the inappropriate choice, though she said, 'Well, we are a bit like parting lovers, aren't we?' I thought, *Are* we? It didn't sound right to me.

She looked, and sounded, extremely grown up. 'I wonder what he will be like. And I wonder if I shall like his paintings. Apparently his studio is very big and I can have a corner of it if I want to. Of course I shall travel about quite a bit too, but he'll be my base, so that's sort of a relief.' She laughed. I tried to but it hurt – I couldn't pretend otherwise to myself.

'That's providing we get on,' she said.

I had no doubt they would. For what father could resist the arrival in his life of a fully grown, beautiful, talented daughter who had nothing to ask but acceptance?' It was a hard notion to acknowledge but there was no point in being sour. Stopping this reunion would have been like trying to stop the sunrise. It was inevitable.

At the end of our meal, I asked, carefully, quietly, my heart constricting, 'What do you feel about him?'

'I feel,' she said, 'a blank page about him. Just that. After all, it's been seventeen years. People change. I wish he had not gone away, I suppose.'

I checked myself from saying that it was the only thing I had to thank him for.

She looked at me strangely. 'And the rest of it is like a Grimm fairy-tale. Horrible but distant. Remote. In the past. I don't suppose he still drinks and drives wild cars. Do you?'

I rubbed my fingertip over her knuckles. 'I hope not,' I said. And I had a sudden foolish premonition. 'Be careful.'

She smiled and looked, for a moment, a great deal older than me. 'I'll wear a seat-belt,' she said. 'Literally and metaphorically.'

I changed the subject. We sipped sweet dessert wine while she spoke with wild enthusiasm about the thousand and one things she wanted to do over there, and as I watched her I thought how much a combination of her parentage she was. In her face was held the image of one I loved, and one I despised, and I wondered if it was that very duality which made it seem acceptable and right that she should go.

Next to us a pair of lovers, not in the first flush of youth, paid their bill with words of regret that the evening was ended. While they waited for their change, he ran his fingers through her stylish grey hair and watched her with great tenderness while she quickly checked her lips in a pocket mirror. She smoothed her hair, smiling into the reflection like a Leonardo, and said, 'He wouldn't want to see me with it all mussed up. We must be careful ...' Then they picked up their briefcases and, hand in hand, went out into the night. Sassy giggled. 'Honestly,' she said. 'At *their* age.'

I felt a little affronted on their behalf. 'They're not exactly over the hill,' I said crisply. 'And neither, for that matter, am I ...'

She looked at me and blinked. 'Oh,' she said in a mixture of astonishment and embarrassment. 'Oh.' And then I could see her rearrange her thoughts. 'But you've got Roger.'

'Yes,' I said, signalling for the bill. 'I suppose I have.' I thought about them, sauntering out into the night holding hands, and was chilled by a definite streak of envy.

Ten minutes later, walking home, also hand in hand, we passed a large red car parked beside Holland Park Underground, and I recognized the stylish grey hair of its occupant. She was sitting, alone, hands on the steering-wheel, staring into the entrance of the station with an expression of deep misery on her face. The chill of envy crept away, suitably ashamed. Who on earth would want *that*?

Saskia said, 'What are you doing tomorrow? After you've seen me off? You should do *something*.'

'Celebrate, do you mean?'

She laughed. 'Certainly not. Not celebrate my actual going – more celebrate the successful outcome of a job well done.'

I looked at her. She was serious.

'Sassy,' I said, 'I don't feel I'm signing off and joining the surrogate mothers' dole queue. This thing will, as they say, run and run.'

'I know that,' she said, 'but the *responsibility* is over. Now it's just the relationship left. It's different.'

'Really?' I said, thinking that youth is infuriatingly black and white.

'Yes, really. You said that ages ago.' She was obliviously positive.

'As a matter of fact,' I said. 'I *am* doing something tomorrow.'

'Oh? What?'

'Well, first of all I'm going to the shop to open up . . .'

'Boring.'

'And then I am going to Mrs Mortimer's will reading. She's left me something and I don't know what.'

That stopped her precocity in its tracks. 'Ah,' she said. 'It could be anything. How exciting.'

'It'll be something small, I expect. Just a token.'

'It might not be,' she said. 'It might be something huge and valuable. She might have left you her entire collection. Or the house . . .'

'And dumped Julius?'

'I forgot him.' She was wistful.

'You may have done, but his mother won't. Nor her grandchildren. No. It will be a keepsake, which is all I expect and is perfectly fitting.'

'You can be really pompous sometimes, Aunt M. Why don't you just say how much you would like her to have left you something really smashing and desirable?'

'Because,' I said, and put my fingers to my lips, then to hers. I remembered how she had looked as a child and how a genius had once captured its spirit on paper.

Chapter Six

And Greasy Joan doth stir the pot, I thought.

In she came. There was that lank fair hair a swathe of
which hung like a curtain over one eye ready for *le flick* – *le
flick* being the occasional sweeping back of its fall so that –
voilà! – the face revealed two eyes after all, but only for a
moment before it flopped down making her a Cyclops once
more. Yet in that time of deliverance, in that short time of
both eyes being out and about, the viewer, me, felt such
relief, such joy, that its loss, so soon, was depressing.

Details, I was in no mood for such details. The early
morning quayside chill had entered what I was thinking of,
disloyally, as my old bones. I waited. I was polishing glass
ready to be slipped into a frame and fixed down. Polishing
has a waiting quality about it. Rhythmic, slow, silent. I said,
'Hi, Joan.'

She said flatly, 'Hi. Sassy get off OK?'

'Yes,' I said, doing soft circles now.

'Good,' she said.

I took the irremedial step. There was nothing else for it.
'How's things, then, Joan?' I waited.

While I waited, knowing the tone if not the content of
what was about to be revealed, I was thinking that she *must*
wash that bloody hair sometimes – but when? Did she rush
home on a Friday night, dunk her head in a basin, spend the
whole weekend looking fresh and shining and sweet, only to
arrive back here on Monday looking stale, dingy and with
the smell of mouse about her? She had worked for me since

leaving school, which was over ten years now, and in all that time I could not recall *once* – I rubbed the glass harder – a shine or the smell of shampoo in her locks. Then there was Reg who did most of the workshop stuff nowadays. He had a wall eye. Was I destined to be surrounded by the unbeautiful? Was I destined to hear their confessions, sigh and shake my head, caught between the rankness of her hair and the insecurity of not knowing exactly where Reg was looking as he spoke? The answer, resoundingly empty, seemed to be yes.

I heard the intake of breath, looked up expectantly, had read the signs correctly. *Le flick, le* preparatory *flick*. And instead of going into accepting mode, as one who has heard its variations over many years, I found myself inwardly infuriated at what she was about to say . . .

'God, Aunt M,' she said. 'Bloody *men* . . .'

Yes, yes. That was it. The usual.

'Do you know what he did on Saturday?' She waited.

And then the most curious thing happened. Instead of Aunt M saying, 'No, tell me, what did he do? Oh, you poor thing . . .' I said none too kindly – well, in fact, *acidly* – 'No, Joan, I don't. What *did* that vegetable head do on Saturday? Microwave the canary?'

She looked at me. *Le flick*. And the look was one of pained amazement. Her mouth was open but no sound issued forth. Very well. I would continue. I felt inexplicably vengeful.

I said, counting on my fingers, 'Joan, I have heard about Sean, Robert, Lucian, Enoch. Now it's this one and he's exactly the same. Let's see. Which one of the many scenarios will it be? He didn't get up until three? He used your bread knife to mend his bicycle? When he *got* up at three, you found somebody else in the bed there with him?' My voice was rising. The hank of hair had slipped back and she was one-eyed again. 'He put on your three-quarters-wired underlift? He wouldn't pay half the telephone? He *ate* the sodding cooked canary?'

Le flick. She spoke. Quietly. 'Yes,' she said. 'He's been having sex with somebody else.' The hair slipped back.

'I'm not surprised,' I shouted. 'You should wash your hair more often.'

She blinked her one eye.

'At least he's having sex. At least *you* are having sex . . .' By now I was getting a bit muddled. 'I bet even the sodding *canary* was having sex before he cooked it!'

The one eye widened. 'Aunt M?' she said uncertainly. 'He didn't actually *do* that.'

'Oh, damn everything,' I yelled. 'It's a great pity he didn't!'

She moved towards me, hesitant, puzzled. 'But I haven't *got* a canary . . .'

'Well, you wouldn't have after that,' I said, half laughing. 'Now, would you?'

She was so woebegone that I felt instantly remorseful. I looked at my watch. Half an hour before I had to leave for Mrs Mortimer's house. 'I'm sorry,' I said. 'I don't know why I shouted. It's probably just seeing Sassy off.' But I knew it wasn't that. 'I apologize. Go and make a cup of coffee,' I said, 'and tell me about it before I leave.'

There is a very tender painting of the Visitation, I think by Tintoretto – or rather, since the picture is in Venice, *certainly* by that fame-hungry, ubiquitous genius of the Veneto – in which the artist shows Mary supporting the stumbling – or perhaps helping up the kneeling – Elisabeth. It touches the mysterious and universal heart of Woman-to-Womanness, as they stand completely absorbed in each other's joy, which could just as easily be sorrow. A saintly pair of men flank the scene and look on, distant and bemused, not privy to the enigma. I remember the tears welling up when I first saw it. I thought of me and Sassy, me and Jill, my mother, me and Lorna. I remembered it and added Joan to the list.

She came back with two mugs and an expression of increased gloom.

I put down my polishing cloth.

'This time,' she began, 'it's worse because I really do love him.'

'Yes, of course . . .' I nodded. She had loved the others too.

'And everything was so good. The sex was still brilliant – even after a *year*.'

I raised my eyebrows. 'Does it go off after a year, then?'

She nodded.

Curiosity overcame the mysterious bond of womanness for a moment. 'If the sex was so good with you, why did he do it with someone else?'

'I asked him that.' She blinked out a tear. 'And he said because he just got bored. But he says he still loves me.'

I kept my mouth very firmly closed.

'And I love him.'

'Well, if that's the case,' I said, with a fatalism born from long experience with her, 'forgive and forget.'

'I'm trying to,' she said miserably. 'Only it *hurts*.'

'Yes,' I said, touching her hair, which felt like oiled rope, 'I should imagine it does.'

And fortunately, I thought to myself, imagine is all I can do, though I wished I felt more smug about my detachment.

Reg appeared from the workroom. He took one look at Joan and me, his eyes swivelling confusingly, and departed again at some speed. I followed him and told him to be especially nice to Joan today. He said, very dourly, that he always was nice.

'How old are you, Reg?' I asked.

'Thirty-four,' he said. 'Why?'

'Why don't you ask Joan out?'

I immediately regretted the intrusion. His eyes moved around dangerously and he changed colour – paled rather than reddened.

'Yes, well,' I said briskly. 'Give me the Adamsons' map and I'll deliver it. I'm going out.'

'Oh,' was all he said.

Was I so uninteresting? Joan hadn't asked where I was going, either.

After I had delivered the map to the Adamsons, I bought a card showing a clump of very pretty pansies, painted with that interesting nineteenth-century combination of botanical exactitude and decoratively romantic form. Jill would love it.

I wrote, 'Get well soon. I'm longing to come up and stay. Maybe next month? S sailed happy. We all missed you all. Now watch this space. Much love, Margaret.' And I posted it off.

Then, feeling curiously fluttery, I set off for that familiar big old house in Parson's Green, almost certainly for the last time. The drizzly damp April weather had given way to a little pale sunshine and everything had that new, washed look about it. I was dreading going back to the street and stopped for a few minutes to look in the window of the Doll's House Shop, a place Saskia used to delight in when she came with me on my visits. There they all were, those miniature little people in their miniature little world, all sitting up neatly or going about their chores in the house. I realized it was exactly the same display of a week or two ago. Nothing had changed nor moved in all that time. They were stuck, immobilized, until someone came along to buy them, rescue them, and move them about. I shivered. The thought was too sombre by half.

In the event, returning to the Mortimer house was not so bad. Julius opened the door to me before I rang the bell, and his two sons, both in their teens, very gravely offered me sherry and cake and showed me into the small sitting-room downstairs. I was glad he had chosen it in preference to the imposing front salon, which his mother used only for formal gatherings and the occasional little exhibition of works in her collection.

The two boys alleviated some of the quiet sobriety of the occasion by just being boyish – trying out the Stanna lift, wandering around with feet still too big for their bodies, giggling nervously when the other sneezed. I was glad of it. Their mother, Linda, having acknowledged me with a half-smile and a nod across the room, turned her back. Secretaries

36

should never marry their bosses, they never feel relaxed about anything. Linda had always been cautious and distant with me. Now she was probably wondering if I would be running off with the family jewels.

About fourteen of us thus assembled, all family save for me, we waited for the Mortimer solicitor to be seated. He made one or two fairly light ice-breaking remarks before he began to read from the will. Pushed to one side in a corner of the room was the electric wheelchair. It did not look entirely empty to me. Full of memories, I suppose. I felt that its owner was still within it somehow, waiting for this last act to be executed in her name before finally going to that great art gallery in the sky.

Chapter Seven

I laughed and laughed. I winked at the wheelchair and
fancied that its very emptiness was a smile. I did this despite
the likelihood of it being considered in bad taste or mad. It
was a friendly piece of revenge, my legacy, a nice joke, and –
let us not mince our words – a fairly valuable one. It was this
last quality that set the not altogether approving whispers
going, I think, rather than its intrinsic worth. I doubted if
any of those assembled had ever seen it: they could not judge
if it were fine or poor, nor its size, nor its style, nor its
imagery. But they knew the name spelled money and the
whispers were perfectly audible.

> To my dear friend and framer Margaret Percy, for her
> integrity on that night and for her being absolutely right, as
> well as irritatingly pompous, I bequeath the portfolio set of
> Picasso etchings entitled *Les Danses de Feu*, in its entirety and
> absolutely. They are in their original box, in their original
> wrapping, in the third drawer down of the yellow plan chest.
> Rhys Fisher has valued them recently and I attach his
> valuation sheet. I hope, Margaret, that you will sell them
> and have a great deal of fun with the proceeds for it is about
> time and long overdue. You might consider a toy boy. I
> wanted very much also to leave you the wheelchair as a
> *memento mori*, or should it be *memento torpidus*, but realize that
> it would be pure indulgence since someone with a real need
> must benefit from it. You will never need such a thing.

There was a codicil, apparently written very shortly before her
death.

Also attached in an envelope is a small and instant gift which I want you to spend straight away on something silly to wear. *Not* leggings, a jumper or anything that covers the knees. I am a connoisseur of legs and you have exceptionally nice ones.

Goodbye my dear and Bless you.

The poor solicitor, looking anywhere but at my legs which were in any case covered by a decent pleated skirt, handed me the envelope with an embarrassed grimace – a smile, I think it was supposed to be. I had begun to laugh at the bit about 'pomposity', reached a peak of amusement at 'toy boy' – where did she get such phrases? – and had calmed a little by the time she complimented my legs. Around me I could hear the whispers, sense the disapproval. *Picasso.* I looked up at the Matisse head which still hung in its familiar place and which would be Julius's now. Ah well, Mrs Mortimer was probably right. As I opened the envelope, I could feel necks craning, lips pursing and eager disapproval in the air. I was glad and relieved to take out four fifty-pound notes. A clever sum. Not enough to make me tremble at the spending of it, not too little to oblige me to buy something tacky. It was a nice in-between amount and I could feel, by the sighs of relief around me, that my audience thought so too. They all smiled politely and the reading went on.

Although there was more sherry and cake afterwards, I stayed only as long as was absolutely necessary to be polite. Just before I left, I went over to the wheelchair and patted its shoulder. I urged it also to have fun.

'She's left it to the Artists' Benevolent Fund to dispose of. Very fitting,' said Linda rather sourly.

'She was full of good ideas,' I said. 'I shall miss her very much.'

'How much do you think the Picasso is worth?' she asked bluntly.

I had the valuation in my bag but did not take it out. 'Oh, quite a lot. More than I or it merit.' I felt my throat

constrict, suddenly feeling the loss of my friend and patroness.

Linda was clearly on the warpath. Her eyes widened.

'We were very fond of each other,' I said.

'Evidently,' she replied, and turned swiftly away.

I went to say goodbye to Julius.

'Picasso, eh?' he said, shaking my hand. 'Never could
stand the fellow. Mother liked you very much. I think she
wished I was a daughter, actually.' He said this wistfully and
I realized he was probably right.

'What will you do with the rest of the collection?'

'Oh, speak to Rhys Fisher first. We'll probably sell the
best pieces and keep the rest for the boys, naturally.' We
both looked across at 'the boys' who were quietly fighting in
the corner, the one putting cake down the other's neck. 'I
expect they'll appreciate that sort of thing in due course,'
said Julius with a sigh.

'I always loved that,' I said, pointing to the Matisse.

'Yes,' said Julius. 'It's rather nice. At least you can see it's
a perfectly normal face and the artist . . .' – he peered at the
picture – 'Matisse . . . hasn't gone and stuck the eyes somewhere else or given it three noses.'

'It's lovely,' I said, and now I did feel close to tears.

'She was eighty-three, you know. Lasted much longer
than the doctors ever said she would.'

'It was the art that did it,' I said, remembering Emerson.
'Passion keeps you alive.'

Julius gave me a sad little smile. 'I expect I shall go very
early, then.' His eyes gleamed suddenly. 'What are you
going to buy? With the cash?' He looked down towards my
knees and then back up at me. The gleam grew stronger.
'Something short?'

It was definitely time to depart.

I walked along Strand on the Green. It was a cool evening
now, slightly blustery with rain just holding off. There were
few people about – the days of warmth and pub-going had
not yet begun. It suited me. I was crying silently as I

walked, the best kind of crying, with large, welling tears, utterly resigned to the cause, totally indulging the sadness. By the time I reached Kew Bridge the tears had stopped and left me with that emptied-out feeling, as if there were space to put in new things, a room without furniture, no longer the static doll's house. I turned around and let my thoughts skim to the rhythm of walking back. Beneath Mrs Mortimer's funny prose lay a sensible message. I stopped walking and bent to raise the hem of my skirt a little, checking the validity of her statement. I suppose they were all right, really, my legs. A man and woman were passing by with their dog. I looked up. My eyes met hers, cool. My eyes met his, appraising. I walked on, thinking harder.

What was my life nowadays? It was the shop, the business my life's blood. I realized, quite suddenly, that it was running very thin. It was Saskia, but she was, quite literally, launched – piloting herself – and would no longer need intensive care. It was a few friends. Jill and David, Verity, Colin were close intimates. But they all had partnerships of one kind or another. Jill and David of course. Verity had met her New Man who brought her flowers and cooked for her and knew how to mend fuses. Colin had yards of young women hanging off him. He said he came to me for a rest. The others were good friends at a distance – theatre, dinner, lunch . . . Mrs Mortimer was gone. Saskia was gone. I was here. I was here, with a good pair of legs, *almost* no grey in my hair and – I stood still, heart pounding – and *money*. A bloody great chunk of potential security was, quite suddenly, mine, whenever I wanted to cash it in. Enough to make my little nest egg look as tiny as a quail's. Now I could do something radical. I *could* kick up my heels a little if I chose. And then I remembered. There was also Roger.

There was also, I realized quite suddenly, *no excitement*. Nothing to make the heart flip, the bone tingle, the mascara go on extra thick. In short, I decided, there by the river, with the seagulls wheeling, the scullers sculling, the flotsam jetsamming at my feet, I wanted some action. Ovid says that rivers do this to the soul because they know all about love themselves, and since his definition of love is generally looser than most, I took it as a sign. That's what I would do, the best thing to do in the rather empty circumstances: I would take a lover. A *lover*. Not a life companion, not a pair of socks required at seven a.m., not a shin-up this ladder to fix my curtains, but a real lover. Orchids and all. And bearing in mind the apparent inevitability of disappointment – what had Greasy Joan said, for example, about sex? – to take a lover for one year would be sustainable, one year would be fine.

It would have been an impossible notion without the security of the Picasso portfolio behind me. Because of that I could take a year's unpaid leave and squander my savings on reckless abandonment – or at any rate, as far as I cared to go in it. Mr Spiteri could trust Joan and Reg and put in his horrible wastrel of a son for a while, something he had always wanted to do. I had no doubt the job would still be there in a year's time. And if not? Why, thanks to Picasso having a creative blip, I would survive. Let others worry for a while. I could just do with a little grape-peeling and satin knickers. And who would it harm? Who would it affect but myself? I didn't even need to tell Sassy – indeed I would not tell Sassy. Given her remarks about those other lovers, she would only worry that we might fall over our zimmer frames while attempting physical union.

At Zoffany's house I had quite made up my mind. The early April light had almost gone now, ducks were tottering around on the pebbly, muddy strand below me, and the cottages across the river glowed in little multi-paned windows. All very familiar. What it needed was something extraordinary, like a huge Oldenberg soft sculpture to come gliding down and land – pouf! – in the middle of it all. A hamburger of velvet with red-satin ketchup perhaps, or a towering pair of latex knees. Jumble everything up, stop the smugness, make the ducks jump, the curtains twitch – something to make *me* twitch. Very well, I was resolved. And it was there by that shifting, oily water that I promised not to renege on the undertaking, for I knew it would be very easy to feel positive, go home, and forget all about it by morning. But not this time. This time I knew what I must do. And the first thing was to

Have lunch with Colin.

Colin was experienced at putting himself about. Colin would be all for the idea of a lover. He had made the suggestion several times both in general and in the specific of offering himself in the role. But nowadays he seemed to find girls ten or fifteen years my junior more desirable. And as far as I was concerned, he was too familiar. I wanted a great big change. Colin was a good friend and that was much more valuable than his body. In any case, now he had a little pot belly in place of the flat stomach I remembered, and his teeth were not entirely his own – I knew he had a bridge though he didn't say so. Nope, if I was going to take a lover, I wanted one who was beautiful. Or if not beautiful, as close as I could get. Roger was not beautiful. Roger was not even a good friend, really. I squared my shoulders. Roger would have to go.

Memento torpidus, I reminded myself, and returned home feeling a good deal more alive than when I had started out that morning.

Chapter Eight

All the handsome ship's officers had to ask the middle-aged
lonely women to dance and then spent the time ogling the few of
us girls under sixty from across a sequinned shoulder pad.
Gross! And now I am here. New York, New York! Hope you
are having some fun too. And thank you, dear Aunt Margaret,
for everything.

••••••••••••••••••••••••••••••

I took Colin to the Kensington Place because I had never eaten there, because it was expensive, and because it was good – but largely because it was expensive. 'I never knew you cared,' he said when I rang him and suggested time and venue.

'Colin,' I said, 'I want to talk something through with you.'

'Fine,' he said cautiously.

My spring wardrobe was not a thrilling one. I had a couple of things I wore for evenings out: some rather dull tops and skirts, a party frock that was more of a dress and the *de rigueur* little black number. Most of my other clothes came from Gap. My summerwear was a bit more interesting, but it wasn't warm enough for turquoise cheesecloth or silk harem pants, and anyway the Kensington Place was hardly a beachside trattoria. I ended up going for the severe look. Hair tied back, a pair of pearl disc earrings – Saskia's – white crêpe blouse and velvet trousers. Colin said I looked as if I were going out for an executive lunch. 'I like the earrings,' he said as we opened the restaurant door. My only borrowings! I nearly snarled.

We both ordered scallops to start. Then steak for him, magret of duck for me, and a bottle of white Burgundy. The place was extremely busy and we were told that service would take a little time. 'Alas,' said the man in the long white apron, 'someone has not turned up in the kitchen and we are at full capacity. I only tell you this in case you have an early-afternoon appointment.' He looked at me when he said this. Colin was wearing a perfectly nice but ordinary crew neck jumper, corduroy trousers and a shirt with its collar tucked in. He did not look as if he had an executive appointment. I smiled at the waiter. 'Not at all,' I said, 'we have all afternoon.' And surreptitiously, after he had gone, I undid the top button of my blouse.

'That's more like it,' said Colin cheerfully. 'A little revealed is more mysterious and intriguing than everything either shut away or completely visible.'

'Is that why you comb your hair like you do but don't wear a hat?'

'Sorry?' he said, smiling away.

'Your scalp,' I said, looking at his hair, 'is just beginning to peek through in one little place. Just enough to be mysterious and intriguing.'

'Is it any wonder,' he said, 'that I prefer my women very young?'

We chinked our glasses affectionately.

'Anyway,' I said, 'I am not sure I want to be mysterious and intriguing.'

'Of course you do. All women do. You're made that way – all hidden and tucked in. It's that mystery in *you* that makes *us* so threatening.'

'I don't feel threatened by you.'

He put his chin on his hand and stared at me gravely. 'I shouldn't go round saying things like that if I were you.'

'I haven't come here to flirt,' I said briskly.

'Evidently,' he said. 'For that would be *two* buttons.'

We had drunk nearly all the wine by the time the second course arrived. So I suggested this time we had a bottle of red. 'Agreed,' said Colin.

He was still looking half amused, half confused by my announcement. 'A lover for a year is a bit like saying a three-minute egg will always be cooked properly. You can't plan the perfect duration, it depends on so many factors – mostly how fresh it is.'

I giggled. 'Very fresh,' I said. 'I want him very fresh.'

'Oh, we *are* talking about a relationship with a male, then?' he replied wryly.

That removed the giggle. 'Colin! You are not taking this at all seriously. I have been having a relationship with a man. With Roger.'

He looked at me above his glass. 'I said a relationship.'

'It *is* – I mean it *was*.'

'It was a disgrace. So tell me.'

'What?'

'What stopped you having a real one?'

'You know about Sassy.' I laughed, slightly nervously. 'You know *very well* about Sassy . . . It was just easier not to, that's all.'

'I think you're still holding on to something that you should let go of. If it's what Dickie did to your sister – that was one man among many – and a very young one too.'

For a moment a shadow dimmed my good cheer. I saw Dickie's handsome, boyish smile, heard Lorna's laugh, saw them arm in arm and then heard the grinding of metal, the howling of brakes. I rejected the image.

'Whatever it was,' I said, 'is over. Besides, I thought you were an Existentialist?'

'So I am.'

'Man's self is nothing except what he has become at any given moment?'

'Exactly so.'

'It applies to women too. Sartre might not *really* have thought so but Simone certainly did. I have been Aunt Margaret. And now I am going to take a lover. And here's to it.' I raised my glass.

He looked serious for a moment. 'It isn't necessarily a

game, you know. You have to know what you are doing. People get hurt.'

'Colin,' I said, 'I am nearly forty. I have had relationships in the past.'

'Me,' he said. 'I was your last. You told me that.' He put up his hand palm outwards. 'Disregarding Roger.'

'Existentially speaking, correct. And now there will be another.'

'And how do you intend to go about finding this For One Year Only stud?'

'Not stud. *Lover*. And I don't know. I was hoping you might be able to advise me . . .'

My duck arrived looking deliciously pink in the middle and I cooed over it. 'Shall we have another bottle?' I said, for the red had gone down quite a way.

'Let's eat a bit,' he replied, 'and then see, shall we? Besides, you've got to get in training.'

I refused to meet his eyes lest he see the panic.

Later, with coffee, he counted off the requirements on his fingers.

'Young.'

'Youngish,' I said. 'I mean, I don't want anyone older than me.'

'Middle-aged, then?'

I stuck out my tongue at him.

'Good-looking?'

'Attractive will do.'

'Solvent?'

'Relatively. And with a view on life. A craft, a skill, a something – even if he doesn't pursue it full time. I don't want a wastrel.'

'Lets me out,' he laughed.

'Certainly does,' I agreed.

'Physical attributes: tall, active – '

'*Active*? I don't want a mountain climber.'

He smiled knowingly. 'Active, my dear Margaret, is a polite way of saying *virile*.'

I put my hand to my mouth and blinked. 'Ooh, I hadn't thought about *that* . . .'

'Well, you better had.'

'I mean,' I shrugged carelessly, or I hoped it was carelessly, 'of course I *thought* about it, otherwise I'd be seeking a friend like you. But I do want a lover – only, *virile* is such a positive word. Isn't it?'

Colin was laughing again.

'Why are you laughing?'

He looked up. I followed his gaze. And stared straight into the eyes of the waiter, who wore an expression such as might append itself to a monkey touching snow – deep interest laced with anxiety. He blinked as our eyes met.

'More coffee?' he said, and his voice seemed to have gone up an octave.

I winced in the sun and Colin took my arm.

'That was a lovely lunch and a very generous gesture,' he said, pulling me across Church Street. 'And now I want to buy *you* something.'

My legs were fine but the rest of me felt as if it were almost floating. A combination of extreme happiness after a very good lunch, and a sense of grand destiny, of taking control of my life – if not my direction at that precise point, for now that we had reached the pavement, Colin was hauling me past the shopfronts aglow with wonderful clothes, and which I wanted to inspect more closely. Eventually he guided me into a shop that smelled of chocolate, chocolate, nothing but chocolate. And a beautiful golden-haired girl, with eyes like a doll and a voice to match, said, 'Can I help you, sir?'

'Chocolates for the lady here,' he said and pushed me firmly towards the counter. I saw him wink at the girl who fluttered her eyelashes and looked at me pityingly. Obviously I was the dull executive wife and he was the dashing Bohemian husband. 'Not *that* Bohemian,' I wanted to say. 'His jacket is Jaeger and he sells ethnic rugs to the middle classes for a living.' Then I jabbed my finger at the gleaming ranks of seduction laid out before me.

Back in the street we ate about three each – no, this is not true: he ate two and I ate four – and then I said, 'Come and help me spend two hundred pounds on myself.'

'Sure,' he said. 'Where?'

I looked up. Next to the chocolate emporium was a shop called Passions. It had lots of frivolous stuff in the window – skin-tight velvet leggings with embroidery, off-the-shoulder tops with bows and glitter, skirts that flared and came nowhere near the knees.

'In here,' I said, and, giving him the chocolates, I licked my fingers and marched in.

There was a very good reason for drinking all that wine. It was called throwing caution to the winds.

Chapter Nine

I fly to Canada tomorrow and he is going to meet me off the plane.
I am so glad to have had these few days here to get used to the
idea. I feel nervous and I think he sounded it too. The Frick
was wonderful – you were right – and that calmed me down. I keep
wondering what to wear which is so silly. As if I am going to
meet a new lover or something! Hardly!

••••••••••••••••••••••••••••••••

Verity has one of those organically created kitchens with
genuine atmosphere. Lots of pine – shelves, dressers, corner
cupboards and a big rectangular table awash with fruit
bowls, paperwork, toast crumbs, flowers and high-quality
foreign white goods that discreetly blend in. It is precisely
what *House and Garden* tidy away when they photograph
those 'country kitchen in the heart of Mayfair' absurdities. It
looks the way it should look if it is to function – a sort of
rustic heartwarmer but underpinned by sophisticated knowledge. Only not pretentious. The clothes cradle attached to
the ceiling holds drying clothes rather than drying floristry,
and the oven is state-of-the-art Neff. I always felt at home in
the place, although I was absolutely certain that if I tried to
reproduce it I would fail. Verity is extremely good at jigsaw
puzzles, which I am not, and I believe this may have
something to do with her ability to make living space look
right. It's called an Eye, and she has it for her kitchen, her
whole house, even her life which always seems to be sorted

out. I have it for frames and pictures and not much else. From the expression on Verity's face as I showed her my newly purchased skirt, very much 'not much else', and I had second thoughts about showing her the top that went with it, which I kept hidden in the Passions bag.

'Mrs Mortimer said I should show my knees,' I said defensively.

'Well,' she said, 'you're certainly going to do that.' Verity pushed the milk bottle towards me, still eyeing the garment draped over a chair back. There were unmistakable signs of it having been purchased *in vino veritas*. She touched it with the very tips of her fingers as if it were leprous. 'It's – well, it's a bit pre-teen.'

'*Pre*-teen?' I looked at it as it fanned out before us. It was some sort of synthetic white silky material, stiffish, with two layers of supportive netting under three tiers that ended above the knees. In truth, *well* above the knees.

I took comfort from recalling Colin's expression when I came out of the changing cubicle. It had certainly been approval. If not downright lust.

'Colin liked it,' I said.

'Colin's a man,' she said. And for the first time I noticed that she did not altogether sound or look her usual bouncy self.

'Exactly so,' I said, sipping my coffee, staring at her over the rim of the mug.

'Why have you – I mean, well, what's it for?'

I put down my mug. Defensiveness bred aggression, as it will. '*For*?' I said. 'What do you think it's for? I'm going to cut it up and use it for dusters of course.'

She passed her hand wearily over her mouth and I realized that its corners were drooping. What with the unbounciness, this all looked suspiciously like depression. 'Sorry,' she said, 'I'm a bit out of sorts . . .' And to prove it she burst into tears. Definitely not the time to bring out the black stretch lace with the drawstring plunge.

'What is it?' I said. 'I'm sorry – should have noticed. Won't you tell me?'

51

'Oh shit,' she said, and buried her face in her hands.

I had never *seen* her be anything but lively, even when faced with any difficulties. Verity with her head in her hands weeping and scatological was something completely new.

I handed her a tissue, patted her hand, waited. Very soon she made a muffled noise which sounded like an apology, for which I said there was no need. After a little more peek-a-booing with the hands, she regained her composure, but still looked – there is no other word for it – grief-stricken.

'Come on, tell me.'

'I don't want to load you down,' she sobbed. 'Not with Saskia just gone and you being so brave – with the skirt and smiling through and everything . . .'

'Smiling through? Verity, I'm fine. I mean I am *really* fine. This is not a brave face. Not even a false face. This is me and I am OK. Sassy had to go, I was prepared for it, welcomed it really.' I threw up my hands in what I hoped was a convincingly cavalier gesture. 'Shit, I even *paid* for her to go. So weep on, speak on – I'm in an absolutely positive frame of mind. I even came to ask your advice on some future little plan of my own' – she showed a tiny spark of interest – 'but it'll keep. So what's up?'

She wiped her eyes, put her chin in her hand and looked at the table. With the damp tissue she pushed the toast crumbs around. 'What future little plan?' she asked.

'It'll keep.'

'No, no. Tell me. It might take my mind off . . .' And the tears spilled out afresh. She gave me a little sideways woebegone look of interest. I took it to mean she really did want to know and launched in.

'OK. Well, this' – I pointed at the skirt – 'and this' – I removed the BSL with the DP from the bag – 'are my artillery. I am going into battle despite knowing it won't win the war.' I smiled, rather pleased with the metaphor.

She stared at me wetly, uncomprehending. 'I wish you wouldn't talk in clichés,' she said, 'and then look smug about them.'

A little dashed, I went on. Putting more of a small-arm than a big gun into the manner of delivery since she was clearly snappish as well as raw. 'I am going to take a lover,' I said. 'Now what do you think of that?'

What she thought of it was surprisingly obvious. She burst into fresh tears and implored me to think again.

Ah well, I thought, as I settled down for a woman-to-woman session in Tintoretto mode, at least I can justify putting off talking to Roger for another night.

Verity had been going out with, or – to use the more mature term – had been the lover of, Mark for about eighteen months. During the course of the relationship she had blossomed, related to everyone over and over again that this was the real thing and we should *all* try it, and since she had never been short of a male or two in her life, I assumed it was. Not only that, but I assumed that, as she was a woman of the world in these matters and I was but a woman of the insubstantial, she would be the right source of guidance on how to find a lover. Since her recommended advice was now somewhere between a world thrust towards gelding and suggesting that the only sensible bedfellow was a hot-water bottle, I realized I had judged wrong. It confirmed one thing, though. A year was the right term to go for.

'It's the first time I have *ever* let something like this get to me,' Verity sobbed. 'Usually I see the signs and I'm off.' She gave a long sigh and paused.

Lord, I thought, this could take weeks.

'We were absolutely fine for the first year,' she said, lacing her tea with cooking three-star, 'and then he began to forget the niceties and I began to tell him he had forgotten them.'

She waited pointedly for my response. 'Only reasonable,' I said.

'And then he said I was being clinging, demanding' – she fluttered her hands – 'but I was in love, you know . . .'

I nodded helpfully, but in truth I was glad to say that I did *not* know, or had forgotten.

'And the more I tried, the more he failed, and then he didn't say I looked nice any more and he started' – a new tissue was drawn into the drama – '*flirting* with other women.'

'At least it wasn't other men.'

'Listen, Margaret,' she said, straightening her back and giving me a correspondingly straight look, 'this is no joke.'

'I wasn't joking,' I said. 'Joan of the hair had one who did that.'

'Really?' said Verity.

'Really.'

She looked interested. It seemed to me that since I could offer no advice or practical help, a little reminder that there are others worse off than oneself, *always*, was no bad thing. Worse off, as I said to her, for one is, at least, equal to battling it out with another woman. But one would not know where to begin the campaign with another man, short of praying for a penis.

Anyway, Verity draws her fictions from life, and by the time I had brought her right up to date with Greasy Joan she was considerably calmer, her eyes a-gleam with the tale's potential – and, alas, quite ready now to tell me about her sufferings in detail. I looked at the clock. Two minutes past midnight. *Definitely* no chance of ringing Roger now. Tomorrow, then. I wasn't looking forward to it at all.

The house certainly did feel empty. The actions I took for granted with another human being living in the same space now seemed empty also. A glass of wine before supper wasn't the same without Sassy sitting there with a Diet Coke, and supper itself had lost its interest too. In place of her prattle, sometimes amusing, sometimes as irritating as a mosquito, was now only me talking to myself. I suppose in my heart I had rather looked forward to this, but the reality wasn't quite as simple as I had supposed. I had no trouble going out but returning to the quiet stillness – no bass beat from her bedroom – was deadening. The pleasure of an early morning of silence and singularity soon gave way to mournful loneliness. I had suspected it might, hoped it wouldn't.

A space within me seemed to yearn for a little friendly Polyfilla. Or more. Despite Verity's tears, a romance with a man seemed the solution. In between her sorrowful outpourings I had managed to slip in the question 'Where did you meet him?' without, I hoped, appearing opportunist. She said, 'The post office', which was not very helpful. The thought of hanging around in a queue for stamps with a seductive smile and a frilly skirt held no charm – a certain surrealistic style, but definitely no charm at all.

Roger had been away overseeing an Easter school skiing trip. He came back looking bright-eyed and healthy with his normally pale face a good deal improved by the snow tan. He came to the house bearing gifts – a bottle of schnapps and an embroidered belt, neither of which I liked. He pecked my cheek and settled himself in an armchair and looked like part of the furniture, which I found intensely irritating.

'She got off OK, then?' he said.

There was a gap between the end of his trouser leg and the beginning of his woolly green sock. This was also intensely irritating.

I sat down opposite him. 'Yes,' I said. 'She seems to be enjoying herself.'

'That's good.'

He had what I can only describe as a companionable smile on his lips as he stared at the fire and began to recount tales of the piste.

'Well, that all sounds very jolly,' I said eventually.

'Pity you couldn't come, really. Maybe next year.'

'Maybe,' I said cautiously.

'I'm going fishing for the May half-term. You could come, too.'

I knew this was extraordinary generosity. Fishing was silent and manful and not at all a social event.

'Oh no,' I said. 'But thank you.'

The flames flickered on.

'So how are you finding it?' he asked.

'Finding what?'

'Being here without Saskia.'

'A bit quiet. Not too bad.'

'I suppose I should move in. Keep you company.'

I suddenly saw us sitting at an eternal fireside together, him dreaming of stench, or whatever those fishes are called, and me dreaming of the one that got away.

'No should about it,' I said briskly.

'We could try it. We get on well.'

'Roger,' I said, 'I get on well with the postman. I just think there should be something more.'

'Bed, you mean?' he said gloomily. 'I suppose we are a bit quiet in that department. But we could improve.'

'I think the rut is too deep.'

'Keep it as it is, then?'

'Well, no,' I said. 'Not exactly . . .' And I took a really deep preparatory breath before saying the rest.

I rang Jill but she seemed dejected – the flu bug's finale – so we talked only briefly. She wanted me to come up on an extended visit, but maybe because of her lowness of spirit or maybe because I had plans afoot, I made an excuse. I was a little more fragile than I cared to admit and wanted to be jolly. Jill was in one of her introspective moods and I couldn't rally to the cause. 'I'm a poor friend,' I said, 'but I've got quite a lot to deal with down here.' Jill thought I meant the business and accepted it, and we finally settled on the end of May. By then, I felt sure, something new would have happened.

'You can bring Roger up too if you like, at least for part of the time.'

'No I can't,' I said, 'I've finished with him.'

She perked up. 'Why?'

'Boredom factor. Fresh start factor. Zen Moment of Right-ness . . .'

'Permanent?'

'Absolutely.'

'Oh, thank God for that,' she said. 'I know he was nice but he was so dull. That's the first cheering thing I've heard all week. Is there anyone else?'

'You'd be the first to know if there were.'

'There will be,' she said, and sighed. 'You are so lucky just to be able to do that.'

'What?'

'Put an end to the boredom.'

'I feel the cold draught of loneliness all the same.'

'Better than the warm fug of interdependence.'

'You are fed up.'

'I'll be all right by the time you get here. Composting does wonders for the psyche – all that leaping about in shit.'

I laughed. It was clearly not the moment to tell Jill about my plans.

The shop was reorganized fairly smoothly. Mr Spiteri said that he wanted his son to learn the business and it was a good time to throw him in at the deep end. His son was a spoilt, lecherous, flashing-eyed twenty-five-year-old who should have been gainfully employed years ago. I did not think he would be over-zealous and I did not think that my position was seriously threatened. Besides, I would be keeping a watchful eye. Joan flicked rather a lot, and Reg swivelled, but on the whole they were for it. Shake hands and come out fighting, I felt like saying, as the two avoided each other's eyes (not surprisingly, I suppose) at our meeting.

Joan and Reg and I went to the pub on my last official day. It was a bright afternoon and we chose the Dove at Hammersmith, where we sat out in the warmish sun. In its glow I began to feel as those old primitives felt about Helios, Apollo, Shamash – that here was a new beginning, something to celebrate, something nourishing coming out of the mystery of it all. *Extremely* fanciful, but there was the river rolling by, sunlight on water, greenery in trees and a new atmosphere of buoyancy after the fag end of winter. That this fresh, bright sunlight would illuminate what I fondly called my laughter lines, was chastening, but, nevertheless, here I was: I had changed course, dammed the river of my life and channelled it towards the brave unknown. And there was always candle-light. I wondered what on earth my companions would say if they could hear my thoughts. After all, I was only leaving my job and taking a lover – not re-creating the universe. All the same, I felt like Woman Reborn and a very good feeling it was too. I raised my glass to the two of them and wished them good luck.

'After all,' I said, 'I shall only be down the road. You can ring any time.'

'We'll need to,' said Joan wryly, 'with Son of Spiteri in charge.'

'You are both more than capable. He knows that, really. It's a token something and you'll just have to bear it. Unite in your adversity!'

Joan smiled and Reg blushed.

'Wartime spirit,' he said. 'My Granny told me all about that.' He was wearing sunglasses, which helped me consider-ably. Why I had such difficulty with him was to my great shame. I suppose that, as they say, eyes are the windows of the soul and I found it disconcerting not knowing which window was open. Joan was still flicking her hair, but somehow it no longer bothered me. There was no doubt that taking this time out for myself was A Good Thing. Who could it harm? And they had two good eyes between them, didn't they?

Taking a lover, I mused on the way home. What a grand, old-fashioned ring the phrase has. But from whence? For such an undertaking is a great deal easier said than done when you have been living in a fairly small world of well-worn friends. The emotional part of me said that I could not dictate such a receptive state at will. The rational in me thought it was a good idea. The rational won and I was suddenly gratified, though somewhat embarrassed, to find myself growing antennae. This is rather an unnerving state for a woman. It may be an unnerving state for a man, too, though I suspect they are brought up to be the hunters and find the role natural. Indeed, if you have ever observed a man being hunted or stalked by a woman you can see plainly that the mode is not conducive – yet – to the feminine. Never mind. I would have to be *subtle*. I pondered how to be subtly predatory, and gave up. It was too puzzling. Instinct would assert itself, I decided. I felt rather tacky about the whole business, and feeling tacky made me choose to keep the whole business to myself until the effort was satisfactorily concluded. Not to Saskia, nor Jill, nor Colin nor Verity would I confess any more than I had already. From now on I would act alone. 'Strangers in the Night,' I sang as I let myself into my empty house.

The telephone was ringing. I picked it up and, still in Sinatra country, attempted a velvety, expectant voice. But it was only Sassy giving me an update on how her first week with her father had gone. Very well, seemed to be the consensus. I thought about *my* news, the news I was going to keep to myself, and felt distinctly better, and managed to sound as if I didn't mind at all that they were getting on so well. He apparently had a demoiselle, half French and beautiful, Sassy said, and only a few years older than her. Typical, I thought. I remembered Roger – half-baked and monotonous – and said through my teeth that I was glad to hear it.

'Maybe you should get a toy boy as Mrs Mortimer suggested,' she giggled.

'Ha bloody ha,' I said when the receiver was safely back in its cradle.

Chapter Ten

*He mentioned my mother for the first time when we went to
Niagara. I could hardly hear what he said in the rush of the
water, but I know that he was meaning to say he was sorry.
There were tears on his face and I know you will say it was the
spray, but it wasn't. The Falls seemed the natural place to say
such things and it was OK. We haven't talked about it again. I
wished you had been there with us.*

•••••••••••••••••••••••••••••••

I confess, yes, that I *did* saunter down to the post office. It
was my first official engagement as predator and I wanted to
see what it was like. I mean, I argued with myself, as I
pushed at the door and went in, even Gerard Depardieu
must post his letters *sometime*.

If he did then he did not choose the main post office
in Chiswick. The queue was long and I stood behind a
cross man in an anorak that gave off the slight smell of not
being quite washed. He had a red face and was talking
loudly.

'Post office. Huh! *Post office*. I tell you, if this was a
business they'd go bankrupt! Ten windows and only three of
them lit. And look at this queue . . .' He gesticulated to his
audience most of whom were finding the carpet unusually
interesting and shuffling their feet like chain-gang slaves.
Too late, I did not swing my eyes carpetwards quickly
enough. Our eyes met. He moved closer. He opened his

mouth to speak and something told me that this was not going to be Depardieu.

'I'm unemployed, I am. Why don't they give *me* a job, eh?'

'Well ...' I said, but of course it was not answers he required, merely encouragement.

'I'm fifty-one – ' he peered closer – '*fifty-one* ...'

I wanted to show him some solidarity. 'I am unemployed too,' I said meekly.

'There you are, then, *there* you are.' He looked over towards the smug, amused counter staff. 'Here's another one for you. Two of us, out of a job, and willing ...' He took my elbow. 'You are willing, aren't you?'

'Oh yes,' I said gamely and feeling an absolute shit.

'Here you are, then,' he called again. 'We'll have six first-class stamps and two jobs please ...' He laughed a bitter laugh.

'Excuse me,' I said, detaching my elbow from him as gently as I could, 'I have forgotten something.' And I fled.

Outside, leaning against the wall, I took some deep breaths. Well, *he'd* have made a lover all right, I thought reproachfully – plenty of time on *his* hands. Good grief. What was I doing? Trawling the post office? Why didn't I just go and beckon superciliously at a selectee from the dole queue?

'Margaret?' said a voice. 'Fancy seeing you here.'

It was Verity and I just about stopped myself from saying, 'Don't tell me you're back on the look-out, too' when decency and a sense of proportion prevailed.

'What a way to spend your day, propping up the post office!' She laughed. She looked better. Not entirely her radiant self of yore, but distinctly better. She held a letter in her hand in such a way that made it seem important. She waved it about. She looked at me pointedly. I was being asked to inquire.

'Who are you writing to?' I asked dutifully, nodding at it.

'Mark,' she said, and with a flourish worthy of Sarah Siddons she dropped it into the box.

We had a coffee. I needed one and I also needed to get

away before my new-found employment agent came out and took me into Sainsbury's for an assault on the checkouts. She needed one because she had, she said, just done a wonderful, liberating, definitive thing.

'What?'

'I have returned the keys of Mark's flat to him. That's what. And that is *it*. The letter says it all. Goodbye and farewell, may you please rot in hell.'

I stirred my coffee. 'You're a poet and you don't know it,' I said absently.

'Oh, those bloody clichés of yours,' she groaned. 'He asked me back, you see.' If ever the light of triumph and vengeance was illuminated in face of woman, it was now. 'And I have told him no. And I mean it. *No!* Rotten, lousy, stinking, opportunist bastard. Pass the sugar . . .'

And we were off.

Or rather she was off. From the nature of her monologue it would appear that Verity was being sensible. Since she had met him she had not worked, had hardly slept, had got bags under her eyes whose luggage capacity would have sufficed for a six-week jaunt to Sydney, and discovered that the true joys of sex required more than mechanical brilliance.

'Snored instantly,' she said. '*Instantly!*' I watched her re-sugar her cup and sip it without even noticing.

'Best off without him, then,' I said, thinking mechanical brilliance wouldn't be bad.

'You bet,' she said.

'I've finished with Roger.'

She put down her cup. '*No!* Why?'

'Dull,' I said.

'Really?' she replied, absently sipping. 'I thought he rather suited you.'

That she meant no malice by the remark, I understood, but nevertheless I had considerable pleasure in telling her about Mrs Mortimer and the legacy, my year away from work and the river of new life – leaving out the bit about the lover, of course. Friendship was restored by her warm and enthusiastic response.

'Well, that's absolutely brilliant. Lovely! Just what you deserve.'

I bloomed in the garden of her delighted approval . . .

'And what's more,' she said, leaning forward so that her earrings tickled her cup, 'I never thought you had it in you.'

. . . and withered, slightly, again.

'*Enjoy it solo,*' she said, 'or you'll waste the whole year just like I have.' She put down her cup. 'In fact, we can be two freewheelers together. Friends in adversity and goodbye to men.'

It certainly was not the right time to tell her that I intended the river of life to flow erotically through my days.

Having sworn a bloody oath across the coffee cups that I would, metaphorically, worship only at Diana's shrine and thumb my nose at Venus, I continued to consider possibilities. When the antennae were sleeping, the fins sent me swimming in search of a good catch. It was all quite unnerving, this heightened interest in the male of the species. I now knew what it felt like to be one of those creeping things that go for it in a set mating season. When both antennae *and* fins were up, it became extremely alarming – even greengrocers' assistants were not beyond assessment. I was appalled at myself. But rather amused too. What I needed was to discover some reciprocal antennae or another set of fins masculine in similar circumstances.

I attempted to damp the mating season down a little by reading *properly* – not the grabbed ten minutes before dozing off. So I decided to investigate the novel section at the library and treat it rather like a delicatessen counter – trying out the unknown and not going for safe old cheddar. It was as I was doing this – running my fingertips along the stacks, assessing a jacket blurb – that I bumped against a suede jacket, beige chinos and an apologetic smile. But instead of giving back a warm and apologetic smile in the vague ritualistic way you do on such occasions, I felt my antennae instantly on the alert. Here was a male. Male singular? How did you *tell*? Very possibly by a wedding ring? I peered. He wore gloves. Our eyes met above the book he was consulting. I remembered that I had barely cleaned my teeth before tipping out that morning (living alone and not working inclines you to great personal laziness), let alone gone in for fin-twitching gear. I looked down again at the book he held and he must have read the hunger for knowledge in my eyes.

'Did you want this?' he asked.

'Is it good?' Quick on the repartee, I thought.

'I haven't actually read it,' he said, a little tersely. 'That's why I got it off the shelf.'

Of course, while I was temporarily engaged in thought, he swam off without giving me a backward glance. End of brief encounter. But the pudding had been stirred, the aroma released, and the fruit was tentatively beginning to show itself. Very possibly this could be *fun*, for each day now represented an adventure. I realized that though I was outwardly nearing forty, inwardly I was once more the woman in her early twenties who had existed pre-Saskia. With the salutary admonishment not to take this too literally and to remember the years bring wisdom one should not undervalue, I inclined myself cheerfully to the hunting down of Aunt Margaret's Lover.

After the library I left all my receiving equipment out – antennae, fins, pricking of my thumbs – and let it ride. I made sure I looked appetizing even before visiting the little run-down corner shop. Most bizarre. But always a little inner voice said, 'You never know . . .' for who might not be found gracing that cluttered emporium with its yellowing boxes of rubber bands and economy lavatory paper? Even Harvey Keitel might need a Lyons fruit pie from time to time.

I began to miss the framers, but when I crept back there on one of my days off from hunting, Joan was extremely proprietorial, quite bustling, and put down the cup of coffee she offered me – *my* coffee – on the customer's side of the counter. I took the point. I had spent long enough being schoolmarmy about how I really wanted them to take responsibility and not keep running to me, so I could scarcely blame them for complying.

'Anybody interesting been in?' I asked, but had the grace not to add, 'Single men for instance?'

Joan said they were doing fine. Business was as usual and Son of Spiteri showed little in the way of damaging interest. He arrived at about eleven, departed for lunch, sometimes came back and sometimes did not. 'Cover for him if his father inquires,' I advised, for he was clearly quite harmless if kept indolent.

I finished my coffee and resisted the urge to do some Florentining on a gold frame. Joan picked up the mug. 'We'll ring you if we need to,' she said. I took the hint. One of the signs of a really good manager is one who can devolve and who has nothing on her desk but a telephone and a picture of the kids. I devolved my way home. Nothing on the answerphone, but on the mat . . . lo! a good-quality white envelope, addressed in pen and ink, Surrey postmark, and an invitation within. It was from Julius and Linda. They were having a small party to 'celebrate my mother's life' and would be 'glad if you could come . . .'

Was this, I wondered, fate? Might not Mrs Mortimer, even now, be guiding me towards a liaison? Apart from this invitation there had been very little social activity in my life. It is not at all easy meeting new people, let alone potential lovers. I began by saying I would be prudent, cautious, assessing, and certainly not jump at the first opportunity. By the end of the first week I would have willingly settled for a vault into the dark with one new male face between twenty and sixty-five and without a wife or a poodle.

Once, in a moment of weakness, I rang Colin, but thankfully he was going away. If I was glad, I was also envious, for he was off somewhere warm with one of his unlined floosies. Where on earth do all those dollies come from? I asked my hall wallpaper after I had wished him *bon voyage* and replaced the phone. *Where?*

Chapter Eleven

His girlfriend, Judith, is also his model but does not live with him in the apartment. We get on very well. He has given me a corner (quite a large one) of his studio, which has pitched me into working straight away. He is extremely disciplined (something to emulate?) and paints the figure, quite obsessively, with great feeling. Are you behaving yourself? Don't go off the rails while I am away, will you?

•••••••••••••••••••••••••••••••

A party! That was more like it. Out could come the knees, the skirt and the drawstring *décolleté*. I cheered up at once and decided on a course of action to repair the ravages of decay. Face packs, hair treatments, emery boards, cuticle stuff and a rather strong magenta nail polish with flecks of gold in it. Special offer. Do I need electrolysis? I pondered, scanning my face in a raking light. I decided not. If a potential lover wished to stand me under the upturned Anglepoise before making up his mind, then he had not the mettle for me. I settled for plucking my eyebrows which made me sneeze, squeak and cry, and after such suffering I felt considerably more worthy to be blessed. No kindly Venus could look down and ignore the agonies of one who has never plucked before.

I was extremely pleased to be able to say to Saskia, when she rang and spoke to me as if I were some aged relative in a rug by the fire, that I only sounded odd because I had on a face-pack.

67

'But why?' she asked incredulously. 'You don't need one . . .'

I couldn't be sure whether she meant, 'You don't need one because you look great as you are . . .' or 'You don't need one because you are past your sell-by date anyway . . .' I took it to mean the former and said that it was nice to pamper oneself.

'Have you been to see the Giacometti at the Tate yet?' she asked.

'Er . . . no,' I said, feeling unfairly ashamed. Truth to tell, I had forgotten it was on.

'But you will?' she said anxiously.

'Of course I will.'

'Then can you get me the catalogue and send it over? And while you're at it, there's the Beuys show at the Whitechapel. But I expect you've been already . . .'

'I can go again,' I said brightly, crossing my fingers.

'How nice for you to have all that spare time to indulge yourself at last,' she said.

Hmm, I thought, my niece seems to have inherited her aunt's capacity for pomposity rather well.

'I'm going to a party,' I said.

'What's the show?' she asked, interested.

'A *party*, Sassy, not a private view . . .'

'Oh,' she said, and immediately lost interest.

'Julius and Linda.'

She laughed. 'Make sure they don't try to snatch the Picasso back.'

Saskia, quite clearly, had no idea that beneath my old sweatshirts and leggings lurked a woman of passion and desire. And knees. I smirked at the thought, which cracked the face mask.

But all the same, if one were seeking a lover, one could do a great deal worse than look in the sympatico world of art. The visually creative male is not the stuff of which husbands and reliable significant others are made – he is, however, inclined to be more red-blooded than most, and not at all bashful at the prospect of a protracted fling. Indeed, flings suit the artistic temperament very well, whereas a mortgage and cosy fireside do not.

Post office, corner shop, library – all were nonsenses when it came to the pursuit of the Male Singular. He would undoubtedly surface, sprouting signs, somewhere that was utterly predictable. Maybe Julius and Linda's party. How apposite, given that the reason for their party was to remember the woman who had caused all this knees-out, antennae-up in the first place. And if not there, then maybe at a private view. It was certainly not going to be on a windswept platform with a bit of grit in my eye.

Jill sent me a postcard of a pair of swans necking. 'They mate for life,' she had written, 'which I used to think was very romantic . . . Looking forward to seeing you. Thanks for the pansies. Very pretty.' What this woman needs, I thought, is a bit of romance in her life. And I smiled. If I ever achieved the quest for a lover, I would take him up to meet her, stay for the weekend, maybe even arouse some tickle of remembrance in David's breast. Yes, but first – first obtain the wherewithal.

About a week before the party Julius rang me. It was during the day and I had just begun clearing out cupboards. I wouldn't have actually owned up to this activity to anyone else – being mindful of my bright burblings about having a year to pamper, indulge, expand, enjoy myself. But as a matter of fact clearing out cupboards was a delightful bit of pottering. So, happy as a babe in a sandpit, strewing about me ancient magazines, strangely shaped tupperware (reconstructed in the dishwasher but never quite thrown away), assorted wellington boots, very odd crockery and carrier bags that would, after all, never come in useful, I answered the phone on my knees and with good cheer in my heart.

Julius said that I sounded very bright and I said that I was. He told me that he was glad I was coming to the memorial party and I said I was glad to be coming too. He asked me if he had interrupted anything special and I said that no, of course he had not. Then there was silence. So I asked him, as one does, how he was dealing with the loss of such a lovely parent and would he like to talk about it, meaning here, now, on the telephone, but he said, yes he would, very much, and could we perhaps have lunch. I said yes, when, and he said, why not today. I looked at my seductive clutter, sighed and agreed. The where was not quite so easy – he coming from Whitehall and me being in Holland Park, so I suggested the Kensington Place again. He had never heard of it. 'Let me educate you in matters of the palate,' I said grandly, to which he said, 'I should like that very much.' I nearly added, 'Cheer up, Cinders, you shall go to the ball' because he sounded so woebegone. That is the problem about flying as high as a Tiepolo angel: you want to take everybody else with you – which is obviously a very attractive trait – but when you come down those you have done your Tiepolo act on generally feel betrayed. I say this only with hindsight, sadly.

I walked to the restaurant since the day was blue-skied and sunny, and the gusty wind sharpened me up. I did not go in executive gear this time but in a black velvet suit of Saskia's which seemed appropriate. I was getting used to giving my legs an airing and to using mascara. I cannot say that I was entirely successful in the use of make-up. After a disastrous session at a beauty counter, where I sat meekly before a Barbie goddess who applied a series of things to my face and clucked a good deal, and from whence I emerged with brick-red countenance and a vermilion lipstick line that nature had not intended, I decided less was safest. And no amount of Mrs Mortimer's shoulder whisperings that I should slap it on persuaded me.

Julius was waiting at the bar when I arrived. He looked uneasy as he perched on a stool in his dull, dark suit and stared into his glass. I gave him a peck on the cheek and sat on the stool beside him. We were knee to knee, mine very much in evidence due to the overstretched velvet. Sassy and

I were about the same size standing up, but sitting down I seemed to have more of a *spread*.

'How charming you look,' he said, brightening.

'Thank you,' I replied, with a regrettable little simper. Oh, how the ritual of the female role has penetrated our lighter bones. To counter this I nodded in the direction of the barman before Julius could do anything like raise a gentlemanly finger.

'I think I should like a glass of champagne,' I said. 'What about you? Will you stick to the same or join me?'

'I'd better have the same,' he said, mournfully again, 'as I have to work this afternoon. Mineral water, please.'

'Nonsense,' I said. 'One glass of champagne won't gum up the telephone lines.' And I ordered it.

One is hoist by whatever the female equivalent of a petard may be – a labour-saving gadget, perhaps? For after the champagne, and once we were seated, Julius seemed to abandon all notion of restraint and drank considerably more than I did. We ate and talked fairly easily at first – about his mother and her life, a little about the art collection, the boys, what was happening to the empty house. Then, over the two slices of mango and an apricot coulis, the tone began to change.

On the subject of the house Julius became mournful again. 'I want,' he said, moving his glass around on the tablecloth, 'to move back into town. Linda wants to stay in Cobham.'

'Why?' was all I could think to say.

'Precisely,' said Julius.

'Schools?'

'The boys are at Minderhurst in Kent. London would be considerably nearer for their trips home.'

'The countryside? Walks? London is a bit congested. Also threatening.'

'Linda's view of the countryside is that it should be kept at a safe distance and surrounded by houses similar to our own. She takes the Range Rover everywhere – everywhere being Guildford for shopping, the tennis club for exercise and socializing, drinks with neighbours, and neighbours' swimming-pools in summer.' He sipped his drink and said with emphasis, '*We* do not have a swimming-pool. Yet.'

'It sounds a wonderful life,' I said. 'Hard to give up. Safe, secure . . .'

He laughed without mirth. 'As to London being threatening – in Cobham we have been burgled more times than I can remember, cars are vandalized as they park in local byways and Simon had his bicycle stolen at knife point last summer.'

'What are you going to do?' I was beginning to feel more than a mite the conspirator, not a role I liked.

'She wants me to sell my mother's house and use a chunk of the money to build a pool. I want to keep the house on and begin to use it during the week. The boys are getting old enough to need somewhere in London as well. I think the whole thing makes great sense.' He took my hand, which was a shock, and said, 'I should value your opinion.'

I winkled my hand free, ostensibly to refill his glass, and then patted his now empty fingers in what I trusted was an aunt-like gesture. I was jolly sorry about the mascara by this time, spare though it was, and the knees.

'I've no idea how much a swimming-pool costs, but I should think selling a few of the pictures you've inherited would cover it. So she can have her pool and you can keep the house.'

'I've thought about that. But I realized, suddenly, after the way you talked at the funeral about the collection and what it meant to my mother over the years, that I should like to keep it intact for the boys. There is something of a need in this decaying world for passing on such a cultivated inheritance.'

'Oh, Julius,' I said, really very moved at the notion, 'I think that's a really wonderful thing to do . . .'

His eyes shone, he clasped my hand again. 'Do you?' he said searchingly.

'Oh yes.' And then I looked into his eyes and read quite

the wrong message. And far too late to do anything about it. Courage and fluency left me and went over to his side.

'Margaret,' he said, 'I am talking about an open marriage. One in which Linda will pursue what she wants, and I will be left free to pursue what I want. Here.'

His fingers tightened around mine. Oh God, I thought, make the waiter come. But just when some waiterly invasiveness was required, none was offered. So we continued to sit, eyeball to eyeball, my hand held in his and me trying hard to recapture the quality of auntness.

'I thought Cobham was the kind of life I wanted . . .' he continued.

A desire to giggle rose and I longed – a little hysterically, I suppose – to add '. . . until I bathed in Badedas'. I forbore.

'Now I realize it is not. I feel redundant there. I want to get back to London, have some life, some love perhaps, some fun . . .'

There was that word again.

'Margaret? Would you come out with me sometimes? Would you let us get to know each other? I have always been very fond of you, and now perhaps it could be more . . .?'

I looked at Julius. He had nice brown eyes, very appealing in their intensity at the moment, and, if a little stuffy, he recognized this and was prepared to act. Here then, sitting opposite me, was the very thing I sought. Frankly I almost succumbed. 'Yes' was not very far from my lips, but something got there ahead of it.

'Julius,' I said severely, 'what would you tell Linda?'

His eyes darkened. 'Nothing. She need never know. I would be in London during the week and go home for weekends. What do you say?'

'I say let's order coffee and forget it.'

'But why?' He leaned back, letting my hand drop, looking slightly drunk and boyishly crestfallen. 'You don't find me attractive, do you?'

'More to the point,' I said crisply, 'I don't find the idea of Friday night to Sunday night alone very appealing.'

'I might be able to stay up for some of the Fridays.'

'Julius, have an espresso and calm down.'

'Well, I'm very disappointed,' he said. 'Very.'

'And I am very flattered to be asked,' I said. 'But what you really need is a mistress, not a lover.' I beckoned to the waiter. 'What fun, Julius!' And I laughed.

Nicely, I thought.

But I also thought what a very silly view of our liberation we women have. Could I imagine myself making just such a proposition to a man and expecting him to oblige? Yet Julius quite obviously thought there was nothing at all odd in having clear demarcation lines and sticking to them. Had he done an Edward Fairfax Rochester and thrown himself at my feet, saying, 'In that case, if you won't agree to a weekday liaison, then I must and will have you for ever, I shall divorce Linda immediately,' I might have listened, or at least perked up a bit, for pride would have been restored, and there would have been the required peck of romance. But clearly real men – I counted Julius a real man – are not so impractical. This is probably why we do so badly. It may well be that Byron is right when he says that 'Man's love is of itself a thing apart, 'tis woman's whole existence . . .' In which case, Margaret old thing, I said to myself, it is certainly time to reconsider your position and break the mould . . .

Chapter Twelve

He showed me some old photographs, including one of him holding me as a baby, with my mother smiling at us, which I had never seen. There was also one of you and him together – you are trying to balance a champagne bottle on your head and he is laughing. I am going to get a copy of it to bring back.

....

Of course I did go to the party, but in sombre clothes and with my antennae as withdrawn as they could possibly be, and not a fin in sight. Fisher, the valuer, was there, and he was a good buffer to stick with. Sharp-witted, amusing, quite uninterested in women and excellent at verbal Rowlandsons.

'See her?' he said discreetly from behind a canapé.

I looked at a woman with blue hair. Not granny rinse though she was granny age, but a very determined cobalt. Her eyelids were a pulsating burgundy as were her lips. She had nails like talons and wore long, clinging black velvet. In what seemed an extraordinary mismatch, she was talking to Linda, who was wearing her pastel Betty Barclay tie-neck, with a look of sweet devotion and dewy-eyed gentility.

I nodded. 'Couldn't help seeing her,' I said behind my glass.

'Lucrezia Borgia minus the poisoned chalice,' he said. 'And *very* hard at work.'

'Hard work talking to Linda? That's a bit bitchy even for you.'

He shook his head. 'I mean negotiating. She's buying for the chap who bought up half of Wiltshire.'

I shrugged for it meant nothing to me.

He took my elbow, moving us out of earshot and further into the L of the room where it was less crowded. 'A rival to the Aga Khan,' he said into my ear. He raised his glass and indicated the wall in front of us. I looked.

'She wants that,' he said.

'Good taste,' I said, trying to be flippant. And then I dropped the pretence and added, 'So do I. I love it. Always have.'

It was the Matisse head.

'It deserves to be loved,' he said softly. Then he drained his glass in unFisherlike abandon. 'She won't get it, I don't think, *La Borgia*.' He looked ruminative. 'Julius doesn't want to sell – at least, so he says . . .'

'He told me the same thing.'

'But there is the question of what Linda wants, too . . .'

'She wants a swimming-pool.'

He looked at me incredulously. 'A Hockney?'

I laughed. It is funny when people are so single-minded about their work. I mimed the breast-stroke. 'Not a painting of one. A real swimming-pool. You know – tiles, sunshades, blue water, expensive . . .'

He raised a scandalized eyebrow. 'A Matisse for a *swimming-pool?*' He drained what little was left in his glass, brushed the sides of his hair with his hands – a curiously masculine gesture, and in this case gladiatorial I was sure – and walked with smooth determination towards the pair of conspirators.

I saw him greet them, smiling with the honeyed lips of one bent on smarm, then put a hand on each of their shoulders, drawing them towards him. I yearned to know what was said but Julius came up at that point. He filled my glass, said very curtly that he was glad I had come, and then went off again. I was cross, because I knew almost no one. He was punishing me by not introducing me, as a good host should, and certainly he knew how to be a good host if he chose. Not very nice of you, Julius, I thought. I looked about me and tapped my glass. At the furthest end of the room was the lone back view of a grey-haired man, quite tall, neatly besuited in dark grey. He was staring at a Victorian painting of a poor but honest cottager and his winsome wife, who in their turn were staring at a ewe and her new-born lamb with tender delight. I found the painting irritating since their cottage windows were significantly cleaner than mine, their fingernails spotless and her well-rounded apron considerably more than a dolly tub white. Oh, those wretched Pre-Raphaelites!

'The message is obvious,' I said to the back view. 'The ewe has had a lamb – symbol of the Redeemer who came to take away the sins of the world. The cottager's wife is heavily pregnant, so the painter is telling us that despite the naughty goings-on involved in her reaching that state, God will forgive . . .' The back view began to turn. I chuckled and added. 'So long as she didn't enjoy any of it, that is, and lay back praying for England throughout . . .'

He faced me and smiled a little cautiously – nervously even – and I realized that his suit was of that particular colour called clerical grey. I realized this because beneath his chin lay the neat white band of dog collar. Quite as Persil-white as the painted pinny.

'Charming,' he said. 'A very charming picture. You know about paintings?'

'Well,' I said, downcasting my eyes, meek before the Lord. 'I know what I like.'

Later Fisher returned and we went for a stroll in the garden. This was almost entirely made up of shrubs, land-scaped lawn, espaliered fruit trees and conifers. Not a surprise in sight.

'A swimming-pool would be an improvement,' he said. 'Pity.' He looked smug.

'What have you been up to?' I asked.

'Oh, nothing out of line. Just muddying the waters a little.' He looked up at the cloudy sky. 'May rain later.'

I stopped walking. 'Oh, bugger the rain. Tell me.'

He smiled skywards. 'I have done nothing dishonourable so far as my profession is concerned. Besides, I am more or less retired nowadays.'

'I never suggested you'd been dishonourable. And *that's* the statement of a guilty man!'

'I told Ms Borgia that I had heard there were several Matisses coming on the market next year. That is all.'

'What does that prove?'

'It proves nothing. Only, as I said when Linda skipped off to get us our drinks, *they* will be top notch.'

'Meaning that Julius's one is not?'

'Only by implication. Any fool could see how good – *exceptionally* good – it is – but neither Lucrezia nor Linda has an eye. I have also advised Linda, who was somewhat hurt when the blue lady departed so rapidly, to wait and see what the market in general does. And that is wisdom, always.'

'It sounds a bit skulduggery to me.'

'Oh, not at all. Look at that blackbird up there. He's warning us to turn back now, I think. Um, what were we saying? No, no, not at all. The point is that the best value in any sale is usually achieved with collections. Mrs Mortimer's St Ives group, her Pop Art collection – thematic, chronological. People like stories. The Matisse sticks out above all the rest – a rogue, a beautiful rogue.' He gave me a sideways glance. We were nearly back at the house. 'Easier, perhaps, to sell the Picasso suite . . .' He opened the door for me. 'Ah, dear, but as Linda said acidly, *she* – meaning *you* – has that . . .'

'I'm putting it up for auction very soon.'

'Do you need the money badly?'

'Not yet,' I said. 'I just don't like the thing. And, anyway, I was *told* to sell it.'

'Withdraw it. At least for the time being,' he said, as Linda bore down on us. 'That's my advice. A *Vollard Suite* went recently and not for as much as it should have. And yours is only photogravure and not good images at all.'

'I know. I wish you'd tell Linda that,' I muttered, stamping a smile in readiness.

He chuckled. 'Say nothing for the moment.'

And before I could be inveigled back into the spider's web, I made my excuses, thanked Linda and Julius, and left, flaying the spotted laurel with my wing mirrors and spraying up gravel in my desire to be speedily free.

There is something altogether irritating about a past lover finding immediate solace in the arms of another. Even if you don't want him. Quite why this is so is one of the mysteries of our human nature. Well might Rousseau argue that man – and woman? He does not say – is by nature good, and politically so he may be. But in the areas of love and emotion I suspect we will always be wanting. A dog-in-the-manger attitude seems to have a universally high profile among separated lovers, and, though I certainly did not wish to eat hay with Roger any more, neither was I truthful when I told him I was glad he had found someone new to root around the byre with.

He came to collect his encyclopaedia of music, overlooked in the general settling up, and whistled in the hall. Roger was not one to whistle. He was also wearing a rather dashing black roll-neck jumper under his old tweedy jacket, which gave him a fashionable air. It transformed the paleness of his face and his rimless spectacles into a kind of casual aesthetic, which the whistling compounded. He called around noon, and after he had taken the book from the shelf and was cradling it lovingly in his arms, I suggested, with what I felt was conciliatory largesse, that he might like to stay and share my lunchtime soup.

'I can't,' he said happily. 'I'm meeting Emma for lunch.' He was near the front door now. 'But thanks for asking.'

'Emma?' I said sweetly. 'A student?'

He smiled. And maybe it was that smile which made my vascular ducts freeze, for it was pointedly *complacent*.

'No,' he said. And nothing else.

Short of realizing the delightful vision of twisting his jug ears off, I smiled too. 'A girlfriend? I *am* glad.'

He smiled. That smile again. And I stuck my hands in my pocket for fear of committing the double van Gogh.

'Yes,' he said. 'Well – lover, actually.'

'Blimey,' I said, restraint fleeing at the sonorous beauty of the word on his hitherto dusty lips. 'That was quick.'

'Would you like to see a photograph?' he said eagerly, and handed me the book while he delved in his breast (perhaps heart is more appropriate?) pocket. He held it up for me. It was a gummy black-and-white shot, head and shoulders only, of a not at all bad looker. More to the point, a not at all bad looker who had probably been in nappies when I took the eleven-plus.

'Gosh,' I said.

'Mmm.' He turned the photograph and looked at it fondly. 'You can't see here,' he said, even more eagerly, 'but she has black hair and blue eyes and a very lovely nature.'

'Well done.' I tried to sound joyous. 'What does she do?'

'Plays the oboe.'

'I mean for a living.'

He looked at me pityingly. 'Plays the oboe.'

'Oh. Ah. Well, that's just up your street. How did you meet?'

Only then did he look a bit shifty.

Part of this dog-in-a-manger attitude is that it can get even nastier: when you spot a weakness you press it home. And much against my better judgement, minestrone spurned, I pressed more firmly. Why should he look shifty if there was no savour to be had in the truth? 'Come on, tell me. After all, it's quite hard to meet new people. Especially' – I nodded at the photograph – 'ravishing young women like her . . .' I would, I knew, be forgiven for overweening. Ravishing she was not, but she was certainly, confound it, more than just presentable.

'Well,' he said, backing a little, holding up the photograph as one might hold crossed sticks at a vampire. 'She sent me this. With a letter.'

'Out of the blue?!'

'Not exactly.'

I waited.

He then took a deep breath, almost visibly threw caution to the winds, and said, 'I put an advertisement in *Music Week*.'

'An advertisement?' I imagined a full-page colour spread. 'Saying what?'

'Oh, I can't remember exactly.' He shrugged. 'Anyway, she answered it and we met and . . . well, that's it, really.'

'What sort of advert? I mean – well, what an extraordinary thing to do.' I was also thinking that it had *worked*. 'Was it expensive? Advertising is usually an arm and a leg. At least when I did one for those pine frames years ago, it cost me at least a couple of hundred.'

'No, no . . .' He relaxed, smiled. 'Not a big ad. One in the lonely hearts column. Eight lines for thirty quid or something. I forget.'

I looked at the photograph. My expectation of lonely hearts was that all the advertisers must be – in the new sensitive parlance – extremely cosmetically disadvantaged.

'I got nine replies,' he said proudly, 'and Emma was the best. There *was* another contender . . .'

Contender?!

'But she was married,' he said peevishly, 'and she only told me on our second date and even then not until the coffee.'

'Were most of them a bit ropey?'

He looked offended, as well he might. 'Not at all,' he said with dignity.

'And you've done all this in just a few weeks? You were shifting.'

'And why not?' He jutted out his chin.

'I'm sorry,' I said. 'It's just a bit – well, very . . . surprising.'

'You said yourself it's not easy to meet new people.'

'Yes, but . . . *advertising!*'

'Well, what would you do? Sit around saying prayers?'

After he had gone I sat in a slump on the stairs for a long time, shaking my head occasionally, ruminating, looking for some reason to laugh the notion out of existence. And could find none. On the other hand I could not quite see myself putting an ad in the lonely hearts column of *Framing Today* (were there such a publication) because the last thing I wanted was to meet a picture framer. Particularly as – I gurgled at the thought – I might get Reg!

I rang *Music Week* and asked if they had a trade counter for back numbers, which they did. So hopping in the car and driving a little less safely than I would have liked, I went to their Marylebone office and bought up the last three issues. I took them to a nearby café, and, while I waited for my tea and scones, turned to the classified advertisements. Bold and upfront as if there were nothing to be ashamed of at all was the heading: LONELY HEARTS. It sounded so pathetic and I had a sudden horrible vision of a shelf of pumping arteries waiting balefully in line.

The waitress brought my order. Instantly I felt furtive and plopped my arms over the magazines before she could see what I was looking at. I sat there, rigid and stupid, like a child in the classroom who does not want her work to be copied. The waitress set down my order in the small remaining space of the table, and when I looked up to thank her she was staring at me as if I were quite potty. Before departing she gave a long searching look at the magazines hidden beneath my arms and then back at my face again. As if, were the police to inquire of my whereabouts, she could be absolutely sure of giving a very good description.

I found Roger's advert eventually, though at first I could match none of the dozen or so entries in each issue with the man I knew. In the end the bit about considering Schubert the greatest composer of art songs the world has ever known, and liking skiing, convinced me it was his. The rest of it was scarcely recognizable and it was only comparing what he said about himself with what the other advertisers said about themselves that made it clear. He had obviously done his market research. But if he saw himself as forty-four, good-looking, fit and fun with *SOH* (what on earth was that, I wondered? Sort of Handicapped?), then what were the ones who called themselves 'presentable, active, mature' like? 'Active', despite Colin's more salacious connection, made me think of pensioners in gardens digging furiously lest the neighbours think them senile and call in the cart.

However, as I idled over my tea and picked around at the crumby plate, Roger's advert inspired disturbing thoughts of how I would describe myself were I to place an advertisement (which, of course, I had no intention of doing) in this column. I came up with some funny notions.

'Maiden (well, I was nearly) aunt seeks toy boy with whom to make sweet music.' I laughed out aloud, which, as the café was now in a quiet period, brought my disapproving waitress back to the table to collect my empty crockery. I considered her as a contender: 'Tall temptress, forty something, into food and Madonna (she had been tapping her foot to the café's tinny radio earlier) seeks mature man to help her fill her sandwiches . . .' I laughed again, left a decent tip, and departed for home.

But it is not a laughing matter, this heart-seeking business. I soon realized, as I began to read the other advertisements, that it is to be taken extremely seriously. Someone who writes, 'Fifty-something lady harp, strings all broken, needs kind, patient male restorer to prepare her for plucking again,' is not in it for flippancy and flings. If I had expected to find some amongst the advertisers who were tongue in cheek, I was disappointed. I was even, momentarily, tempted myself to answer the chap who wrote, 'Guitarist, classical. Lonely male, forty, seeks female companion for forthcoming South-East Asian tour, Sept/Jan. Considerable free time together for sight-seeing, hugs and possibly more. The lady will be N/S' – N/S? Near-sighted? Not slovenly? – 'cultivated, attractive, with SOH. And under thirty-five.'

Pride would not let me answer and pretend I fitted the age category, though I did feel like writing to say I considered it very ageist of him to want a woman younger than himself, and *so much younger* than himself.

I idled around the kitchen until about six and then rang Verity. She sounded morbid. Very well, I thought, this will cheer her up. And clutching the magazines and a robust red wine, I went up the road to visit the patient.

Things were obviously not going well in the 'I did the right thing' department. Verity had the slump of an ageing and discarded courtesan about her and she was wearing black from top to bottom. The only bright moment in the proceedings was her face when she saw the bottle. It lit up.

'Oh good,' she said, 'I could do with a drink. I've made a rule to only drink with someone else present, otherwise I should probably become an alcoholic. And all for a man . . .'

She grabbed the Côtes du Rhône and had the cork out before I could say something suitable like 'Pen the men'. And she was halfway down her first glass before I had even smelled mine.

'I should have brought one each,' I said drily.

'Never mind,' she said in innocence. 'We can always go to the off-licence for more.'

Realizing this was serious I shoved the magazines, open at their relevant pages, towards her. She read them gloomily, slugging away at her glass, the very picture of dissolute woman-hood.

'Christ!' she said. 'What a depressing scene.' She pushed them away. 'It's hard enough to get shot of the buggers without advertising for another one. Who in their right mind would do that?'

I put on an air of mature indifference.

'Quite so,' I said.

She looked at me suspiciously. 'So why did *you* get them?'

Smooth as water I said, 'Because Roger has done it – apparently successfully – and I wanted to see how.' I pointed out his advertisement. She read it, peering with astonishment, mouthing the words. And then she threw back her head and hooted. I felt, oddly, offended.

'I suppose it *is* rather amusing,' I said, attempting mature indifference again. Despite my rejection of him, I didn't take kindly to seeing someone else ridiculing my ex. After all, by association it was ridiculing me for having been his woman.

'Good-looking?!' she spluttered. 'On a dark night with the gas turned down!' She poured some more wine. I felt like my smile had got stuck somewhere between my nose and my eye bags. 'Fit and *fun!*' she went on, still hooting. 'What arrogant shits the entire bunch are. You must have had a real laugh when you read this lot.'

She looked at me.

I gave as hearty a guffaw as I could muster. And changed the subject. Verity's views on the notion of lonely hearts advertising were clear and unequivocal. She, being of sane disposition and sound mind, despite the temporary hiccough in her love life, could be speaking only for the majority of personkind. I replaced the magazines in my bag and we talked about her erstwhile lover for about two hours. Pretty well non-stop. And then I went home. I tried to put the magazines in the rubbish sack, but they intended, and succeeded, in staying on my kitchen table. Then I went to bed, fell into a troubled sleep, and dreamt I had brought my harp to a party and nobody had asked me to play.

My first thought on waking was unpleasant. It was: the year is slipping away and you have made no progress in finding a lover. What are you going to do about it? I got up, went to the kitchen, ground the beans and, while waiting for the coffee to brew, idled through those tantalizing advertisement pages again. But I didn't *want* a musician. And then another advertisement, in a display box, caught my eye. 'If you do not find what you want here,' it said, 'try the dating pages of *On Sight*, the weekly magazine for Londoners.'

Whatever I was going to do, I decided, wincing at the memory of Verity, I would definitely keep it a secret. Women may be women's best allies if Euripides is to be believed, but I was fairly convinced that the Elizabeth and Mary sisterhood would always stop short of a man. Pity, a thousand pities, but there it was . . .

The coffee was cold by the time I got back. Nevertheless, I sipped it, my heart thumping strangely, as I opened the pages of my new purchase and began running my finger down the column headed MEN.

They were an interesting and assorted bunch. There was the chap who very nearly stole my heart after two jolly lunches, but who announced after the second that he was, er, actually still *in* a relationship of sorts.

'How "of sorts"?' I asked primly.

'Well, we're not married.'

'But you live together?'

He nodded and suggested that, surely – and he put his hand very lightly on my waist where I felt it like lead – it need not matter.

'Refer to Julius,' I said, then skipped off, leaving him puzzled and cross.

His view, apparently also shared by some subsequent encounters, was that he needed a fulcrum to leave his dead relationship and so had advertised in the hope of finding one. Honestly, when will the chaps out there learn that it is *all right*, it is perfectly *OK*, living on your own? And considerably better than staying on in the yoke of vapid unlove.

Loneliness is a rite of passage, but it passes once you get the hang of social individualism. I was hardly going to stand in line for a man while he made up his mind whether or not to go. And if he *did* go, the chances were there would be ordure in the cooling system to which I would, one way or another, be recipient.

In any case, experience and observation have shown me that there are very few genuinely dead relationships unless one or other partner has found someone new. Refer back to me and Roger: there is always the dog-in-the-manger problem: galling to see what you could not make work, work well with another. And the better it works the more inclined the dog in the manger is to become an albatross. I am inclined to think that ex-wives and mistresses are worse than their masculine counterparts at not letting go. Practical dependency rather than an emotional one, perhaps? Who will mend my washing machine now that he has someone new?

So of course I wanted someone who was completely free. I might require a lover for only one year, but I jolly well wanted him to be a full-blown lover and not some 'Now you see me, now you don't'. He had to be prepared to enter the game fully and openly, or not at all. If I had gone for that fulcrum seeker, it would have been like going into a china shop wanting a jug and coming out with half a teapot. Not what I wanted and completely useless to me. And, knowing my luck, one that was minus the spout.

After that near miss I tried to be more discriminating. I bought the magazine, read through the advertisements, circled any that appealed – I had to keep them hidden from Verity, under my pillows, so they became as seductive and secret as pornography. I soon learned to go for those who were looking for 'fun, romance, good company', rather than those who said they were serious and wanted a relationship and perhaps 'more' – presumably marriage and children. Anyone who advertised for a 'broad-minded woman' was definitely out – I was all for a decent sex life, but *not* hanging upside down from a chandelier with yoghurt smeared all over me. I also ignored those who said they had SOH, Sense of Humour, because anyone who has to advertise that he has one, probably hasn't. You have to be firm in these things. I then wrote out a letter introducing myself and saying what I wanted. A lover for one uncomplicated year.

I enclosed quite a nice photograph that Sassy took of me on holiday last year, which showed the knees and my sunny smile but not much else. I gave only my telephone number and my forename and sat back waiting for the phone to ring. And ring, it most certainly did. Pretty well constantly. I was glad I had sorted out all my cupboards and given up my job for a year in order to pursue this notion, because its pursuit took up almost all of my time. It never occurred to me that the whole thing was distinctly bizarre.

Chapter Thirteen

Verity is talking to her wall. Since she took out the video of *Shirley Valentine* she considers this to be an OK thing to do and not an occasion of madness. In the first few weeks after giving Mark the boot, she used to mutter her way around the house, embarrassed to be speaking out loud at all, and remembering that in her childhood it was considered certifiable. *Shirley Valentine* has released her from that fear. Rather like discovering that all the other private and quasi-sinful things she thought only she did were fairly standard to her sex, talking to the wall now feels All Right. She is beginning to develop a relationship with some of her consumer durables, too.

Today is Thursday. She has done a fair morning's work at the WP. Nothing great but she's keeping her hand in. Aunt Margaret's story of Joan's bisexual lover has been rewarding in the creative sense and she has nearly completed a treatment for a three-part mini-series based on the theme. Now the afternoon looms and every time she sits down to read, or lies down to snooze, her heart suddenly pounds as she remembers some betrayal, some loving phrase, some painfully magical moment with the out-booted Mark. She makes tea, dutifully, then forgets she has and pours a very weak gin. To the Italianate ochre walls of her kitchen she says, 'Well, Wall, what the fuck am I going to do with the rest of my life?'

The wall does not respond.

'Answer came there none,' she says disconsolately, and

then apologizes to Tuscan Glow. It never said it would reply, after all. But at least – unlike the friends she needs to be with her and who are not – at least it is there and constant. She knows she has bored the knickers off three or four women who have their own married lives to think about as well as children, which she has not – children who, despite their smallness and one would have thought simplicity, seem to take up a damnable amount of caring time that could be spent sitting with her in her kitchen going over her pain.

She sips the gin. It really is almost tasteless, so she adds some more.

'Well, Wall,' she says, 'at least Aunt Margaret has time on her hands. At least she isn't bogged down with getting on with life and preparing the way for the new generation, while I'm stuck here attempting to climb out of the pit. It's a question of what you miss about being with a fucker like him, and what you are glad to get away from. Together she and I will survive.'

The wall seems to glow at the suggestion.

She sips again ruminatively. 'Or not make any more relationships ever again. I don't much care which. Aunt M manages it. She's even got rid of Roger – not that you could think of him as a *relationship* . . .' She giggles behind her hand and gives the wall a wicked look. 'Not with those ears . . .' She sips again. The conversation, though one-sided, is warming up. 'I suppose jug ears are like small dongers really; only acceptable if your name is Rothschild. Do you agree?'

If the wall does, it chooses to keep the accord to itself.

She taps the glass against her teeth and rearranges some dried herbs hanging above the hob. These make her weep silent tears, which dribble into the glass. 'What is the point, Wall,' she says, 'of having dried fucking herbs when there is no one to enjoy' – she picks up a leaf or two of rosemary – 'roast lamb?' She chucks the dried spears away and snaps off a piece of basil. 'Or pasta?' She consigns the basil with the rosemary. The tears are flowing copiously into the glass, into her mouth. She crosses to the wall and lays her cheek against it. If she closes her eyes and really concentrates, the flat, emulsioned surface could be his cheek returning the compliment. For some reason she sees not Mark's face, but Roger's ears, which makes her smile. He was a prat. Mark was a prat. They are all prats, every damned one of them. 'Women are best,' she murmurs to the little bit of Italy beneath her cheek. 'Aren't they, Wall? And you are feminine too. The French say you are and they should know.' She laughs. 'Roger's ears. *Dear* Aunt M. Haven't seen much of her this last week, come to think of it . . .'

Verity drains her glass and puts it purposefully into the dishwasher, wagging her finger at it – she has got quite good at liberating herself from reality in the matter of addressing inanimate objects – and saying, 'You stay where you are. I do not need *you* to survive this blip in my life. After all, what are human friends for?'

She perches on her high Victorian bar stool, takes the phone from the wall, and taps out Aunt Margaret's number. She waits. It is answered very quickly by a female voice which seems to have been steeped in rich cream before being poured over velvet.

'Hello,' says the voice. 'This is Margaret Percy speaking.'

There is a pause. Margaret Percy speaking is clearly waiting for her caller to articulate, and her caller is clearly trying to come to terms with getting the name right but the voice so completely wrong.

'Hello,' repeats the velvet cream. 'Hello?'

'Um,' says Verity. 'Aunt M? Hello?'

Verity is much relieved to hear that the velvet cream was only a figment, for her friend's voice resumes its pleasant, familiar ordinariness.

'Verity,' she says. 'How are you?'

'Miserable,' says Verity. 'Can you come over?'

There is a tiny sigh at the other end of the phone. 'I'm a bit busy,' says the ordinary voice. 'Can I come tomorrow?'

'How can you be busy?' says Verity crossly. 'You don't do anything nowadays.'

Now there is no hint of the velvet cream, only the frostiness of an ice-lolly or two. Even Tuscan Ochre has a stern look about it. Verity realizes that she shouldn't have said something quite so querulous and insensitive. It was the gin, she tells herself, and the Wall, and prepares for contrition.

'Just because I don't go to the shop doesn't mean I sit in a heap all day.' The justifiably cross implication is that Verity does this, Margaret does not.

'I mean you are wonderfully free nowadays.'

'Mmm,' says Aunt Margaret, more like ice-cream but ice-cream which is inclined to melt.

'Can you come tonight?'

'No, I'm going out.'

Verity waits to hear where: the normal passage of conversation. Where is not forthcoming.

'Where?' she asks.

Aunt Margaret's voice freezes again. 'Just out. For a drink.'

'Who with?' asks Verity, thinking she might come too if it is someone she knows.

Aunt Margaret says, 'What is this? The third degree?'

Verity is puzzled. 'I just wondered,' she says. 'Well, can you come round afterwards?'

'No.'

'Why not?' says Verity peevishly.

'Because I'm doing something else.'

'Well, *what?*'

'Going for another drink somewhere else.'

'Blimey,' says Verity. 'You're boozing worse than me and you haven't got a broken heart to justify it.'

'I am not boozing, Verity. I am going out for a drink – *two* drinks at *two* different venues. That is all.'

'High life,' says Verity mournfully. 'Can I come?'

'No!' Aunt Margaret's voice explodes. There is silence. And then, quite suddenly, as with the breaking of a storm, she resumes her normal manner. 'Sorry,' she says. 'Sorry. Didn't mean to be so . . . But you can't.'

91

'Is it men?' asks Verity, aggressively. *I have no longer got one*, resounds in her head.

'How have you been?' her friend says at last – just the question Verity wants to be asked.

'Grim.'

'I'm sorry,' says Aunt Margaret.

'Yes, well, it goes like that.' Verity's voice quivers slightly. 'Aunt Margaret?'

'Yes?'

'Whatever happened to After Mark Anonymous project?'

'Sorry?' Aunt Margaret sounds abstracted.

'You know – what you said last time. You said if I ever found myself reaching for the telephone to dial his number, I should talk to you first. Like the AA. Don't reach for the whisky, reach for a friend?'

'Well – are you feeling like calling him?'

'I'm *always* feeling like calling him. The telephone is like a sodding quart bottle of gin stuck on the wall.'

'Poor you. Can't you find something to take your mind off it?'

'I have. It's called gin. I think my liver has probably gone to live in a squat with a bunch of drunks where it's safer . . .'

'Oh, Verity.' Aunt Margaret sounds more peevish than sympatico. Verity, at the centre of her pain and anguish, steps it up.

'I've read *Madame Bovary* and I'm halfway through *Anna Karenina*. Need I say more?'

'Verity, are you blackmailing me?'

'It is not inconceivable that I could top myself.'

Silence.

'Are you dumping the project? Do you know what you are suggesting? You are suggesting that I resume the yoke of destruction, just because *you* are too busy to give me a few minutes of your time when I need it and –'

Aunt Margaret capitulates. 'Sorry,' she says, reminding herself that to have a friend you must be a friend. 'Slip over then. Just for half an hour.'

Verity puts down the telephone, clasps her knees to her chest, and looks pleased. At least somebody thinks she is important. 'See you, Wall,' she says cheerfully. 'Who needs a brute of a lover when they have a friend to see them through?'

'I'll do the same for you one day,' says Verity, plonking herself down on the sofa.

'I sincerely hope you won't have to,' says Aunt Margaret.

'I will if you are going out with men.' Verity narrows her eyes. It has not escaped her notice, despite her grief, that her friend is looking well turned out. 'You have a new hair cut. It suits you,' she says.

'Thank you,' replies her friend, patting it, a spontaneous gesture. Verity narrows her eyes some more. 'And you have painted your nails.' Aunt Margaret looks at them as if she is surprised to find them growing there at the end of her fingers. 'Oh yes. I have.'

'You've got on sheer tights and you've had your legs shaved . . .'

'Waxed,' says Aunt Margaret pleasantly.

'You are wearing a little black woollen number that I haven't seen before and *high heels*.'

'Only little ones,' says Aunt Margaret calmly.

'Mascara? Eye shadow?' Verity leans forward, her eyes no more than bright little slits in her face. Her voice rises. 'Foundation? Rouge?' She sniffs. '*Perfume?*'

'Would you like to see my underwear too?'

'Black? Lacy?' asks Verity.

Aunt Margaret laughs, 'Nope. White cotton. With that vital, generous gusset.'

They both laugh.

'Who is he?' demands Verity.

Her friend and counsellor smooths down her frock. The telephone rings. Saved by the bell.

Instead of taking the call in the hall, Verity is surprised to see those little high heels previously remarked flashing up the stairs, two at a time, to the bedroom. The sound of a closing door tells the listener below that this is to be a very private conversation. She is intrigued. She sits back in the sofa and her eyes re-form their normal ellipses. Above her she can just about make out the muffled sound of a voice. Up and down it goes, pausing and beginning. A laugh. A silence. And then nothing.

The bedroom door opens, the little high heels come down the stairs in orderly fashion, and Aunt Margaret's face wears a look that says very clearly, 'Do not ask who it was.'

Verity says, 'Who was it?'

Aunt Margaret frowns. 'Nigel,' she says, a deal too carelessly, shrugging her shoulders as if to dissociate herself.

'Who's Nigel?'

'Hey,' says Aunt Margaret, looking at her watch. 'You came here to talk about you. I've got to go out soon.'

Verity also looks at her watch – with surprise. For nearly five minutes she has forgotten to think about the ghastly Mark and her heart, such an aching thing, has been pumping away quite normally and without pain.

'Drink?' says Aunt Margaret.

Verity nods. 'Diet Coke,' she says unexpectedly. 'If you've got it.'

'In this house,' says her hostess, 'Diet Coke is not a problem. Saskia left cupboards full of it.'

'Miss her?'

Aunt Margaret ponders. There is an irritating little half-smile about her lips, which Verity notices. 'Not as much as I thought I would.' She hands Verity the fizzing glass.

Verity narrows her eyes. 'Other fish to fry?'

'Just keeping busy. Now, come on, tell me. Talk away.'

Verity begins. Her heart resumes its aching and the tears flow from her wide-open eyes.

Chapter Fourteen

*At first after I arrived I felt guilty because I have no anger
against him and I felt that I should have. I told him this and
he just said that anger was destructive, necessary for war but
not for peace. And that he hoped this was a protracted peace. It
is hard to equate this man with the one I was afraid I would
meet. He is quite philosophical really. I don't suppose the two
of you will ever meet? I'm sure you'd be surprised and pleased.*

••••••••••••••••••••••••••••••

Jill is talking to boxes of leeks but not out loud. She cannot
talk to them out loud because she is surrounded by her
employees – doughty countrymen all, in mud-encrusted wellingtons and ancient thornproofs, the backbone of rural
England and already suspicious enough of her femininity without seeing and hearing her perform such a patently gender-
brained foolishness.

Jill is telling the leeks that if it weren't for them, and the
carrots, she would be off down to London to stay with her
friend Margaret, who would *understand*. Nobody up here
understands. She is not sure that she does, really – and a
session or two with Margaret would probably clarify things,
or put them in perspective, and all those other consoling
phrases which represent the comfort of women. She straightens her back and looks around. The sky is heavy with rain
and the air is raw despite its being nearly May. Up here in
this wild north early summer means nothing and the air does

not warm up until August, if then. Jill loves it all – the seasons, the mountains, the clear streams, the contrasts. She looks at one now, clumps of speedwell glowing among the ragged grass at the edge of the field, the humble germander a brilliant David to that Goliath of a sky. If only she could keep all this, but transport herself – transport *her* David for a while – she would be perfectly happy. Possibly.

'If I . . .' she says out loud, and fiercely, and then recollects herself as she sees Sidney Burney looking at her expectantly through his bushy brows. He removes the disgusting thing he keeps in his mouth and calls a pipe and grunts questioningly.

She pushes a strand of hair from her face to give herself time to think. What can she invent to say? She has to match the fierceness. 'If I had known how long this was going to take . . .' she says, hoping it will be enough. But it never is for Sidney.

'Yes?' he says.

'I'd have got another lad.'

He returns his pipe whence it came and nods sagely. 'Cost you,' he says.

It is a conversation they have had before and with which they are comfortable.

'You could go in now,' he says, bending low over the earth.

Jill remembers that Margaret describes her workers as van Goghs: one of her birthday presents was a beautifully framed reproduction of an old woman bunched over the stony earth, grimly absorbed in her task. It came from the museum in Amsterdam. One day Jill would like to go and see the whole collection for herself. David keeps saying, 'Yes, old fruit,' but then never has the time. She could make time, she supposes, but to go alone would be too sad somehow. Not much point in suggesting to Giles that they might meet up there. What son in his right mind would prefer to accompany his mother on a trip to Amsterdam when he can go with a crowd of mates? Giles is stuck in the flat Dutch countryside for most of the time and when he gets away to the delights of the city, he is hardly likely to want to hot-foot it to a museum.

Maybe she should go down to London? She really could do with a visit. But she can't leave this lot. Not yet. She straightens her back again and grunts. They all do that, the men, and she has long learned not to care if they find it unwomanly in her. She stands hands on hips, feet apart, readjusting to being vertical again. Around her the greyness deepens so that even the half-budded trees seem monochrome. It is a breathtaking piece of magic once the summer colours everything green, but not yet, not yet. Up here the gradualness of it is something like waiting for a birth. All very D. H. Lawrence, Margaret says of the wildness. Usually she finds that it calms her heart.

Well. Jill looks from the grand mountains and the lowering sky to the men around her. Not much likelihood of finding a Mellors among them. Jill sighs. Fat chance. They are all either well over sixty, or the same age as her son. Apart from Sidney, the leader in all things and Jill's right-hand. Though possibly in his fifties, he both looks and smells like a potato which has been left in the soil too long. He sucks his pipe, not female toes, and takes his sandwiches well away from her when the time comes to eat, keeping his nose in a book and his cap well down over his eyes. No. Nothing of Mellors material there. He just so happens to be the backbone of the business.

'Do you think we should get another hand?' she asks.

He pauses, considers, removes the pipe and says, 'Maybe, See how we do to the end of the week.'

She nods, bends again and resumes her task. A business acquaintance of David's once told her that her men would achieve a higher productivity if she didn't work alongside them but was seen to be doing all the powerhouse stuff. 'Managers manage,' he said, 'and workers work.' Jill has never liked businessmen. If she had known – she pulls aggressively at the harsh green frond – if she had known that David would turn into one, she would most certainly have thought again when he snapped open her bra after their third date.

She stops what she is doing reluctantly. There is something soothing about the rhythm of pulling leeks, a sense of healthiness, the body in action, the mind left free. There is no doubt that this kind of work keeps her fit without her having to cavort around in overstretched pink Lycra or punish herself on the tennis court. She stands upright again. This time her grunt is valedictory.

'Better go in and sort out a bit of paperwork,' she says, and plods back over the fields. One part of her casts a calculating eye over the carrot tops, the bushy greenness of the potatoes, the misty cucumber frames; the other part muses on the sensual effect of spring.

David had certainly responded to the sap rising last night. While they were breathing and touching and rolling she had had the most wonderful fantasy that she was half woman, half tree. Like Diana – no, *Daphne*. But she could not remember *which* tree, so without thinking she said to David – who happened to be above her just then, although they were quite liberal in their sexual roles – 'Was it a laurel or a rowan tree? I can't remember.' And a pair of very surprised eyes, which had hitherto been bathed in that faraway ecstatic light of yielding to lust, refocused, looked down at her and blinked, and said, with just a peppering of peevishness, 'What?'

'I was wondering if it was a laurel or a rowan.'

She caught his look. The peevishness had deepened. His eyes opened and closed in a momentary gesture of irritation. 'You aren't bringing the bloody garden centre into bed with us now, are you?' He had never forgiven her for once mulling over expanding into peas in a post-coital state of clarity. David called the market garden a 'garden centre' only when he was sorely tried.

She began to explain the fantasy and then decided that she could not be bothered. Not be *bothered*? That was seriously worrying. They could, of course, have had some fun speculating which bits had turned into tree and which were still her and where the squirrels may have put their nuts ... But instead she just clamped her mouth shut, closed her eyes and indulged her fantasy alone. When he said a little later, urgently now, kneading and stroking her flesh, 'What are you thinking?' she just smiled and said, 'Roll over and I'll show you.'

Leaving her boots at the door, she pads down the hallway, stopping to pick up a couple of letters from the floor. Both have familiar writing: one from London, Margaret; one from Somerset, Amanda.

Guiltily she opens Amanda's letter first – not from motherly impatience but to get it over with. Once a week her daughter sends her a letter which contains everything a grandmother might wish to know about her distant family. But it is the kind of letter that an ex-patriate might send to friends in the home country, with a request to 'pass it around when you have finished with it'. Impersonal. Jill could not find a way *in* to her daughter, or rather, she suspected, there was nothing *in* her daughter to find. Amanda was happy. Extremely happy. She was dull, safe, kind, organized, calm and *happy*. She was David. It was hardly fair for her mother to go probing around looking for something that simply wasn't there.

The Irish are giving British mushrooms a hard time, Amanda writes, and she is doing a course in child psychology – Jill's heart sinks – and they have finally got round to buying a camper van. Maybe Jill and David could come along some time? They are thinking of a holiday in Wales – doing the castles with the children. Jill's heart spreads around her on the floor. Time for an ally.

She picks up Margaret's letter for relief but it is curiously devoid of intimacy and reads – unless it is Jill's state of mind – not unlike Amanda's. Bright, breezy, full of details about what she has been doing, but feelings? That incisive observation of the strange ramblings of life? That *personal* touch? No. Not about her, nor about what Jill might be feeling. She puts the letter down and sighs. Ah well, it must all be very strange now that Saskia is away. Perhaps Margaret is in

99

even lower spirits than Jill and doesn't want to burden her. More than likely. She stands up, makes two flasks of coffee, which she sets on the table with several chunky white china mugs. (Should a manager make hot drinks for her employees? Yes, she says defiantly to the sleeping cat.) It is not as if she does not have friends up here – she does, but they are not pals of the heart, and everything in their lives looks reasonably rosy, secure, proper. Although Jill knows this cannot be so, that 'All human life is there' must extend to the north of England too, she has not penetrated anybody enough to find out. The market garden has saved her from idling decay, but distanced her from the kitchen tables round about.

She takes her own coffee into her office, which makes her feel a little better. At least there is her business. This is something she has achieved, despite David at first saying it was nonsense (he is very supportive now, except occasionally when he gets into his cups and little spurts of primal resentment burst out). She opens a couple of envelopes left over from yesterday. One contains an invitation to the opening next month of an organic farm shop near Otterburn. The high life, she chuckles. Pity it's the week after Margaret is coming. A bucolic jaunt like that would have had them both giggling like schoolgirls. It would be so nice if she could live up here all the time. It has always been Jill's fantasy that her friend will find true love here among the Cheviots, and settle near by.

She places the invitation from the organic shop on her desk. Pity, she thinks, for Margaret might have met the man of her dreams there and never gone home again.

Chapter Fifteen

I have been painting away – some good, some very good and some complete failures. It's encouraging to have Dad alongside. He doesn't say much unless I ask him a direct question, and then he is forthcoming and quite didactic. A sort of parent/ tutor. It's a funny thing, the blood bond, but our signatures are almost identical. He signs his 'Richard Donald' and says the days of 'Dickie' are long gone. He showed me a beautiful drawing of my mother and me when I was asleep in her arms. It is very tender. He has given it to me. What are you doing over there? I have heard nothing for ages.

....

Woman, 39, seeks lover for one year. I offer good legs, bright mind, happy disposition, in return for well-adjusted, solvent male between 35 and 40. April to April. No Expectations.

The male population singular's view of age seems to be a broad canvas. Rather as in the old days, I suppose, when if woman say no she mean yes, now in the new days if woman say she want a man between thirty and thirty-eight, really she mean between school-cap and prostate operation.

I went with the ageist flow. I saw the point. It is shopping and you aim to get what you want, So, feeling somewhat sweaty of palm and with a hint of humiliation about me, in went my advertisement, age range and all. In a way it seemed One For The Girls ... Heaven knows there were enough advertisements from active chaps of autumnal hue for beautiful women with brains, legs, solvency and half their age.

But consequently, at the beginning of the Pursuit I wasted a lot of time having jolly lunches with the 'I may be fifty but I can act like I'm thirty' types, or 'I may be an inarticulate twenty but I can roger you rigid with my fabbo joystick'. Neither of which was remotely what I had in mind. So I learned to be quite crisp on the subject of age, even more on the subject of status. 'Just what exactly do you mean by "sort of" married, squire?' And very firm on the year's duration. An apparently callous sifting but, since the response to my advertisement was in sackloads rather than handfuls, a necessary one. I could not afford to waste time – theirs or mine – and most went into the bin.

I became acquainted with the mystery of physical chemistry: a conventionally handsome contender left me cold, while a chap with a broken nose and eyebrows that met in the middle gave me quite a frisson. Alas, this latter loved sailing and fishing, both of which activities either required a lover who would be permanently available for splicing the mainbrace, or ready to do battle, wreathed in loving gratitude, with a sharp knife, rubber apron and fish guts.

In the first week I saw sixteen different men so that my days became like the dear Queen's – lunch here, drinks there, dinner somewhere else – only I had no equerry to steer me through. In this business you are very much on your own with no consultative body to advise you. It certainly streamlines your response and removes the pleasures of prevarication. I might arrive in a restaurant looking for a 'handsome, successful lawyer of thirty-seven' only to find a crumpled or defiant-looking individual some twenty years older and heavily into Grecian 2000. I would be polite and then something glaring would happen. 'Remember Alma Cogan's frocks?' he might say and our eyes would meet across silence, saying it all. Or there were the bright-faced babies of tender years who wanted an older woman, and the prospect of instructional sex and having to be powerful all the time left me cold.

The following week was much the same, full of dates, empty of success and I began to worry that I might be getting high simply on going out with a new man every night, rather than conserving my energy and judgement for the right one. It began to feel rather hopeless – the sort of thing Angela Brazil used to call 'madcap' and which was perpetrated by girls with fresh faces, turned up noses and names like Molly. I did not want to be like a Molly – I wanted to be seductive and be seduced in a grown-up manner that had nothing to do with japes in the dorm and being called Molly.

Clearly, I could not talk to Verity about this, since she was in no state to join in the plot with rapture. Nor to Jill either, because she would have been horrified at so pragmatic an approach to what she stoutly believed should be left to Fate. When – *if* – I ever achieved my goal I should have to invent a moonlit story about how we met. She had always wanted me to get a *proper* – she really meant *improper* – man into my life, perferably one from up there, probably in the same village and quite likely from the house next door. But *advertisements*?

Never!

Thus, when I was not in a whirl of nail-painting and eyelash-curling, and seriously considering changing my hair colour to Gloriana's auburn for a while, I wandered around pondering the problem alone.

Shuffling rather aimlessly around the local bookshop, I began a close inspection of the jacket blurbs and found, rather dauntingly, that most books of any literary merit with heroine protagonists are either about how to keep a man once they have got him, or how to get away from him when it turns sour. Or lovers just fall, plop, into your lap. So where were the hunting heroines? Was this, I wondered, the result of thousands of years of being hunted? Was it truly not credible or seemly for a woman in print to set out deliberately to find a lover?

Elizabeth Smart did it, of course, but it was more like dementia than fun and ended in a pool of tears at Grand Central. Many heroines, Zen-like in their innocence, got their lovers without expecting it – Emma, Jane Eyre – and in most modern stuff the heroines are, somewhat understandably, attempting to be individuals rather than couples. Deliberately seeking a lover, rather than a husband, protector, father-of-my-children, was a rare concept between bindings. I read Marguerite Duras' *The Lover* in hope, but her heroine is a schoolgirl and, if laconic later, begins life by being extremely surprised to find herself with a lover while she is still in ankle socks. He just seems to drop by the school gates one day and that's that . . . I could not find one heroine who from page one declares that among her various life pursuits she intends to find herself a suitable lover to go with them and who, without a lot of mordant angst, goes out and gets one. I was still stuck on page one myself – yearning to break the literary mould but with no success.

Surely there was somebody out there with a like mind? Between thirty and forty, prepared to be transient, solvent but with free time, cultivated, attractive to me, reasonably virile, socially adept, single . . . As I ticked off the requirements my heart beat a little less confidently, for it suddenly seemed a very tall order, not unlike requiring some fantasy hero from *True Romance* to be made flesh. Never mind, I told myself firmly. Buck up and keep plodding on.

After all, the Brazil madcaps always did. *And* they won through.

I decided to abandon my own advertising in favour of answering advertisements instead. Perhaps that would yield better results. But before I gave my telephone number, or any way of being traced, I would request a photograph from them first. The way we perceive a good photograph of ourselves can be very telling – my chirpy smile and my knees for instance – and maybe that would help. Something had to, for I was beginning to feel quite desperate – time ticking away and all that – and also the longer the hunt went on, the more likely my friends were to find out. If I harboured unliberated prejudices about the method, what would *they* think? I could imagine introducing him (when I found him) and them staring at him silently, as if he were an exotic fish.

Not only was requesting a photograph before committing myself a good idea, but it was also sensible given my vulnerability. Apart from the one in a million chance of a correspondent being Jack the Ripper's great-grandson, there was also the possibility of an unwelcome correspondent turning up on the doorstep . . . 'Hi, I was just passing by on my bike en route for Spud-U-Like and I wondered if you'd like to join me. My name's Kevin and my hobby is breeding goats . . .' But if I wanted a photograph I would no longer have the protection of a box number. I would need a forwarding address. I pondered. I decided. My poste restante victim just had to be Colin. And just for once, I would play him at his own game. We sat in my postage-stamp garden which was looking springlike and sweet and I put him in the canvas director's chair because I thought it would make him feel superior. It was about six o'clock and warm, with the last rays of sun playing on some pink azaleas and a feathery-white spiraea. All very feminine, I thought, and prepared to be all very feminine myself. Colin always *said* I should try harder. The director's chair was placed next to a viburnum which had caught enough warmth during the day to give off a rich vanilla scent, and a clump of tall, golden lilies near by decided to match this with a heady aroma of their own. I had dabbed Chloë behind my ears and was prepared for a bit of eyelash fluttering. I sat in a chair slightly lower than his so that I could gaze up at him, and handed him just about the wickedest Martini I could bring myself to mix. Despite Mrs Mortimer's ethereal voice in my ear saying, 'Just wave the vermouth bottle vaguely in the direction of the gin,' I never quite could. Just as well, because he took one gentle sip and then exploded.

'Jesus Christ,' he said, though not entirely unadmiringly, 'have you heard of vermouth?'

Flutter, flutter, I went.

He sipped again. He gave a small grimace which erred on the side of appreciation. He looked at me.

I smiled a smile that revealed the depths of my interest and friendship.

'You want something,' he stated.

'Haven't seen you for ages,' I shrugged. 'I just wondered how the holiday was.'

'The holiday was fine. Very good in fact.' He allowed a faintly lecherous light to enter the remembering look in his eyes. Normally I would have kicked him.

'Good. Nice place, was it?'

'Oh, nice enough.' He sipped again. His eyes held the unmistakable expression of one who expects to be kicked. 'We didn't go out much . . .'

'Oh,' I said. 'Hotel had lots of linen cupboards, then?'

That caught him. Somewhere between a laugh, a snort and a sip of his drink. He patted his chest, his eyes watering. When he had recovered, he said, 'And what have you been up to?'

I kept my even smile, my depths of interest and friendship. Later, when all this was over, I would tell him how close he came to being tipped out of his chair. It was bad enough, heaven knows, when my father used to come home from work and say the same thing. And I was only twelve then . . .

'What *have* I been up to?' I tapped my teeth with the glass. 'Very little really.'

'You've been out a lot.'

'How do you know?' I forgot to flutter.

'Out a *lot*.'

'Oh,' I said airily. 'Not really.'

'Where?'

'Oh, here and there.'

'Not much here.'

'What is this, Colin? Meet the Neighbourhood Watch?'

'Out a lot and *touchy* about it.'

'Not at all.'

'So you've found a lover?'

For a moment I forgot our lunch conversation and thought he had discovered about the advertisements. Though part of me desperately wanted to confess, most of me wanted to keep silent. I mean, love is supposed to be for ever, isn't it, according to received wisdom? As they say of marriage, so read for love, it is the triumph of hope over experience – you are not supposed to go advertising for it or giving it a deadline. All I wanted was to treat a love affair as a holiday. Book in advance, go for a limited amount of time, have as much enjoyment as you can get and leave in good spirits. As I looked at Colin, my inner bravado left me. If he knew what I was doing, he would have a joke over me for ever.

He was looking at me expectantly, his head inclined slightly. The air was slightly damp now and the chill seeped into my bones. I poured the rest of the rocket fuel into our glasses and tried to recover my calm and flattering disposition. I needed this man, or rather I needed his address. I revived the hamster image and prepared to be gently dismissive. Indeed, given the Martini, a beguiling chuckle was playing about my throat. At least, I hoped it was.

He still looked expectant, though the whites of his eyes had turned a little pink.

'Hooked one, have you?' he said, clearly wanting to throw down a gauntlet.

It was a gauntlet to which I should not have risen. I should have brushed my hair back delicately and replied with sophisticated calm. Instead, instantly on the defensive, I said, 'No, I haven't!' with the indignation of a Victorian virgin.

'Hold on,' he said, 'I was only inquiring. I thought you would have done by now.' He looked smug. 'You're taking your time to get started.'

I let it pass, temporarily. But vowed to get even some day. A photograph of Colin next to a picture of a hamster with the caption 'Can you tell the difference' loomed comfortingly large.

'How do you know I've been out a lot?'

'I've rung. Quite a few times.'

'You didn't leave a message.'

He sipped. 'I couldn't,' he said.

'Oh, why?'

'Because every time I heard your voice on the answerphone I just fell about.'

Some kind spirit put a small but strong rod down my back. I straightened, grew six inches in my chair, and our eyes were practically level. I put false *bonhomie* into mine.

'Why was that, Colin?' I asked.

'Well, go and listen to it. *Have* you listened to it? You sound like a cross between Mae West and a madam. Talking of which' – he raised his nose and sniffed – 'this garden smells like an Egyptian brothel.' Clearly amused, he smiled at a lily head, reaching out to touch it so that it nodded acquiescently. 'Sexy flowers,' he said, taking the nodding acquiescence in his hand and peering into the private waxy depth. 'All you'll need is a red light.'

'Who? Me or the lily?'

I was about to forget the friendly flattery and the forwarding address and tell him what I thought of him when his arch expression gave way to a sudden softness and the hand that had touched the lily touched my cheek.

'Margaret,' he said, 'if you go putting out a message in that voice you're asking for trouble. I mean, I *know* you, so I don't find it a come on, but somebody else – anybody male – hearing that kind of up-front allure, might get the wrong idea . . .'

Up-front allure? I thought. I was impressed. However, the rod came out of my back and spinal curvature renewed itself. It had never occurred to me that I was being naïve.

'I know about things like provocation,' he continued, far too pretentiously. 'After all, I *am* a man.'

'No you're not,' I suddenly giggled. 'You're a hamster.'

108

And while he was looking puzzled and a little anxious about that statement, a shaft of wondrous deceit hit me.

'Colin,' I said confidingly. 'You are right. I have got a lover. Only he's married.'

'Why a hamster?' said Colin wonderingly.

I waved my arm dismissively. It had goose bumps. I had to move swiftly before the dropping temperature restored his vigilance. 'The thing is, he doesn't want to have any connection with my address here in case his wife is using a detective. You know. They can' − I thought of V. I. Warshawski − 'they can trace anything. Even post. So I wondered if I could use you as a safe letter-box. You know. He could send his letters to you and I could come and collect them.'

He stared at me, then rubbed the tip of his nose thoughtfully. I waited. He said nothing.

'Oh, go on,' I said. 'You can't go getting all moral about it, considering your checkered past.'

'Two things,' he said, extending the correct number of fingers. 'One: why a hamster? And two: you want me to be a holding address so that when the crap hits the spinometer I get the knock in the night? And for ever after get branded as a covert homosexual?'

'I thought you were liberated. You read the *Guardian*.'

'Honey, I am liberated. If I *were* gay, I would tell the world and celebrate it if necessary. But I'm not. And I don't think my . . .' − he paused, looking worried now − 'my women would be impressed.'

'They wouldn't know.'

'Try keeping women away from scrutinizing incoming mail.'

'OK,' I said, prepared to be kind. 'Tell them.'

He scratched his head in genuine confusion. 'This just doesn't sound quite right to me. I mean, it's a hell of a lot of subterfuge. What is he? The Prime Minister or something?'

Deceit has a way of enticing us further into wicked abandon. 'Nearly,' I said. 'He's a diplomat. A very high-ranking diplomat. *Now* do you see?'

'What's his name?'

By now I was clone of Mata Hari. I looked down at my empty glass wistfully. 'I can't tell you that,' I said.

Which was true.

He agreed, if slightly fuzzily, and so, fluttering femininity over, I slipped into Mama Pasta mode. 'What you need is something to eat.'

He stuck out his underlip. 'Why a hamster?' he said with an insistence that brooked no denial.

So while I chopped onions and garlic and he mashed up the basil leaves, I told him about what Saskia had said.

'That child always had the devil in her,' he said fondly.

I felt a sudden pang. 'Yes,' I said, chopping more fiercely. 'It came from her father's side.'

'I thought you had let all that go,' he said, pushing all the greenery into the sizzling pan.

'I think I have. I think that was a Pavlovian reaction rather than what I feel now. Time heals and I can't hold on to hatred for ever.' I could use strong words like 'hatred' because that was how I had felt and the Martini countered caution.

'How's she doing?'

'She is doing fine. She writes me long, long letters all about Canada and the people she's meeting and little snippets about the different ways of living and looking at things – it really has worked so far as broadening her out. She's in Quebec at the moment for the ice hockey which is *very* exciting . . .'

'And the other thing?'

'You mean Dickie? Or *Richard*, as we are supposed to call him now.'

I paused. I realized that I had not really thought about it properly. Afraid it would hurt, I suppose. Curiously it didn't. I turned down the flame and folded my arms. I looked at Colin and felt an immense rush of gratitude for his friendship. Being a friend, he could touch these sensitive areas without appearing obtrusive.

'She and he,' I said, 'are quite clearly made to love each

other. And reading between the lines, she wants me to love him too. Of course I can't. But I don't begrudge her the closeness of a father. So long as he stays over there and out of the way. She's painting a lot, which is what she wanted. And she's happy.'

Colin pulled a cork out of a bottle of Merlot. 'You've changed your tune,' he said. 'There was a time when you considered him entirely evil. In fact you built your whole life around that notion.'

'It's only for a year. I can't deny genes after all. I only hope she's got the few good ones he may have.'

'Well, well,' he said, sniffing the cork. 'Aunt Margaret *resurgat*. Pity it's with a married man, though.'

'What are you talking about, Colin?'

'Your new lover,' he said, eyeing me over the bottle.

'Oh, that. Yes.' I sighed as convincingly as possible. 'Well, who knows where love will lead us?' I turned back to the bubbling pot.

'Indeed,' he said, in a tone that made me feel like kicking him again.

'Glasses?'

Chapter Sixteen

*Dad has gone away for a week with Judith, so I have the place
entirely to myself. I could do with a bit more twentieth-century
stuff out here. You don't send me any news of the London
scene. Isn't there an Auerbach show open/opening soon? It's at
the Hayward, I think. Can you get me the catalogue? You've
been out such a lot that I feel a bit guilty. Is the loss of Roger
hitting you? Dad and Judith have been a bit fraught recently,
hence the holiday. Your answerphone voice is disgusting. Why?*

....

I had given myself until the end of May to meet Mr Right so
that he could be with me when I visited Jill. There were
about three weeks to go. Or to be precise, two weeks, since
we would need at least a week beforehand to ... um ... get
to know each other a little first. Hardly fair to meet him in a
wine bar and tell him to have his bag packed – a little time
was necessary. Also I didn't want to make any bloomers at
Jill's. I could imagine it:

Jill: How did you two meet?'
Me: At a party.
Him: Through an advert in *On Sight*.
Jill: Is that a joke?
Me: Yes.
Him: No.

Jill was clearly fed up and I hoped that she would get some

vicarious pleasure from my happiness. She needed occasional reminders that the world could, indeed, be frosted pink and sweet to the lips occasionally, but David seemed increasingly unable to provide such reminders. There really are virtues to the life singular. Maybe Jill and David had grown apart because the children had left home, for the family unit had been their lodestar. With just the two of them now, all the flaws took on a sharper edge. But it was hardly fair for Jill to expect more pink fluff from a man who had never claimed to have any in the first place. So, I decided, she could turn to me. If Jill wanted candyfloss, why then I would provide it – in abundance if the lover was willing – the darlings and endearments dropping like dew from a rose leaf.

Verity was seriously absorbed in what was going on in my life. She did not approve and felt that I had let her down, but I calmed her by saying my various dates were just dates and nothing more. But she would come round on any pretext early in the morning and look pleased if I were still in *déshabille* – quite often bounding up the stairs, two at a time, to peek through the crack in the bedroom door, no doubt to behold some tousled head still breathing satedness into the pillows. She said it was jest. I knew it was not. Why, she had already given me a serious, low-voiced, gimlet-eyed chat about *condoms*, Margaret, *condoms*.

'Tom Cruise has just gone,' I would shout. 'But Eddie Murphy's just called to say he's on his way.'

'You should be so lucky,' she would say, coming down the stairs with a faint leer on her face. And since I had probably had a date with nothing resembling either of them the night before, I was inclined to agree.

'But where do they all come from?' she asked me peevishly on one such occasion, and I have to say that pride upped and pinched me. *Where do they come from*, indeed! Anyone would think I looked like a Troll.

'They come from their mothers' wombs, Verity,' I said. 'The same as you and me.'

'You know what I mean,' she said waspishly. 'Where do

you pick them up?' The urge to denounce myself as a hooker and say 'King's Cross and environs' was delightful temptation. Instead I patted my hair and pouted into the mirror, saying, 'Oh, here and there, you know.' A secret, significant little smile reflected back at me. 'Here and there.' I knew that would infuriate her. There was no doubt that while Verity was absorbed in my life and romantic interludes, she felt much better. Her weight had returned to normal (perhaps this was not a credit, since about the one thing she could celebrate in all her sufferings was that she had got back into her ten-year-old jeans without dieting), her eyes were bright with life rather than gin, and she was less and less inclined to speak with poetical, tear-stained yearning of the absent Mark. At this stage I still had plenty of time for her and I was sure she'd be more or less cured by the time Mr Right came along. Fondly, I saw again the *tendresse* of Tintoretto. Two women: one stumbles, one saves. Despite Saskia's going away, life could be fun after all.

Did I hear the echo of a ghostly chuckle?

One morning the doorbell rang and it was not Verity but Colin. A grinning Colin, holding out three letters. 'Well, well,' he said, his eyes gleaming dangerously. 'A clever cove this one. Writes you three different letters, from three different addresses, and in three different handwritings. My, my – his wife *will* be confused, never mind MI5!'

It was a fair cop.

I took him into the kitchen, shoved a bowl of muesli under his nose, told him I hoped it choked him, and while I made coffee explained everything. I also told him that if he broke my confidence and anyone else found out, I would consider it my duty to the feminine cause to make his future participation in muesli in my house a dangerous form of cereal roulette.

Women are the only *true* romantics. They understand the dimension of the spirit which drives the soul towards the sublime and are quite ready to be pragmatic about it. They know that as the melting splendour of a perfect soufflé requires some shit-hot elbow time to make the conditions right, so romantic liaisons will not arrive in their laps unless they prepare the ground. Prepared ground can be anything from fancy clothes, scented cleavage and a Marks & Spencer's dinner for two on Wedgwood, to an inner belief, en route for the canning factory in a dawn-damp overall, that today might be the day.

Colin's bleating indignation at my calculated methodology would have made a grown feminist weep. 'How . . .' he said passionately, indeed, with more passion than I had heretofore experienced in his pronouncing presence, 'how can you set out with such a cynical undertaking?'

What on earth *is* it about this 49 per cent of the world's population that when a woman says 'I know what I want and I know how to get it', she must immediately be suspect? The virtue of patience, with all its attendant passivity, is considered suitably female. To the man falls the much more muscular and outward-bound virtue of endurance. Thus, of course, did Boccaccio's final tale turn the legend of Job, who endured the wrath of a psychopathic *God* and was rewarded for it, into the disgraceful episode of patient Griselda, who was accorded the mere domesticated trials of a psychopathic *husband* to prove her worth. God, presumably, felt it was beneath him in her case. Job Endured, got rid of the boils, collected fourteen thousand sheep, six thousand camels, a thousand yoke of oxen, a thousand she-asses and one hundred and forty years of fulfilling life, in which he produced seven sons and three entirely marriageable daughters, and finally retired, without the need of a hip replacement, to sit on the right hand of God in virtuous splendour.

And patient Griselda? Well, you don't see her in the likes of the Sistine pecking order. *She* got back her supposedly murdered children (having just got through personal growth therapy to deal with their loss perhaps), her home – with the neighbours all pointing their fingers and knowing – and a complete nutter of a husband. Thank you very much.

'Why hang around,' I said perkily, bearing all this in mind, and with perhaps a degree too much bravado, 'when it seems to be working so well?'

'It does?' he said, supping his hamster food. 'But you haven't even opened them yet.' He pushed the envelopes across the table at me.

Resentment rose in my beating breast. Just because bloody Colin was willing it all to be misguided, I was allowing myself to be cornered. And I was about to say so. Indeed, I was about to give a little speech, the gist of which was that I did not need his presence in order to open my mail and discover whether within there nestled the fulfilment of my cause. I was about to be terse, to tell him it was all *my* business, to say that if this batch of potential lovers was not suitable, I would wait for another lot. I would get it right. I would not be judged, it was for me alone to judge and he could just piss off. I would say this, I would, I *would* . . .

And then I did not.

For it came to me in a shaft of glorious understanding. This was exactly the spur I needed. All those weeks of meeting men and rejecting them. Too old, too young, too fat, too thin, doesn't like Cézanne, can't take a hot curry, uses a biro – why, it could be endless. I could go on for ever like that, and then, suddenly, Saskia would be home, Mr Spiteri's son would be propping up a business meeting in St Tropez, and the whole delicious game and adventure would be lost. So I decided, there and then, and with gratitude towards Colin in my heart, that *one* of these three would be He. And who knows if it was that decision, made in a moment of true psychological surrender, which brought me, unquestionably, to the right choice.

I sat down opposite Colin and reached for the envelopes, pulling them towards me. The atmosphere between us was as charged and electrical as in that sunbaked Western street in *High Noon*. Everything was suspended. Colin's spoon was midway twixt bowl and lip, the milk dripping into the muesli below. My hands rested lightly on the three contenders. The clock ticked, Gary Cooper walked. It was irresistible and I hummed the theme. *Do not forsake me, oh my darling . . .* Colin put his spoon down. He tugged at his hair. 'Open one for Chrissake,' he moaned. So I did.

At first I thought there was nothing inside. Further investigation revealed that there was – a humiliating something. It was a short note, to which was clipped my own photograph. It said, 'Very nice picture and I hope you find what you are looking for.' It was signed 'Advertiser'.

'Well?' said Colin.

I put the envelope to one side. A certain number of dolorous bells began ringing in my ears. 'Not for me, I fancy,' I said brightly. 'A bit short.'

One sentence, to be be exact. Never tell a lie if you can equivocate.

'Can I see?' He held out his hand.

'Certainly not,' I said and picked up another letter hurriedly. Two choices left. Fear gripped the soul. Once you set yourself on a certain course of action, you are best advised to adhere to it. One of the remaining two would have to be *He*.

For a close-up it is not a good idea to be photographed from slightly below centre face. You get quite a lot of nostril involved and nostrils are, perhaps, the least appetizing portion of the human visage. My second possibility seemed all nostril and not much else, and though I was willing not to be prejudiced by this fact alone, his attached letter had a certain nostril quality, too.

In my letter I had stated what I wanted clearly. So it was *very* frustrating both to know what I wanted and to have said it and then, having done so, to be told that I actually, really, deep down, wanted something else. Someone to have a bit of romantic, full-blooded fun with for a year, I had stipulated – a serious commitment to this, rather than to a life partnership. I had given a list of my interests and characteristics, and a list of what, approximately, his should be. I had written a humorous but not unfeeling letter. It was bold, brave and rather derring-do and left no room for a sub-text. Nostrils had other ideas.

I put the letter and the photograph to one side and Colin grabbed them. He stared at the photograph intently and then pronounced its subject as looking like a serial killer. I had a feeling that if it had been a snapshot of the Greek ideal he'd have said much the same. I snatched back the letter before he had a chance to read it, because this was, after all, the open-hearted offering of another human being and I didn't see why Colin, who ventured so little bravery in his relationships, should get the chance to laugh at someone who, though pedantic, arrogant and nostrilly righteous, was prepared to stand out there in the marketplace and expose himself.

'What does he say?'

'Basically that he cannot believe I know my own mind.'

Colin laughed, 'Can't believe it in the literal sense, or can't believe you're sincere?'

'I think he thinks I'm playing a game, carefully structured, in which the prize is him for life.'

Colin looked at the photograph again. 'Poor sod,' he said.

'Don't be patronizing; he isn't a poor sod at all. He's ventured, knowing the rules and the risks, and he'll venture somewhere else.'

'Why on earth did you reply to him in the first place?'

'Because he sounded all right.' I paused. 'And because he's got a Ferrari.'

Colin stared at the picture anew and the compassion faded from his eyes. 'He'd need one looking like that,' he said.

I patted his hand sympathetically. 'It was the Ferrari, wasn't it?' I said. Which made us both laugh.

He reached for the third letter and began opening it impatiently. I took it from him and made the most of doing the job neatly. I took my time. There is enjoyable power to be had even in such little things. Also, I was really worried by now. I mean, supposing this one had the body of Woody Allen, the brain of Rambo, the face of Andrew Lloyd Webber and Kevin Costner's sense of fun? I delayed. Colin hunched nearer across the table, staring at the envelope as if it were an Academy Award. Why had I used *his* address when, I suddenly realized, I could have used the shop? His breath was on my hands.

'Oh, open Sesame!' I said, and reached within.

Chapter Seventeen

Dad and Judith are back but all is not well. I hope it isn't because I am here. I do miss London. He says that he does too. Please send Auerbach catalogue to cheer us up. How are you passing the time?

....

We sat in a pub near Oxford. It was a midweek lunchtime so not too crowded, though there was the usual collection of braying salesmen and hunched locals giving out the hostile stares of those who wish they were still tugging forelocks, using spittoons and keeping the pub to themselves. I had arrived by myself, clutching a photograph surreptitiously in one hand and wearing what I hoped was an expression of complete cool. Of course everybody looked because the door banged loudly, which did for the complete cool rather well. I sometimes wonder if the masculine frequenters of rural pubs are aware that we women have the vote and are therefore allowed to enter the hallowed den of the beer pump unaccompanied and without a veil. The shadowy stares seemed to think not.

I advanced. It would take a moment or two for my eyes to accustom themselves to the dark surroundings and make out whether he was there. Small English pubs in the heart of the countryside tend to be dimly lit affairs. You arrive in the light of the day, push open a door, and enter a twilit world of shaded faces, smoky air and talk, which immediately banishes the reality outside. The best way to counter this almost mesmeric quality is to march up to the bar and buy a drink. In this way you shed your guise as female stranger invading the community with dangerous whiffs of outside and receive a more benign acceptance. Once you have sat down with a glass in your hand, you become just another member of the Chorus. The assembly breathes easily again and goes back to its desultory ways. So for the bar I headed.

Of course there *were* women in there. Two – one on each side of the bar. She of the customers' side had the look of one who seldom gets off her stool and for whom chatting to besuited chaps while sipping gin and tonic is a way of life. She was, as they say, of a certain age, but this had not tamed her approach to colour. My lemon-coloured jumper had seemed quite a singing affair when I donned it new that morning, but next to her sunset lips and nails, her unapolo-getically tangerine top and her gilded head, I was nothing more than a jeans and jumper wimp. Despite my drear aspect, as she shifted to let me near the barmaid, she gave me a lovely smile. I moved closer. I saw why. With a chest like hers you could afford to smile. It was the kind of promontory upon which you become fixated while wonder-ing how it ever stays up – sort of wonderful, really. Waiting for my change, I became fixated on it and it was in that state that I felt a hand at my elbow and a voice in my ear say:

'Margaret?'

To which I said, 'That's me,' and blushed to be caught in such compromising contemplation. I had planned to be sitting, calmly sipping a white wine, cool and at ease. Instead I was caught, bolt-eyed, staring hard at another woman's breasts.

He was much as his photograph had shown. Fair hair, lively face, no Schwarzenegger but no string bean. Around my age – and a good deal more relaxed about things than I was.

'Shall we sit down?' he said, sliding amused eyes from mine to the tangerine chest and back again. It was quite clear that he had noticed how mesmerized I was by what I had seen. Probably the whole pub had. When nature has endowed you with only a pair of cherry pips you are inclined to be fascinated by dramatic mammaries. And they were definitely arranged for showing. She smiled at me as I squeezed past. It was a smile that quite clearly said she took deep pride in her equipment. So the best defence was attack.

'*What* an amazing bosom,' I said as we sat down.

He laughed, rubbed his nose, picked up his glass and said, just a little cautiously, 'Well, yes. Unmistakable, certainly.'

I soldiered on. You know that awful moment when you feel yourself hurtling down a path you do not wish to take but can't stop yourself? Hurtle, hurtle, I went. 'I've always wanted a large chest,' I said, conversationally.

He thought for a moment, contemplating his glass quite gravely. My entire body went slack. How could you *say* that? asked the remaining sensible bit of my psyche. He was by far the best bet of all my dates so far, not least because I had decided he would be, and now I had shown him in one moment of creative delirium that I was completely batty.

He looked up from contemplating a half of bitter and said, also conversationally, 'So have I.'

I stared at him for a moment. And then he laughed. Just a little. One of those laughs that is not sure if it should have been born. And then I laughed just a small laugh – before putting my hands over my face and saying through my fingers, 'Shall I go out and come in again?'

To which, very nicely, he put out his hand and removed mine, looked at me and said, 'If it's any help, I'm feeling a little confused about all this too.'

I don't think there could have been a better thing to say in the circumstances. The hurtling ceased and I put my chin on one of my hands, while extending the other. We shook on it. 'I don't normally go round staring at women's breasts in pubs,' I said. 'Nor discussing them.'

Pushing a puddle of beer with his finger, he laughed again, a good deal more easily. 'Women's bodies are just extraordinarily beautiful pieces of design. Everything about them seduces the eye.' He gave a sideways glance back at the tangerine chest. 'And those are – well, very . . .' He was stuck for words.

'Big?' I said helpfully.

He gave a capitulating nod. 'Big,' he agreed.

A lecher or Nietzsche's nephew? Neither, I decided.

'End of subject?' I asked.

'End of subject.'

We both leaned back in our seats, able to relax at last. There were some ham sandwiches on a plate in front of him.

'Shall I get you something to eat?' he asked.

'Later,' I said. 'Shall we talk *properly* for a moment?'

He agreed, straightening his back, as if getting ready for an interview.

'You first,' I said.

Until this point our contact with each other had been minimal: the initial letter with his phone number, the brief message I left on his answerphone leaving my number and the even briefer message he left on mine arranging to meet at this pub. It had all been very strange after the wealth of literature received from my others. He also gave the telephone number of an architectural practice in Holborn, in case I should want to check his credentials as a man of honour. His name was Simon Phillips, which was quite acceptable. After a Jason or two anything was quite acceptable.

I doused the madcap Molly of the Fourth in me, who wanted to say, 'Is it true that all architects are failed artists?' and clamped my jaw shut, nodding at him to begin. After my blisteringly wonderful opening, I simply did not feel safe.

'Shall I tell you about myself or do you want to ask me questions? Or would you prefer to tell me about yourself first?'

I had a terrible urge to say, 'Well, Doctor, it's like this . . .' but managed to control it. We sat there, with our drinks and his plate of sandwiches, and I thought that in my whole life I had never felt more unreal. But I argued with myself that you could meet a chap at a party and get to this point. All we had done was meet through an advertisement, and, really, going to parties in hunting mode and all dressed up was no different from advertising your availability in writing.

Then I said, straight out: 'I just wanted some fun for a year. A bit of a fling with no commitments beyond that. And no expectations. *Absolutely* no expectations.'

'Are you . . .' He played with the puddle of beer again, considering what he was about to say. 'Is it . . . rebound?'

Rebound would do, I thought. I nodded. 'Sort of.'

'You were very positive about it being for a year?'

So I told him all about Saskia's going and about Greasy Joan and Mrs Mortimer – even the Matisse. But not about Dickie. I was looking forward to being free of that piece of history so far as the next year was concerned. I had already made up my mind, you see, that he would do very nicely. And despite the tangerine hiccough, I hoped he felt the same. He seemed to. At least, he showed no signs of repugnance. I was fed up with the hunting – women are *not* good at it – and just wanted to get on with having some *fun*.

'So you are an independent woman of wealth,' he said.

Sounded good.

'I suppose I am. And you?'

'I'm a partner in a fairly humble outfit, but I do very well considering the state of things nowadays. I have a fair amount of free time. I'm intending to wind down quite a lot over the next few months.'

'Are you on the rebound, too?'

He thought, and then shook his head. 'All sorts of reasons for doing this. Mainly because it was suggested to me by a friend. And because until three years ago I was married – no children – and since then I have had the odd one-nighter or two but nothing else. And I don't like one-nighters particularly.'

I felt a sudden disappointment and leaned back, sighing. 'Look,' I said in my best schoolmarmy voice, 'this sounds dangerously like someone who wants to settle down into a long-term relationship.' I took up the puddle-of-beer method of emphasis and stabbed my finger into the little wet dots. 'Commitment, expectations and all ... I am absolutely serious. I don't want that. In fact I so don't want it that I would be prepared to get out next year's diary, if I had one, and write on a given date next year, "Affair Ends Today." And if that sounds hard, then' – I shrugged – 'I'm sorry.'

He put up his hand. He was smiling quite peaceably. 'How about April the ninth?'

I stared. 'What?'

'April the ninth. How would that do for a closing date? That's always supposing we get on well enough together to sustain it for that long.' He gave me a critical look. 'I think we might. Unless you have any peculiarities of an untenable nature – which I don't think you have. I mean, you appear to be a warm, rational, attractive human being with a point of view.' He paused, the critical look deepened. 'You're not a racist? Or a supporter of capital punishment? Or – God help me – a *vegan*?' He laughed. 'No, no. At least I know you're not that.'

'How? I might be.'

'Because you've eaten most of my ham sandwiches.'

I pushed the plate towards him. Only one little piece remained. There is a creeping selfishness when you live alone. 'God,' I said, 'I am sorry.'

He stood up. Just for a moment I thought he was going to depart on the grounds of my heedless greed. I mean, how would I have felt if *I* had bought a plate of sandwiches and *he* had practically eaten the lot at our first lovers' rendezvous? Surely, at the beginning you were supposed to be on best behaviour? Munching my way through his rations without so much as a polite request was hardly that. 'I am truly sorry,' I said, half seriously. 'Truly, truly sorry. It won't happen again.'

'So I should think,' he said, and, picking up my glass, he went over to the bar.

I breathed out, relaxed as much as I could, and realized

that I had scarcely looked at him. I suppose if anyone had asked me for a split-second summation I would have said friendly face, comfortable person, and neither a blazer nor a pair of well-creased flannels to mar the effect.

I sat and stared at his back view. Grey jumper, denim shirt, navy cords, deck shoes. Perfectly reasonable. But unfamiliar, the clothes covering an alien body of which I could not imagine the texture or true shape. What was his smell like, his habits, his gestures, his requirements? I went cold. This was all completely potty. And what were we going to do now? Walk out into the Oxfordshire countryside and bonk? Immediately? Walk out into the Oxfordshire countryside, get out our diaries and choose a suitable occasion some time hence when we would bonk? Anyway, I didn't *want* to bonk. I wanted to . . . well, not *bonk* exactly . . . and have hot sex certainly, but with a bit more than – well, with a relationship attached. Just not for ever. Oh, the whole thing was more than completely potty – suddenly it was *impossible*. And dangerous. He was clearly no philanderer – he was bound to want the normal human thing of moving from affection into love and from love into for ever, with all its sorry disillusions. No. *No*. This had gone far enough. It was hopeless. It would not work. I prepared myself to say this when he returned. The barmaid was handing him some change. She was saying she would call him when the sandwiches were ready. He was turning to come back . . . And then, as he returned, negotiating a way around the tangerine top who smiled up at him carnivorously and spoke, he glanced from her shelving bosom to me, winked, said something to her, and was back sitting down. And I thought, *To Hell with it*. He *will* be my lover. I vowed to go home that night and read my Ovid *avidly*. He is a wonderful antidote to romantic love. With Ovid, as with life, it always ends in tears.

'What did she say?'

'She said they'd be ready in a minute.'

'I don't mean her. I mean the tangerine Exocets.'

'Oh. *Her*. She said that I had a nice bottom.'

'She did?' I was struggling between a desire to appear unconcerned and an already and pronounced territorial instinct. 'And have you?' Was all I could think of to say.

He chewed the remaining sandwich and grinned. 'That's for you to judge . . .'

I was about to reach for my glass but thought better of it. In the entire time I had known him, biblically and otherwise, Roger had never said anything to give me a comparable frisson. I smiled unaffectedly and said to myself that one always played games with lovers at first – one certainly didn't let out all the secrets straight away. I didn't want him to know he had scored a bull's-eye in the frisson department.

He continued to chew for a moment, thinking. I was desperately seeking something for my hands to do, but he had taken the last sandwich and I didn't quite feel up to holding a glass straight. It seemed best just to keep them hidden under the table. The way I was feeling I might end up chewing the empty plate. What is it about men that they always manage to hide strong emotion? There he was, just having floated a most suggestive statement, and he was eating as if he had only said, 'Fine weather for May.' Should I have brought up the subject of bonking there and then? I mean, what was the form in these matters? Keeping an unaffected smile firmly on my lips, I said, 'Why April the ninth?'

'Well,' he said, 'that's the day I head off for Nicaragua.' He leaned forward. 'But not for a holiday.' His eyes had become much more serious. 'I'm going out there to work. Taking my engineering skills to a far-flung corner from which I may never return.' He drank some more of his beer, looking at me over the rim of the glass.

'Well . . .' I said, a bit at a loss, 'that sounds very . . . um . . . exciting.'

He leaned back, put down his glass, smiled at the beer puddle. 'Oh, it is, it is. And dangerous. Unpaid, voluntary and extremely right on. It's a commitment I made to some people I know over there – can't be got out of. That's why your year thing was so tempting. I have to go, no matter what. I am shit-scared and I expect to die in the jungle from snake bite. Or a shot from a CIA gun. Or maybe just swamp fever. Anything really.' He shrugged with artificial nonchalance. 'Suicide mission. Call it that.'

'I will not,' I said, suspecting I was being played with. 'You're talking as if you've come out of a nineteenth-century novel. Haggard or somebody.'

'That was Africa.'

'Marquez, then.'

'Right continent at least.'

'You are being extremely patronizing.'

He slapped the table with his hands and laughed. 'I am. But look at it from the Nicaraguan point of view. Torn apart by civil war, racked by poverty, disease, corruption, which has been made only worse by the West – and you sit in an Oxfordshire pub and can't even get the continent right.'

'Well,' I snapped, 'with all that going on I should think a Nicaraguan would be far too busy to notice.'

Our second order of sandwiches was waiting on the bar. The barmaid called to us and Tangerine top looked over at our table laconically. I got up quickly and collected them, giving her an affordably friendly glance as I passed, holding my head and the plate high as I sailed back to harbour.

'Well,' he said, 'that was our first lovers' quarrel. How did you like it?'

'Loved it,' I said. 'Have a sandwich.'

'I don't want to get too heavy about all this,' he said. 'I'm not a tub-thumping individual, nor a crusader, and I would be just as happy – *prefer*, perhaps – to leave that side of things alone. It's a decision I made, I'm going to go and I've done most of the talking about it that I want to do really. What I'm hoping for is a bit of fun until then, and a nice easy ride . . .'

I dared to pick up a sandwich. 'Do you mean that emotion-ally' – I bit – 'or sexually?'

For a split second he paused, stared, looked unsure. Good. I thought. If we were battling for control here, then I wanted, at least, to show I had some artillery. Then he began chewing, swallowed, picked up his glass, drank, put it down and said, 'Both.'

At which we each gave in and exploded helplessly with laughter.

If I had felt unreal before, it was as nothing to this – I mean, we hadn't even held hands. But then, no one had said it was going to be to formula.

He looked at his watch and for a clammy atom of time I thought he might say that he had half an hour and how about it, but he was only checking the date. 'It's my birthday on Thursday,' he said. 'Shall we do something together? I like pasta. How about you?'

Today was Tuesday. One evening to assimilate, one day to be nervous, one day to be *really* nervous and then we would meet again. 'I'd love to,' I said, and I meant it. Which was a nice surprise.

Without thinking too much about the metaphor, I decided to take the bull by the horns. 'Well,' I said, with a great deal more confidence than I felt, 'what *about* the sex thing?'

He looked serious. 'Well,' he said, 'how desperate are you?'

Agrippina could not have been more indignant if someone had suggested she didn't know her poisons. 'I'm not at all desperate. Not at all. I just thought we ought to . . . um . . . well . . . *discuss* it.'

'Are you for or against?'

What a very silly question. I was a liberated women of independent means, wasn't I? 'I'm *for*, of course – but that certainly doesn't mean that I'm *desperate*.'

'Well, I'm for, too. So' – he shrugged and his face bore the slightly perplexed expression of one whose lights have fused – 'it'll happen, won't it . . .?' He gave me a look that made me feel that being caught staring at another woman's breasts was as nothing. 'After all, this is only our first date.' He was right, of course. Possibly it was time to cede a little of the control to nature.

Then somehow all of a sudden we were behaving naturally. As if we *had* met at a party or something and this was our first date rather than the pre-determined unromantic result of forethought. We talked about art, of which he said he knew very little but which turned out to be a good deal more than many. He favoured buildings rather than paintings and his hero was Corbusier. Expressionism was more in his line visually because, he said, it reflected the turbulence of the age. How he managed to say such a thing without being pompous I am not sure, but he did. I told him about framing and how it felt almost godlike sometimes to be adding to and enhancing an already perfect piece of art. How I managed to say that without curdling his blood I don't know, but I did.

Having got our pomposities out of the way, he then said a very nice thing – which was that Inigo Jones began life as a picture-framer. Something which I did not know and which I squirrelled away for the days, those long dull winter days, when I would be back at the shop twixt Reg's eye and Joan's *flick*. I could ponder on being made Court theatre designer by Charles III and thereafter designing temples to ecology . . .

Film interested him more than theatre. Cars not at all, which he regarded simply as things to drive around in. Friends were few and very dear, acquaintances more thickly strewn. He was happier in town than country, though not averse to rural ways. He was neither a gourmet nor a cook, but liked simple food, simply served. And he never wore suits. There were a lot of places he wanted to visit here and in Europe during the year, some alone, some with company. He lived in a flat which he did not own in Clapham.

So banal really, yet so important, all these beginnings.

I was glad that he really was going away. His personal details sounded far, far too appealing. Mind you, anybody's can before you come upon the smelly socks under the bed.

One other matter (besides sex) needed raising. 'We should,' I said, 'discuss money.'

He was struggling not to laugh. 'Oh,' he said. 'Are you going to charge?' He gave me a far too innocent stare. 'I didn't know that.'

I waited.

'I leave you everything in my will,' he hazarded, draining his glass.

'I accept.'

I couldn't decide whether to be offended or not. So I sat it out.

Eventually he said, 'Money?'

I nodded. And waited again.

'You mean who pays for what?' he said.

'Yes.'

'I hadn't thought about it. What's your view?'

'I think we should go Dutch – mostly.'

'Agreed. That sounds fine. Very practical.'

Somebody's got to be, I thought. I stood up. 'And now let me pay for half of our lunch.'

'No, no' – he pushed at my purse – 'have this on me.'

But I insisted. You can have your knees sliced from under you on matters of money in relationships and it was best to begin as equals.

We paid and left. The May sunshine was still very bright as we walked towards our cars.

'This is all very bizarre,' I said. 'Isn't it?'

'It is,' he said solemnly. 'Look on it as an adventure.'

On the whole it seemed the best approach.

'We mustn't forget the romance,' I said, half teasing, turning from unlocking my door.

'Women never do,' he said, and he kissed my cheek.

I jumped about a foot. God knows what I would have done if he had suggested a quick one round the back. The ten-second mile?

'Bye, then,' I said, awkward as a teenager, as I got into my car. He stood there waving as, a little confusedly and in the wrong direction, I drove away. I found myself looking in my mirror to check that he would not slip back into the pub for an assignation with Miss Bristols. But only a moment later I realized, with a wonderful flash of pleasure, that jealousy need never be part of this accord. We had struck a Chinese bargain, one that did not need lawyers or even to be written down, for it was of equal benefit to us both and therefore as binding as law.

By the time I had righted my course and reached home, I was beginning to feel quite thrilled. Something is happening at last, I told myself and Mrs Mortimer. In the hall mirror my eyes looked very bright and my cheeks quite pink, which was exactly right. I could almost see the damp hanky and the tear in my eye as I waved him off to Nicaragua next year ... *Nicaragua* of all places – and I wondered why. Just a *Boy's Own* sense of 'outward bound' tinged with politics? Or something more profound? Not my business. Wonderful liberation. I did not have to find things out. A great relief. It would happen, he had said – and that applied both to sex and to other things. Let it be.

I made up my mind not to tell Saskia what was happening. This was purely for me – if she got wind of it she would hammer it to death. Besides, I felt uncomfortable talking to her at the moment. She had stepped up her campaign about Dickie coming to London one day and I thought I would stick to letter-writing for a while. Letters were much easier to control. Blessed are the peace-makers, perhaps, but I was quite at peace *not* seeing Dickie. Saskia had to respect that.

With my mind a jumble, which was reasonable, I could not settle and went out again almost immediately. I called in at the shop. It was nearly closing-time. Reg was out delivering and there was no sign of Spiteri Junior. Joan looked just the same and it gave me the grimmest of satisfactions to watch *le flick* from the safety of the other side of the counter. It being Tuesday the lankness was apparent but it had not yet reached devastation point. Beneath its haunting shadow I detected a welcoming smile.

'How's it going?' I asked, *bonhomie* oozing from every pore.

'Dreadful,' she said. 'Dreadful.'

My stomach turned over, or whatever really happens to make the midriff lurch. I had promised Spiteri Senior that if the shop got completely out of hand I would come back – if only until a replacement was found – and, heart, blood and soul, suddenly I really, *really* didn't want to.

'Where is the brute?' I asked.

She raised her arms in despair, flicked back her hair again and eyed me balefully as the hank slowly descended. Automatically I reached for the small jam jar on the counter and took out a rubber band, handing it to her without a word. Automatically she took it, also without a word, and put it in her hair.

'In the cells,' she said.

I saw stars. '*What?!*' I screeched. With no protective covering Joan's eyes blinked like a startled owl's. 'What on earth for?' Had he been embezzling? Assaulting the female customers? I saw my delightful days of sunshine and fun evaporate. I heard Simon's voice say, 'I've got a fair amount of free time . . .' My heart sank. Bloody Spiteri Junior. In the *cells*?

'He stole a car and he had some hash . . .'

Not, surely, things that would take him away from framing for ever? Wishful thinking. 'Oh, God.' I slumped down. 'That's it, then. I'll have to come back.'

Joan looked even more startled. 'Well, not necessarily,' she said. 'I mean, I'm coping fine here and Reg is. We're on top of it. Manos is a bit of a pain but he does his turn. We manage . . .'

'Manos?'

'Mr Spiteri's son . . .'

'How on earth can he do his *turn* if he's languishing in cells and reeking of pot?'

'Oh, Aunt M!' Joan was laughing. 'It's my Charlie who's in the nick. Not Manos.'

'*Charlie?* My God!' I said. 'You went back with him . . .?' But I very nearly kissed her.

'Mistake. Never again,' she said grimly.

'I'm sorry,' I said. She shrugged. On the whole there was not the usual look of crushed worm about her. 'Despite that you look well, Joan.'

'So do you.' She looked me up and down. 'In fact you look terrific.'

'Well, that's what a few weeks off the treadmill can do' – I leaned forward – 'and no love troubles to get in the way. I'm sorry about Charlie.'

'Oh, it was over and done with, anyway. Think I *will* give it all up for the time being.' She sighed as she replaced the right-angle samples neatly on the display board. 'It just never works out, does it?'

'Not if you hope it will,' I said, perhaps a little too happily. 'Lower your expectations, and it might.'

I bought a card for Jill on the way home of a simpering Edwardian couple standing in a rose bower, she parasoled, he bare-headed and bewhiskered, their hands about to touch as they reached towards the same bloom. The caption was 'Love blossoms'. Feeling a bit wicked, I added, 'But watch out for pricks,' which I thought was quite witty. I sent it off with a little message to the effect that I would ring her very soon to confirm the weekend arrangements for the end of May. Oh! I thought after I dropped it in the pillar-box. *Arrangements*. Like a double bed? I thought with passing regret of the pretty little room I usually occupied, with its flouncy curtains and broderie anglaise on the single bed, where I had always felt like an indulged child. Well. 'There sleeps Titania some time of the night/Lull'd in these flowers with dances and delight.' Hmm, and we all know what happened to her . . .

Tomorrow I would go to the Auerbach show and get Sassy's wretched catalogue. That'd shut her up. She could be extremely tenacious sometimes. As I wended my way home, I thought, Now there's no going back . . .

Chapter Eighteen

Dad and Judith are separating for a while. It is so sad and I feel very bad about it because, apart from that, I am extremely, extremely happy. And still waiting for that catalogue! What's the matter? Don't you care about me any more? We paint away like mad. I'm learning a lot. He's nicer than you could possibly imagine. Hope you are having a good time whatever you are up to!

••••••••••••••••••••••••••••••

Verity, who is working on a script treatment based on Joan's experience – very loosely based since she has re-invented her heroine as extremely beautiful, extremely rich and extremely powerful – is feeling pretty fed up again. She is drinking mineral water laced with a few drops of lemon juice and, although it makes her feel morally superior, it is no compensation for the buzz of alcohol. However, she has vowed to abjure it, and abjure it she has. Even when Mark rang and said that he was about to ask someone else out but before he did he wanted to know if Verity really meant it was over between them. She had put her knuckles in her mouth while he was talking so that any sobs or gasps would not transfer, and she said brightly when he had finished his little speech, 'Yes, of course. I hope it works out for you.' He had not sounded too sure that it would, nor pleased to be given her blessing. As she put the phone down, she said to the handset that at worst he was game-playing and at best he meant it. Either way it showed him up for the shit he was. Why couldn't he just leave her alone?

She has stomped back to her word processor and written a highly satisfying dialogue between her heroine and her hero in which he abjectly apologizes for everything. The abject apology goes on for quite a long time and turns into a lament for the honour of done-unto women. Verity knows that it will all have to be cut – the whole point is that he does not excuse himself for the way he is made, nor for being in love with both her and the other man. It is a play for the caring nineties, which is how she sold it, and any hint of prejudice will have to come out. Nevertheless, the scene has been a satisfying exercise. She might keep it for the next opus. With the dead way she has been feeling, by the time she comes to *write* the sodding next opus it will be out of the caring nineties and into the terrible twenty-ones – castrate the deviants and women should be seen and not heard . . .

She looks at the screen. 'That is quite enough for today,' she tells it. She knows that she will descend into cynicism if she continues. Tomorrow is another day. Oh *God*, why did she go and say *that*? She could weep. Well, she decides, if she is going to weep, she is not going to do it alone. It is six-fifteen, sun definitely over the yard-arm, and unless she is out, Margaret will be in. Verity finds her friend's burgeoning interest in the opposite sex fascinating, enlivening and – Verity is quite sure – doomed. When the doom finally reveals itself, Verity will be able to sit with Margaret and talk about it in five-minutes-for-you five-minutes-for-me style. It has always irritated her that her friend had avoided such emotional pitfalls. Female normality was to go into battle, win a few, lose a few, and then retire from the war to convalesce with an equally shell-shocked pal. Usually of course another battle soon follows, but in this case, Verity thinks to herself as she swings through Margaret's gate and up the path, she, Verity, will never start another one again. She doubts if Margaret will, either. Maybe it's the lemon juice but Verity is feeling extraordinarily sour.

While she waits for the door to be answered, she looks at the little front garden, which bears unmistakable signs of

activity. Not particularly attractive activity, but better than
none. Verity's garden, like her house, is individual and
stylish – stone urns, well-matched flowers and shrubs throughout the year, window boxes that do not wilt, interesting
varieties. The weeds gave up long ago. Margaret has shown
little inclination to garden beyond the most basic weeding,
so it comes as a surprise to see haphazard polyanthuses
dotted about the front patch, with slightly startled-looking
salvia plonked down between them. Margaret has selected
from the full range of polyanthus colours available, which is
rather a lot; not all of them are complementary.

Margaret opens the door. She has on a bathcap, leggings
and an ancient white T-shirt which shows sign of bloody
battle. As if somebody has attempted to cut her throat. The
mistress of the house is not – quite – looking her best.

'I saw it was you,' she says, reaching out to hoick Verity
in, closing the door swiftly.

'You've been gardening.' Verity says it as if it is an
accusation. Then she sniffs the air. 'What a beautiful smell.'
She looks about her. The Hoover, clearly in the process of
being used, lies in the hall, and everything has an air of
neatness and cleanliness – even the hall table is polished and
clear of debris save for a large blue and white bowl. Verity
peers in, sniffs again. 'Wonderful,' she says.

'Pot-pourri,' says Margaret absently. 'Verity, have you
got anything to unstop wastepipes?'

Verity taps the pockets of her jeans and her shirt. 'Must
have dropped it on the way here . . .'

'Be serious,' says Margaret. 'The downstairs sink is
blocked.'

'Bleach? Soda crystals?'

'I don't have either.'

'What's blocking it?'

'Grunge – tea-leaves. I don't know. Don't just ask the
quality of my blockages. *Do* something.'

Verity is frogmarched into the kitchen. Here it is not quite
so pristine. Indeed, here there are signs of dementia – open

cupboard doors; pans, bottles, brushes, screwdrivers all over the floor.

'Have you got a plunger?' Verity asks.

'Of course I've got a plunger.' Margaret hands it to her as if it were an ill-deserved bouquet.

Verity presses up and down at the sink. There is a rank smell and not much activity from the suction. She continues while looking over her shoulder, 'Why have you got blood dripping from your ears?'

Were it possible for someone with a hatchet in the head not to notice until a kindly neighbour pointed it out, Margaret's surprise would not seem so odd. As it is, Verity is amazed to see her friend put a hand up to her head, pat its bath-hatted horror once or twice, wail, '*Oh, my God*!' and vanish from the room.

Verity goes on using the plunger for a little while but to no avail. She gives up and starts hunting through the floor's detritus for something suitable to poke down the hole. And in her innermost secret musings she wishes she had a man with her to do this sort of thing; in her inner innermost, secret musings she is perfectly willing to acknowledge that they are better, much better, at tasks like this. During this secret betrayal of hers the doorbell rings. Verity is encouraged by a strangled, faraway hostess's voice to 'see who the hell that is'.

'We've met, haven't we?' Colin says, coming into the hall.

'We have,' says Verity firmly, tugging him in the direction of the kitchen, 'and we need you.'

Colin looks pleased until, as he reaches the open door, the pot-pourri's scented delight is replaced by something altogether more unpleasant.

Margaret, her towel-dried hair standing up in spikes that have a certain orange quality to them, comes into the kitchen to find Verity leaning on the sink unit, the doors of which are open to reveal the lower half of a man lying on his back with his legs stretched out.

'Oh,' says Verity, 'you've gone orange.'

'Orange-ish,' says Margaret peevishly. 'I was hoping it would look like Gloriana – a big fiery halo of auburn.'

Verity looks her usual doubtful self. 'More like London Brick Company.'

Gloriana refuses to be drawn. 'Damn stuff. I'll wash it again in a moment.' She advances, looks at the legs, cocks an eyebrow at Verity.

'Colin,' mouths Verity.

Margaret smiles. 'Colin,' she says cheerily, bending down and peering into the cupboard, 'I'd recognize that lower half anywhere.'

His upper half is crouched around a bucket and the whole makes a picture of which Dali would approve. His smile is a grimace.

'If you're going to get yourself a man,' he says acidly, 'you might get one who's good at this sort of thing . . .'

Margaret kicks his ankle, apparently playfully.

Verity says, 'Get a man, did you say, Colin? She's been getting them – loads of them. Why stop at one? And none of them lasts. Too picky, you see!'

Colin chuckles. '"Selective" is a kinder word, perhaps.' His voice is muffled and he is clearly straining to undo something. He continues, 'I didn't actually come round here to do this. Get off, you bugger, damn thing. I came to – ah, good, it's coming now – I came round to see how you – one more turn, I think. Don't turn on the water . . .' He laughs. 'To see how you made out with that Oxford date? The one who sent you his – I SAID DON'T TURN ON THE WATER, YOU SILLY COW.' But Margaret has. Only a little. Just enough to cause a diversion. She hands him a length of kitchen towel, bending over the open door, and puts her hand over her mouth quickly to stifle her laughter. She apologizes as convincingly as she can. Colin's face is bespattered with unpleasant, unidentifiable liquid matter. She gives him a warning look which is wasted since his eyes are closed.

'What on earth did you do that for?' asks Verity. But she suppresses her own laughter. In fact, both women, confronting each other's suppressions, can sustain it no longer. They hold their sides in silent, uproarious mirth, bending from the waist, trying not to catch each other's eye. Margaret tries to form words of more abject apology but each attempt explodes.

Well, she counsels herself, she *told* him to be discreet. Now, as he sits up and picks U-bend detritus from his eyebrows, he will realize she was serious.

Verity is not to be dissuaded. She knew all those dates of Margaret's were more serious than she said. Verity's heart sinks. She has a nasty feeling the blood bond has completely fallen away. Clues? Margaret doing garden. Margaret cleaning house. Margaret dyeing hair. Verity smells man, and man of duration.

'What happened in Oxford?' she demands, once Colin has righted the plumbing and gone upstairs to wash, muttering about women's incapacity for technological understanding.

'Hang on,' says Margaret. 'Colin will need something clean to put on.' And she runs up the stairs after him.

'I can give you one of Roger's old shirts,' she calls through the bathroom door. 'Open up.'

He does so. She takes his dirty linen and hands him an old schoolteacher check. Through tight lips she hisses that if he so much as breathes a word about advertisements and photographs to Verity she will never forgive him and nor will he get his own shirt back, which she will tear into strips and use as bunting for the day of his funeral. Colin, disadvantaged with soapy face, grunts agreement and closes the door.

'Shall we have tea?' she says, switching on the kettle. While they wait for it to boil, she asks how Verity is. Verity says she is much more keen to know how Margaret is and what *she* has been up to – that irritating little phrase again that turns every sodding activity into playgroup stuff – but Margaret insists that Verity start first.

Although Verity is keen to know about Oxford, the bait proves irresistible. She tells Margaret all about Mark's latest sally, which they both agree is not on.

'Just tell him to leave you alone,' says Margaret.

'I have,' says Verity. She always feels a lot stronger about it when in the company of her friend.

This is their usual opening conversation on the topic. Margaret then goes on to say, 'Well, you've got to say it and mean it.' She is about to do this when Colin arrives. Counselling is immediately forgotten as Margaret crumples with laughter. 'Oh God,' she says, 'Colin, you look strangely different . . .' Roger's shirt has defeated Colin's usual stylishness and made him look like a harassed history master. Margaret laughs again.

'What do you think about lonely hearts columns?' Colin asks Verity very politely.

Margaret stops laughing instantly and says, 'Colin, your exceptional sense of elegance is not at all diminished by my ex-lover's garment.' And she keeps her face straight after that.

'Colin?' says Verity. 'You're a man, aren't you?'

'Well, yes,' he says, amused but cautious.

'I mean – why do you all do it? Why, when you have a perfectly good relationship with someone, do you *still* go and flirt with other women and eye them up and down and then forget to tell the one you are with that she looks nice so that the whole thing disintegrates, and when it *has* disintegrated, then you want the original back?'

Colin puts up his hands. 'Whoa there,' he says. 'That's a hell of a lot packed into one sentence.' He pauses, thinking. 'I don't think all men do those things.' He thinks again. 'Do we?'

'You certainly did most of them,' says Margaret, pouring out the tea.

'What? To you?'

'Well, no. Not to me. You didn't have time to get around to it. But you did it to your wife and presumably' – she hands him a mug – 'you continue to do it since you go through women at a rate of knots . . .'

'*You're* not doing so badly,' says Verity.

'I mean *he* does it when the relationship has been going on for some time. Don't you?'

They both look at him. He is faced with two pairs of wide female eyes whose wideness requires an answer.

'Perhaps I am just looking for the right woman.'

'For fifteen years? Oh, come on, Colin,' Margaret snorts. 'Some of them must be coming round for a second inspection.'

'What was it you accused me of?'

'Well, not you in particular – just men in general.' Verity counts on her fingers. 'One. You flirt with other women even while in a stable and happy relationship. Don't you?'

Colin sips his tea. He thinks. Eventually he says, 'Yes.'

'Well, why?'

There are those eyes again.

He shrugs. 'I don't really know. Because it's fun.' He nods, as much to himself as to them. 'That's it. It's fun – and it's harmless.'

'How can it be harmless if it upsets your partner?'

He shrugs again. 'That's her problem.'

The two pairs of eyes engage each other; if eyes could sigh despairingly, these would.

'What about eyeing women up and down? You know – sort of sexual assessment? All men are potential rapists?'

Colin puts down his mug and looks unamused. 'If you are going to get all strident feminist about this, I'm not playing. I'm attempting to answer your questions honestly and just because I, or the men I know, like to look at other women, it does *not* mean we're bent on violence. Frankly I can't think of anything worse than a frightened, unwilling woman. I like mine very confident and very willing. Most of us do.'

Margaret feels a little buzz in her middle anatomy. Very confident and very willing, she thinks. *Oh crikey*, as Madcap Molly of the Fourth would say. She meets Simon tomorrow and it is his *birthday*. For some reason she remembers the old joke about men, birthdays and sex. According to Max Miller and his comic descendants, a chap in a long-term, last-gasp marriage can still expect a birthday coupling even if his wife continues to read her Jackie Collins over his shoulder while complying with natal indulgence. And like any comedy, Margaret is sure, the joke contains a grain or more of truth. If Andy Capp expects it then a new lover must certainly expect it too. They are going to do It tomorrow, without a doubt, and she had better be good. What did Colin say? 'Confident and willing'? She doesn't feel it. She wonders if Simon feels a bit nervous too. She doubts this. He didn't seem the sort who would.

Beyond her thoughts Colin and Verity are still going at it.

'We are built to be permanently aware of sex,' says Colin.

'Would you,' Verity asks, her eyes wide and swimmy, 'flirt with other women in front of your lover of only a year?'

Colin, being a man and good at this sort of thing, takes a sharp right-hand turn. 'Mine never last that long.'

'That's probably why,' says Margaret waspishly.

Verity continues. 'And would you forget important things, like birthdays, anniversaries – that sort of thing?'

'Anniversaries,' says Colin, 'are strictly for married couples. I don't hold with them. Birthdays – well, I agree, that's a bit different. They are special.'

Margaret's heart sinks. Very definitely they will have to do It tomorrow. Where? Here? There? – Wherever 'there' is . . .

Somewhat absently she says, 'Do you expect sex on your birthday, Colin?'

He laughs uncertainly. 'This year's in particular? Or generally?'

'Generally.'

He thinks. 'That's an odd sort of question.'

'But do you?'

He thinks some more. 'I suppose, now you come to mention it, I probably do. If I'm going out with someone' – he allows a modicum of immodesty – 'which I usually am. Why?'

Margaret adds water to the pot. She can feel that both

Verity and Colin are looking at her expectantly. 'I mean,' she says to the kettle, 'what if it was only your – oh, I don't know – let's say *second* date?'

'No point in hanging around,' Colin replies. 'All this wooing stuff went out with the ark, or should have. You can't have it both ways. Either you want the hearts and flowers treatment and are prepared to continue in second place to us, or you come up front and be counted. And that applies to all things. Not just sex.'

'You're getting pompous,' says Margaret.

'Second date?' muses Colin. 'Oh, *I see*. It's Oxford's birthday next time ... Oh well, then. I think in those circumstances I'd expect it even more. After all, you've dispensed with the uncertainties. You've offered yourself to be an item straight away. So why hang around?'

'Who *is* this Oxford?' asks Verity.

'Colin,' says Margaret, 'are you serious?'

He has the grace to look a little humbled, but only a little. 'Sort of,' he says, but there is an edge of teasing in his voice.

'Margaret,' says Verity, 'are you going to tell?'

'There's nothing to tell, Verity.'

'Well, is it a man?'

Margaret nods.

Verity tries to look pleased. She fails. 'Where did you meet?'

Margaret realizes that if she wants to remain on good terms with her neighbour and friend, she must be more informative. However, she can equivocate quite easily. Fortunately, Verity has not asked how she met him, only where – and that's easy. She moves to the kitchen table. Verity, following like a hungry cat, sits down opposite her. Colin, being male, continues to stand up. Endurance.

'In a pub in Oxford,' says Margaret.

'A pub in Oxford?' Verity exclaims, as if Margaret had said a strip joint in Tooting. 'What on earth were you doing in a pub in Oxford?'

'Meeting someone?' offers Colin.

'Shut up,' says Verity to Colin. She turns back to Margaret. 'Hmm?'

Margaret shoots Colin a look of serious warning. 'Oxford has a very good museum,' she says. Which is quite correct.

'I wish you'd told me you were going out for a jaunt to Oxford,' says Verity wistfully, 'I'd have loved to come.'

Colin guffaws. 'Now *that's* a thought . . . Why didn't you take your friend? Old meanie.'

Verity gives Colin a grateful look. 'Well, it's too late now.' She returns her gaze to her friend. 'So, you went into this pub in Oxford, and there he was and . . . what?'

'Well, that's it, really. We talked, had some sandwiches together, and then he asked me out on his birthday.'

'When?'

'Tomorrow.'

'And you're going to have sex with him? Just like that?' Verity is aghast. She puts her hands under her chin and lowers her voice to what she assumes is a confiding and counselling tone. 'You really must be more careful. I mean, you don't know anything about him . . .'

'By gosh!' says Colin. 'That's true. You should ask him to write it all down for you, send a photograph – check his credentials. Never thought of that . . .'

'Colin,' says Margaret, 'haven't you got a home to go to? *Now?*'

'No, he's right,' says Verity. 'You need to be really careful nowadays. I hope you're meeting him in a public place?'

'He's coming here to pick me up. Look, what is all this? I am almost forty, you know.'

She twirls her mug in her hands. She knows she has a perfect right to tell Verity to stop the third degree. She's tempted to tell her the truth, but Verity's reaction to this apparently common or garden pick-up is bad enough. If she were to know how Margaret had really met Oxford – the name might as well stick – she'd go into orbit. Margaret has quite enough on her mind with regard to the morrow, without dealing with all that 'How could you not tell your best friend?' stuff. Verity plays the 'best friend' card when she is down, but it is little in evidence when she is up again. With Tintoretto in mind, Margaret does not feel bitter about this – only aware, which saves her from the blackmail.

Margaret looks at the clock. Half past seven. This time tomorrow, she thinks, he will be ringing my doorbell and we'll be off the starting blocks. She wishes she were more elated, but she feel distinctly nervous – and neither of her visitors is helping. One more sally from Colin, she promises herself, and he'll get more than a few tea-leaves up his nostrils.

Verity says, 'I can't believe you've done that. You've actually told him where you live and you're going to let him come here.'

'Yes,' says Margaret. 'At half past seven tomorrow, actually. It may be the last you ever see of me.'

'And how do you know he isn't a rapist?' asks Verity, dismissing the attempt at humour.

Colin is torn between making another ironic quip and speaking up for the male of the species. Fortunately for his nostrils, he chooses the latter. 'I think that's tabloid hysteria.'

'Nuts!' says Verity. 'Tell that to Rape Crisis.'

The kitchen is looking a mess, the upstairs isn't Hoovered (Why the upstairs? she shudders and asks herself), the bathroom needs cleaning and the back garden looks like a Paul Nash view of Ypres. There is much to be done.

'He isn't a rapist, Verity. He's an architect,' says Margaret. 'And I think he's very nice.' Both statements are true, which is heartening. Margaret will fight back. 'Besides, *you* met Mark in the post office and – as I recall – your bedroom curtains didn't open very early after your *first* date . . .'

'And look at me now,' moans Verity. Which somehow seems to be relevant, but isn't.

After they have gone, Margaret continues to tidy. She has reassured Verity, she thinks, and Colin's knife-edged taunts have died down. As the house emerges into a fresh and neat appearance, Margaret feels better. Mustn't forget to change the bedding, she thinks, and to put on something more stylish than the faded roses on beige from Barkers which were in their sale, draped in the window, and so cheap it was impossible not to buy. Roger had never minded them, but Oxford undoubtedly would. She recalls his perplexed look at her mention of Sex. 'It'll happen . . .' Ah, she thinks, one thing for him to say that in the desensualized atmosphere of a lunchtime pub and mean it – quite another after wine, good food, a celebratory 'Where's my birthday treat, then?' atmosphere, and the presence of one who has advertised for a lover. With Roger it had been easy: sometimes the bed didn't even look disturbed.

Verity shakes hands with Colin at Margaret's gate and saunters off home thoughtfully. Colin drives away feeling that all this talk of sex has made him a little warm around the trousers. He might just call in on the girl from the chocolate shop whom he has seen a few times. Then he remembers, looks down, shudders . . . He is wearing Roger's old shirt. Home and change. Then out into the night. Hunting and fun. Advertising? Who needs it?

Chapter Nineteen

We should make a date to speak on the phone. Either I'm out
or you're out and you never say where. I'm thinking of you.
I'm also determined to get Dad a show in London. Any ideas
for venues?

••••••••••••••••••••••••••••••

I found myself skirting round the bed as if it were a monster,
beds being so blatantly symbolic. I suppose it *is* the best
place for sex because of its comfort, softness and convenience
for sleep afterwards (if not during, with reference to my
immediate ex), though it seems to me a curiously domestic
item on which to begin rampant carnality. Mine was about
five years old and apart from a few limp tusslings with
Roger, had led a blameless life.

I duly changed the bedding to something less floral, eyed
its square familiarity, and shook my head. It somehow didn't
look the part. Well, I thought, seated at my dressing-table
with about half an hour to go, if *it* didn't, *I* had certainly
better. Much smudging and wiping followed to no avail –
my face looked as much a palette as a painting. So I washed
it clean and, with about five minutes left, just bunged on the
usual. Besides, I didn't need too much makeup, given that I
was wearing the Very Not Much Else Pre-Teen Frou-Frou
and the BSL with the DP. And my hair had changed colour
radically. I put out of my mind the London Brick Company.
Sour grapes. It was the aureole of Gloriana to my mind –

and, anyway, his letter hadn't said, 'No redheads,' had it?

We had spoken on the telephone briefly to confirm everything. He had said he was looking forward to seeing me again. I said ditto. The word itself: *ditto*. Not exactly romantic, I thought as I put down the phone. Only out of practice, I counselled myself. You'll get better at it. At what? Oh! At the whole desirable thing. The notion that it *was* a desirable thing required some work because it was beginning to feel more like a pretty dreadfully contrived thing. Ah well, cold feet were inevitable, I suppose . . .

I put my mind to something else while I waited. During the day I had been to the Auerbach show and met Fisher there. He was all smiles but not very complimentary about my hair. 'A little bright' was the way he put it. But as I pointed out, compared to some of the Auerbachs, it looked quite subdued.

'I'm having a relationship,' I said rather proudly. 'And I want to conduct it in much the same way as Elizabeth Tudor – hair and all,' I added defiantly.

Fisher is very good at not looking surprised at anything. He merely said, 'She was the quintessential baroque masterpiece – all ornament hiding the structure. A rose-tinted dissembler with a will of iron.'

'Exactly,' I said.

'Who's playing Essex?'

I tapped my nose.

We walked around for a while. It was a good show and Saskia had been quite right to remind me to go. It would not do to lose sight of the person I would always be underneath all these metaphorical ruffs and farthingales. While we walked, Fisher told me, with an extremely wicked look on his face, that it was all-round stalemate on the Mortimer collection and that I was not to do anything with my Picasso portfolio for the time being. I must do nothing until I had consulted him first.

'In every respect?' I asked. 'Or only in the matter of my pictures?'

'Life, art – I deal in them all,' he said wryly. 'And nowadays it seems there is a monetary value attached to both. In the old days, you know, I not only bought and sold pictures, but I matched what I sold to the client. No use selling a Rembrandt etching to a woman who really wanted something with blue in it to match the curtains, however rich she might be. Nor a lyrical Lanyon to somebody living in immaculate high tech. And so on. It was as much that side of things I enjoyed as seeing the noughts on the invoices. Now we have cheque book dealers and collectors who view things as investments. Valuations are much less painful than seeing a beautiful, let us say, Matisse scooped up and hung on a wall for the chattering classes to admire for its record price and then ignore over dinner. I should say Mrs Mortimer was one of the last few collectors with soul. And I'll be damned if Linda and Julius will mock that.'

'You've seen them?'

'Oh yes. I'm a friend of the family now.' He laughed at my expression. 'I *love* the home counties in spring . . . And, as I said to Linda only the other day, as we prune in the garden, so we can prune an art collection to make it better and stronger. I'm cataloguing and considering and taking my time. I have her in my palm.' He held it out flat and then suddenly squeezed it tight. 'Swimming-pool – really! Silly woman.'

'You sound positively venomous.'

He took my arm and led me towards a series of later Auerbachs. 'He goes on in strength to the end,' Fisher said, pointing at the series, 'and has the courage aforethought, or simply the need, still to take risks.'

'I'd rather have these than my Picasso,' I said.

He tapped my arm again and smiled his wicked smile. 'Ah, now you are being greedy. *That* I cannot do . . .'

We walked on.

'I've heard from Saskia,' he said. 'She's bent on getting Dickie a show over here.'

I inspected the paint on a canvas a little more closely than was strictly necessary – a thing only nervous amateurs do at exhibitions.

'It'll die down,' I said. 'Once she's back.'

I bought the catalogue for Sassy and posted it with a short, uninformative note. *Any* daughter would think her father's work brilliant. It didn't mean that it was. Fisher would soon sort it out. He had lost interest, more or less, in the contemporary art scene. Oh yes, she would forget all about it once she was back. April was a long, long way away. Meanwhile – there was some fun to be had. Oxford, Essex – it was all the same – and I liked the idea of baroque.

At about three minutes after half past seven the doorbell rang. I noted the three minutes because such things were small clues to the persona I could expect. Have no expectations, I reminded myself, as I walked fairly casually down the stairs, the skirt rustling above my knees and the stretchy lace clinging perhaps a little too tightly. Have no expectations.

I opened the door. Had I been the owner of expectations, I would have been forced to let them go. For standing on the doorstep, along with Oxford, and slightly in front of him, looking distinctly *resolute*, was Verity. At whom he was smiling politely.

'Hello,' she said gaily, 'I've just introduced myself.'

I grimaced at her, righted myself, and smiled warmly over her head. The smile was returned, all innocence. How could he possibly know what Verity suspected of him?

Now, here is a conundrum. When your new man is standing next to your friend, how do you manage to be unwelcoming to her so that he doesn't think of you as some kind of treacherous monster? Of course, I wanted to say, 'Piss off, Verity,' but instead, for the sake of my standing in Oxford's eyes, I smiled sweetly and said, 'Come in' to both of them.

I held open the door. Oxford passed by first, but before I could hiss a valedictory message over my shoulder at Verity he turned round to say something complimentary. I had no idea what he was complimenting because my brain was entirely engaged in hoping for Verity's demise. Also because she was hissing at me that I was showing too much cleavage, which is a bit thick coming from her. Her breasts seem to start just below her collarbone in a decent set of half grapefruits, and she's never been backward in showing the pips.

By the time we were in the sitting-room Verity was a fact of life and I had to introduce them. Verity smiled, shook his hand and scrutinized him closely.

'You have a mole on your left cheek,' she pronounced and scrutinized it as if preparing an Identikit.

I left them to it. 'Just going to get my *coat*,' I called as I made for the sitting-room door. 'Verity, did you want something?'

'Well, I wouldn't say no to a drink,' she said, which was not what I meant at all.

Neither would I, I thought. I fumed on the stairs and kept my voice light. 'Simon?'

'No thanks,' he called cheerily. 'But don't let me stop you.'

'I think we ought to go,' I said when I returned with my coat on. I sounded horribly like a henpecker, and I added that it was Simon's birthday. Verity, if you please, said that she already knew this because I had told her yesterday. Then, if you double please, she fixed him with a chirpy look and said that she and I had no secrets (That's all you know, I thought) and she knew *all* about him.

'Did you want anything?' I asked her again pointedly. No, she was just passing and had been alerted by seeing a man on my doorstep, she said. 'We are very Neighbourhood Watch here,' she added significantly.

Somehow I managed to get them out of the house. But Verity stuck close and it seemed not impossible she was going to join us. But when they shook hands, I said a very firm 'Goodbye', which gave her no chance.

Even so, before going, she did a circuit of Oxford's car, an unobtrusive kind of vehicle, and made of it what an archaeologist might make of calcified Dinosaur droppings.

'Hmm,' she said. 'Renault, silver grey, H reg.' She read out the number-plate slowly. 'Easily remembered,' she said to him, gimlet-eyed. He looked rather blank at this but showed himself to be game by saying, 'Yes, I suppose it is.' And I dived into the car.

So much for the beginning, I thought, though I was rather more worried about the ending. Verity was perfectly capable of borrowing a ladder and popping her head round the bedroom window. I didn't think I would be able, if asked, to keep my mind on rampant carnality *chez moi* that night. Sometimes, despite myself, I yearned for Verity to get back with the dreaded Mark and just leave me alone.

I gave him a small book of Inigo Jones sketches, usefully on sale at the Hayward that day, and a card of Turner's *Tintern*.

'I'm touched,' he said.

'They'll be a bit out of place in the Nicaraguan jungle.'

·'They'll be a bit of England.'

'Wales, in the case of *Tintern*.' And then, because I could not resist the poke, I added, 'Right continent at least.'

Conversation was a great deal easier this time around, though a little probing about his marriage elicited a rapid shut-down. Quite nicely done, skilfully in fact, but a shut-down nevertheless. Same for 'Why Nicaragua?' Fair enough, I decided. I would not pry. This was a jaunt for a year, not an invitation for life. So I could just sit back and enjoy the simplicity of it all.

'I never married, for which I am jolly thankful,' I said. 'Given the ratio of misery to happiness.'

'And so you select a lover like this whenever you feel so inclined? That's enviably positive.'

'Oh no. This is the first time. You see before you a lonely hearts virgin.'

He laughed but with a distinct edginess.

'I mean that I've only had one bash at it . . .' Too late, I winced inwardly at the romantic delicacy of my words. In these gauzy days of first love here I was sounding like an old colonial major. 'And you?'

'You are the only one I have met. I liked your smile.'

'What if I'd turned out to be horrible?'

'I'd have gone for no. 2 reserve.'

I felt a nasty bristling sensation around the back of my neck. Damn Darwin. I concentrated very hard on the froth of my cappuccino, running the spoon back and forth – a very soothing motion under the circumstances. Despite everything there is that residual worm of possession. I had no idea what my voice would come out like when next I spoke – somewhere between a hiss and a squeak, I suspected.

'Hmm,' I said, noncommittally, sipping the coffee.

'Anyway, here we are.' He raised his glass. 'I don't like that side of things. A bit like a cattle market.'

'Catalogue,' I said. 'And you have to assume that the people who go in for it are as tough as you are.'

He nodded. 'To the year ahead.' He smiled. I smiled. 'May we both get what we want.' We chinked glasses and drank. The hackles went down a bit.

We lingered over more cappuccino and I asked him if he had ever read Ovid on the matter of lovers. He looked a bit taken aback, as people often do when asked if they have read Roman poetry. I really do not see why. After all, there is great comfort to be had, when you are floundering around feeling like the first ever twerp, to find out that people were doing and feeling exactly the same two thousand years ago.

'He's very funny about it all – how to get the girl, how to keep her, what she's probably thinking, how to go about giving gifts and what to expect in return, *quid pro quo* . . .'

'Sounds very cynical.'

'Not at all. It's a blueprint and honest. He says what's in his mind really, as opposed to what others pretend. In the erotic poems, he gives away great chunks of advice which is both hilarious and painful at the same time. Like if you have a married lover and must dine with both her and her husband, when it is impossible to touch or speak of love and you are on fire, you must devise a system of body language instead. He says,

> '"When you are thinking of the last time we made love
> together
> Touch your rosy cheek with one elegant thumb.
> If you are cross with me but can't say so, then pinch the
> bottom of your ear lobe . . .
> When you yearn for your husband to suffer some well-
> merited misfortune
> Place your hands on the table as though in prayer . . . Slip
> neat wine in his glass if you get the chance . . . If he passes
> out comfortably, drowned in sleep and liquor,
> We must improvise as occasion dictates . . ."'

He leaned forward, interested. Ovid always interests people – he's so wicked. 'Could you remember to do all that? I mean, suppose you got something wrong? Pinched an earlobe when you meant to make praying hands?'

'Doesn't matter, really. The game's the thing.'

'Is it?' He was looking at me very steadily.

'It is,' I said firmly.

'We understand that?'

'We do.'

He leaned back, just about as relieved, I should say, as I was. 'Well one thing's for sure,' he said, as our bill arrived, 'you can't go touching your rosy cheek with your elegant thumb with me yet.'

As Aurora Leigh, that talented orphan girl with the creditable pen, observed, 'We have hearts within/Warm, live, improvident, indecent hearts . . .' Well might she say it – and Ms Browning report it – for despite our *knowing* for a medical and biological *fact* that hearts are no more likely to be the seat of emotion than ankles, nevertheless – and at this particular moment I could vouch for it – they *certainly* feel as if they are. Mine went another one of those almighty bumps and my thumb felt several stages short of elegance. As for my rosy cheek, I had absolutely no doubt it was iridescently puce as an Auerbach.

Lord, *Lord*, sex is such an item . . .

We held hands walking back to the car, which felt all right if slightly teenage. And I suppose because the Pinot Grigio had been as good as the company, I felt emboldened, and a little vino-veritassed, to say, 'You haven't commented on how I look. My hair, for instance . . .'

He stood still and stared. 'Oh yes I did,' he said, 'but with your friend there I don't think you heard. You look . . . um . . . very bold.'

'Bloody Verity,' I growled, and the Pinot Grigio loosening the treacherous monster's tongue at last. 'She's so *nosey*.'

'She certainly took a lot of interest in my car,' he said. 'Odd for a woman. At the risk of being sexist, you're usually concerned with more interesting things than tail-lights and number-plates . . .'

'Oh,' I said, 'Verity's a *writer*.'

That seemed to satisfy him.

'She was very much in evidence,' he said cautiously.

'Ah well,' I said, 'the thing is she doesn't exactly *know* about the advertisements. She thinks we just sort of . . . met . . . in a pub. So she's a bit suspicious. Hence turning up on the doorstep, and all that stuff about your mole.'

He laughed. 'Why don't you want to tell her?'

'Because she will disapprove. Because it will spoil the game.' I sounded exactly like a petulant child but couldn't stop now. 'Part of the game is that everybody else must believe in it. They really won't if I say I got you out of a catalogue. Even *I* might not. There's something about being surrounded by believers. You catch their faith – like measles and Billy Graham.'

Why did I say that? What on earth did the Evangelical movement have to do with anything? I was appearing about as romantic as yesterday's cold crumpet. But you know how it is – here comes that incautious hurtling again. 'And then there's Jill – the one we're going to stay with . . .'

'We are?' he said.

'Sorry. I haven't told you about that yet. But yes. She's my oldest and dearest friend and she lives in Northumberland and is a total romantic. This . . .' – I gestured – 'this could probably kill her . . .' I bent my elbow against the car and leaned my head in my hand. 'Well, not exactly. But it would seriously dent her.'

'Surely not?' he said.

'You don't know her. She has a market garden and thinks that baby leeks are the offspring of two adult leeks who are deeply in love.'

He laughed as he kissed me, which is quite a strange physical arrangement. However, putting out of my head the thought that the kiss might be a way of shutting me up and that a restaurant car park was not exactly Venus's shrine, I responded gamely and it was a success. I got that melty feeling inside that you are supposed to get, and – perhaps the best test of all – I was sorry when it was over. Funny how men, even quite ordinarily weak men, go all strong when they clinch. It must be the muscles seizing up in reaction. I didn't mind being held tightly because my ear was against his chest and I could feel his heart doing an Aurora Leigh too. It had been very nice, producing enough glowing embers for a good blaze ahead. I was perfectly happy to stay like that for a while. So why, *why* did I say, through the intimate beating of his heart, 'Well, thank God that's over . . .'

Not unnaturally he stood back and stared at me in wonder.

I explained as best I could that I had meant only that it was yet another hurdle between us negotiated. He replied, not unreasonably, and after which I felt suitably chastened, that he had not thought of it as a hurdle himself, more as an erotic part of the ritual . . . I agreed, very lamely, and then looked up at him. We stared at each other very hard, real deep-eyed stuff, forgetting the asphalt, the headlights, the accelerating cars.

'Are we ready for this?' I asked.

His eyes, my eyes, both held hesitancy. He thought for a bare wisp of time and then said, 'I don't know. Are you?' To which I said the same. And we went on staring at each other until suddenly he stepped back and looked me up and down, from frou-frou to *décolleté* to *les cheveux oranges*, and said, 'You look' – he touched my neck, which made me shiver – 'very fuckable.'

'Yes,' I said, looking around me suddenly and realizing we were in a car park, 'but not here.'

Of the blaze ahead we said little. In fact, driving back we said little about anything. Not a frosty silence, merely a thinking one. Once he asked me how I felt and I said the truth, which was that I felt nervous. 'Me too,' he said. I then came clean and told him all about the mundanity of my bed. It sounded extremely weird to my ears but seemed to make sense to him.

'We do have time,' he said.

'Yes,' I agreed, but I was sitting bolt upright, tense as a cat in danger.

When he stopped the car at my door, he turned to me and was smiling again. 'Perhaps we'd better knock on your friend's door – to show her that you are whole and unharmed.'

It seemed a much funnier and more welcome thing to do than pile into my house and my clean, brooding bedding. But not really practical. So into my house we went. And I suddenly realized that the problem *was* the house, although I was not at all sure what. Maybe it just wasn't romantic enough? Could it be something so silly as that?

'This is a very prosaic setting,' I muttered, turning on the kitchen light, thinking that at least Verity's kitchen had an aura about it. Mine really did look dull. I turned to him. 'Know what?' I said, 'I think I have just discovered that I'm a romantic.'

He laughed and sat down at the table. He put his chin in his hand and looked at me, very sideways. 'Well,' he said, 'you could have fooled me.' A response which, given my record to date, was hardly surprising.

'All the same,' I said, sitting opposite him, emulating his pose, 'all the same, I am.'

The upshot was that we had more coffee, talked some more, kissed and fumbled around a bit, let Verity speak into the answerphone – I knew she would call, I just knew it – and he suggested that since we were apparently going away to Jill's very soon anyway, we could stop off on the way at a fancy hotel. *His* choice. The implication was that, since I had committed him to going away without so much as asking if he wanted to (which he did), at the very least he should decide the right place in which to begin our loverhood in earnest.

In earnest, I told the chaste pillows as I pulled back the duvet later. Silly cow, I told my reflection as I undressed. All the same, I was glad. It seemed much more of an adventure like this. And if there is one thing I do know from my experience of hotels, it's that they are very sexy places: you can be thoroughly irresponsible, quite anonymous, and somebody else has to wash up the glasses and remake the bed. As I slid off to sleep in my solitary fresh-Persilled mound, I found that I was smiling. If he didn't get sex on his birthday, then I should make sure he got a birthday of sex some other time and soon . . .

Chapter Twenty

It was lovely to talk to you at last. You are probably right to be only cautiously optimistic about getting a show together for next year but I mean to try. Have a good time at Jill's. I had a sudden tickle of homesickness at the thought of the season over there. I bet you're feeling quite lonely really. You could come over here. You could see for yourself how nice he is then.

••••••••••••••••••••••••••••••

Verity gave me a long, long lecture on how I should be cautious – to the point of not seeing Oxford any more. I got the distinct feeling that she preferred me as a female guru of the 'single and loving it' kind. I decided that the best thing would be to show her how it can work and be good, encourage her to unfold her wings and dare again. After all, even if love was not for ever, it could be good in its allotted span. I had no expectations, I told her, none whatsoever. She said, 'Hmm, I bet,' so that it was on the tip of my tongue to come right out with it and say *why* I had none. We reached a stalemate, or compromise, depending on which side of positivism you choose, and the days very nicely flashed by. This, suddenly, was living.

By the most curious quirk of female response I found that romantic excitement led to an outbreak of housework fever, and I spent a lot of my time tidying up. At first, I worried that it was a sign of the nesting instinct, but then I decided that it probably had more to do with clearing out the past.

It was as if I had been asleep for many years and had to start from scratch. Pregnant air – the house contained it. The house, a somewhat prissy individual, was sitting back on her matronly bottom and waiting for me to strike at her heart. I was extremely glad to be able to report to her that at least the first night of Picasso-type romping would not take place in *her* admonishing lap.

Saskia had left her room in immaculate shape, uncharacteristically, and I had only to water the plants or open a window for the new spring air to sweeten its staleness once in a while. The photographs that she had extracted from me sat in homely display on her shelves and I looked very hard at one or two of these. Somewhere my psyche seemed to sense a rush of air – as if a great and ponderous bird were slowly beating its wings, about to take off and swoop down on me. I had felt its first faint flappings when Saskia decided to meet her father, heard as well as felt its beat as her letters and phone calls multiplied, and I knew that when she returned here, the beaten air would go swirling round, churning things up, settling them all back in a different and dangerous order. Dangerous? Why did I think it could be dangerous? To what was the danger? Stirred air settles again, in time, and leaves no trace of its motion.

In one of the photographs of Lorna I used to see a plea for vengeance – if not a characteristic of hers in life, then certainly one that I allowed to her in death. Now, suddenly, I saw Saskia's eyes in hers – not surprising since they were now not far apart in age – and Saskia's eyes were pleading for something altogether different.

No more housework today, I decided, and took myself out into the fine warm air instead.

Colin and I had lunch in a pub by the river. I said that the metaphor it presented of the flowing water of life was made more appropriate by my sitting with one old flame and discussing the new. 'Come off it,' Colin replied, with a dismissive – and offensive – wave of his hand. 'You can't dress *this* up so lyrically.'

I reminded him that Ovid had used a river several times to illustrate just such a fantasy, and that he had been among the most pragmatic of poet/lover combinations going.

> '"Rivers know all about love themselves.
> Inachus pined, we're told, for Melia the Bithynian
> At her touch his icy shallows thawed."

'He gives a whole list of tough cookies whose lives are reborn by the eternal water's flow.'

'Knickers to that,' said Colin, raising his manly pint. 'All I'm saying is that you got this man out of a newspaper and you can't go turning the prose of that into poetry. You can try' – he swigged again – 'but even you won't be able to succeed with that. *That's* poetry, *this* is life.'

'I can succeed with anything, Colin,' I told him, 'because this is my fantasy. And since this is *my* fantasy – ' I stared out over the water, gleaming seductively in the sunlight, the brightness hiding any noisome objects that dipped and bobbed through its surface – 'it will be exactly as I say.'

'It'll end in tears,' he said defiantly. 'You should come a little more up to date in your literary leanings and think about Emma. Couldn't see the wood for the trees.'

I laughed. 'Do you mean Roger's new lady?' I asked innocently.

'I mean Jane Austen's female blind spot. As well you know.'

'You just don't want me to be any different from you and the hundreds of others who just muddle through instead of taking their destiny in their own hands and doing something *positive*.'

'Emma Woodhouse,' he said. 'Would you like another half?'

While I waited, closing my eyes to the warm sun and feeling very much better now that I was out and about and not up in Sassy's room dealing with history's dust, I suddenly thought about the Nicaraguan question. There is absolutely no point in a man telling a woman that there is something pertinent to his *modus operandi* which he is obliged to keep from her. She may well sit there and nod sagely and appear to keep thinking only of the lasagne verde, but eventually she will be mighty curious, as I was now. What happened to his wife? What made him choose to go to the very depths of hell like a character out of Waugh? He was so *nice* – such an ordinary seeming man, really. So what could it be?

Colin's advice was to forget all about it. Concentrate on the here and now. If he was going, he had a reason. If he didn't want to talk about it, he also had a reason. I envy men their simplicity. He was right, of course, and to concentrate on the here and now was exactly what I aimed to do.

'Talking of which,' Colin said, 'how is the here and now?' He winked across his cheese roll. I told him that we were saving that for a more romantic setting, so that we got it absolutely right first time. He stopped chewing and eyed me in amazement.

'You've gone soft,' he said.

'Romantic,' I corrected. 'And in a relationship between two *mature* people, it's perfectly easy. It's only when you mess about with giggly things fifteen years your junior it gets messy.' I leaned across and fixed my eyes on him. 'Why not try someone a little nearer your age? It could be fun. You could advertise. It does work . . .'

Colin's eyes bulged. 'Not on your life,' he said. 'I'm staying just the way I am.'

'You'll be wearing a condom in your nineties,' I said scornfully.

'I certainly hope so,' he laughed. 'And I am not being Emma Woodhoused out of it.'

When I got home, I wrote to Jill. Because I didn't want to lie to her, my letter was fairly restrained. There was a new man in my life and I was bringing him up with me. I knew she would be pleased. Then I lay on my unseductive bed watching television, feeling pretty smug. It was nice to have a man out there for a while. And Colin, content in his bimbos, was absurd. Emma Woodhouse, indeed. I was surprised he had even read it.

Chapter Twenty-one

*It isn't very pleasant but Judith and Dad are just about
managing to do it gracefully. All her things have been collected.
What went wrong? Judith says he just never let her get close.
Dad just smiled when I asked him. Things move on, he said. It
doesn't seem to affect his work. Nothing does. Now there is a
lesson.*

●●●●●●●●●●●●●●●●●●●●●●●●●●●●●●

Jill stands, holding the letter, staring out of the window,
dazzled by the morning sun. David puts his head round the
door and says that he is going now. Back at seven. Don't
forget the oil in the car. She hears the door bang, watches
this husband of hers walk across the gravel of the drive, open
his car door, struggle with it slightly in the fierce wind, sit,
close it and start the engine. Gone at last. She sees the fields,
the new growth, buffeted and sparkling in the cold, sharp
sunshine. Beyond their land the sheep track up the mountain
is clearly delineated, as if spotlit. 'Might go for a walk this
afternoon,' she mutters to herself, putting the letter down,
scratching the back of her hand, which does not really itch.
She looks out of the window again and shivers, for although
the month is May, it is cold out there. I will remind Margaret
to bring warm clothing, she thinks, and she will have to
remind *him* too. She dials her friend's number. She puts the
phone down before it can be answered. No, she does not
want to talk to Margaret yet. She must assimilate. The tone

of the letter has the half-suppressed excitement of involuntary delight – as if it were written by someone who could say more but daren't. In fact it is both half-suppressed and bald in its information. 'I met him very recently,' it says, 'and I think he is A Good Thing. I think you'll like him, and David as well. And – yes – we sleep in the same bed! Just to save you asking. I thought about putting you through the embarrassment of deciding what to do etiquettically, but didn't think it was fair on him. Well, you old romantic, what do you think? I think he's someone you'll approve of at last. He makes Roger look like what comes out of the tap when the washer's gone . . .'

Jill ponders this last as she zips up her anorak and slips her feet into her wellingtons. She does not want to go out there today, she really does not, but the activity will be good for her, help her to think, help her to come to terms. Ye gods! she thinks, as she strides across to where the others labour, what have I got to come to terms *with?* This is my friend, this is my friend who has been lonely, unaroused, self-sacrificing, afraid, and who has now, finally, found something romantic and exciting. So why do I need to come to terms? I'll get over it. It has just been a bit of a shock, that's all . . . How cleanly these carrots come out of the ground. As she moves along the line, bending low, grunting, feeling the satisfactory ease of the culling, she tries to put out of her head thoughts of being unaroused, lonely, self-sacrificing . . .

Gradually, as she moves bent-peasant fashion, she catches up with Sidney. 'Just damp enough, the ground,' he says, and she watches his huge raw hands which work swiftly at the task. If only he were less bucolic, more rugged, she might be able to have some kind of fantasy about him. She agrees the ground is easy today. And then finds herself saying, because she is still puzzled, 'What comes out of the tap when the washer has gone?'

He looks at her. More woman's madness, she reads in his face. He sucks his pipe. Humour the boss. He would much rather work for a man. He considers. Then says slowly as if he were Solomon, 'Drips.'

She stares. Of course. *Drips!* How very, very funny. She stands up and laughs and this time she makes no excuses for herself. Let them think what they like. It *is* funny. That is precisely what Roger was – a drip. She returns to the soil. I wonder, she thinks, what this one will turn out to be?

Later, after supper, when David is sitting in the settee – she considers it as 'in' instead of 'on' because he sort of sinks into it and becomes a living extension of it – she tells him about Margaret's news. David's first and only question is 'What does he do?' And on hearing that he is an architect, David says, 'Good. I can ask him about that pitched roof on your storehouse.' He is satisfied with that. What Jill thinks is that while the men are off doing men's things, she will be free to discuss this new and interesting phenomenon with her pal. She has put off telephoning her for some preliminary discussion – the normal procedure – because she wants to sound full of enthusiasm and approval, and she hasn't quite got there yet.

'They sleep together,' she says to the newspaper.

David reveals himself and laughs good-humouredly, but he doesn't close the pages, merely peers over them. 'I should bloody well think so. Better put them next to Giles's room or they'll be keeping us awake all night.' He laughs again and folds the paper ready for the crossword.

'They've only known each other a short while.'

'Earplugs then,' says David.

He is nice, thinks Jill. My husband is a very nice man and I am very fond of him. She goes and sits beside him and they peer at the clues.

'Some G & S to get you in the mood for housework?' he says.

'Pinafore. Clever me.'

He pats her shoulder. 'Woman's clue,' he says.

She checks his expression. It is *almost* innocent.

'I'd better go and get their room ready.'

'Whose room?'

'Margaret's . . . and . . . er . . . his.'

'Bit soon, isn't it? You've got over a week. Do we know his name?'

'Simon. But she seems to call him Oxford.'

David does not look up but he says, so that she could smack him for his percipience, 'You don't sound as if you approve. Anything's better than that other bloke.'

'Roger.'

'I shouldn't think he *could*.'

'Could what?'

'Roger,' said David smugly.

'Oh, you only didn't approve because he showed no interest in the Flymo.'

'Rubbish. Besides, *everyone* likes riding on the things. And a help with cutting the grass wouldn't have come amiss. No spunk. What's feminine and royal in pink beads?'

'Pearly queen.'

'Where would I be without you?'

But she has already gone, out of the door, padding up the stairs, into the large bedroom at the back of the house, window half covered with cautiously budding wisteria that trails its tendrils in the wind. The room smells of old rose petals from the dish by the bed. The coverlet is smooth, dark red silk, something someone brought back from China, inherited from David's grandmother. It was their first double-bed cover, now relegated to the spare room to make way for the new Italian print from Conran. She runs her fingers over its cold sheen. It feels infinitely sensual. She bends her head and touches her cheek against it. The nice thing about this kind of silk is that it doesn't show the creases after lust, she remembers. It billows like a conjuror's robe and lies back smooth and flat and innocent afterwards. She had forgotten that. She goes to the top of the stairs and calls her husband. 'Come and help me test something out,' she says, and goes back into the room to lie on the bed. The scent of the petals is erotic, so is the touch of the silk and the memories.

Downstairs the telephone bleeps. David answers it and she can hear the resonance of his voice. She lies there, waiting. When the resonance has gone, she lifts her head and listens. Far away she can hear the tinnier sound of the television. She draws up her knees and lies there for a while longer, staring at the ceiling, smelling the scent of the petals, trying to think enthusiastically about Margaret's lover, until David calls to her that the news is on.

Chapter Twenty-two

Judith wanted to know about Dad's past because, apparently, he would never speak about it. I decided to respect his silence. He's making some curious paintings at the moment, really exuberant and colourful, with a lot of joy about them. He says they are to do with me. Also lots of drawings.

....

It was a very funny hotel. A bit of a risk, he said, but we agreed afterwards – or was it during? – that it was worth it. An old manor house just south of Hexham and Corbridge, set in (according to the guide book) an area of outstanding natural beauty. This part was true; it was the description 'hotel' that was eccentrically wanting. For the place was much more as if we had stumbled upon a country house weekend. As new – or prospective! – lovers, it was not the place to choose if you had the hots.

All the things that Oxford had chosen it for were correct – the view from the bedroom, the four-poster bed, the antique furniture and paintings, the good food and wine served in an oak-panelled dining-room, its individualism – but we were more like guests in the true sense of the word than anonymous arrivals who had come here for a romantic coupling before paying and passing on. This helped to heighten the anticipation of our lovers' denouement. We were kept on our toes from arrival to bedtime, and opportunities for groping or game-playing were few.

We arrived later than intended because of a puncture. That neither of us got cross boded well. He got out and got under while I sunned myself at the side of the Al and read up on Hexham Abbey and Roman Corbridge, just supposing we had time to go there ... Part of me, watching him perform that quintessential male task, was titillated – God knows when liberation will truly overtake the soggy inner pleasure of being looked after – and part of me was embarrassed, for he had removed his shirt and lay on a rug. I kept turning my eyes from Hexham Abbey's Saxon crypt and fifteenth-century paintings to his chest, ribs and hairy bits, and I couldn't help but think that soon they would be less a distant view and more a sensual fact ...

Our conversation going up was fairly general. We talked about the hospital project he was working on in Oxford, joked about Verity, pointed out things of interest along the way. For some of the time we listened to *Tristan and Isolde* – not very appropriate perhaps, but beautiful. The weather, which had been sharp and cold and blustery, had turned kind and there was an air of holiday happiness about the jaunt. At one point, after we had been stuck behind a pig truck for several miles and he demanded that I held his nose, the laughter nearly made me say, 'Lovers who laugh together stay together,' but I stopped myself just in time. No doubt Mr and Mrs Crippen shared a few jokes in the early days ...

'How are you feeling?' he asked, as we turned left at Darlington. 'Fine,' I said, and wished I could add, 'Except for the tom-toms in my solar plexus when you ask me questions like that ...'

Probably the only irritating aspect of our journey northwards was that he seemed to be a great deal more relaxed about everything than I was. Something to do with having taken control, I suspect. So when we finally arrived and stood holding hands and staring at the ivy-covered frontage of Marston Manor, I was amused to see erupt from the peaceful portico a tall thin man of latter years, in tweed jacket and beige cavalry twill. He rubbed his hands and strode towards us, saying, 'Welcome, welcome. Bit late but never mind, never mind . . .' Then he extended one of the rubbed hands to shake Oxford's, then mine, and to take finally both our overnight bags. True, I thought, as I followed his jolly gait into the building, the sign saying 'Hotel' was very small and discreet — but this was much more a scene from Brideshead than a touristical exercise.

Oxford signed us in and mine host led us up the heavily carved staircase to our room, called by him the oriel room, which was more like a dowager's boudoir than a guest room. The bed was a tapestried affair and had certainly not been bought at recent auction. The two armchairs matched the hangings of both bed and window and the walls were panelled. Panic set in that we were not going to have a bathroom but the heavy wooden door to this was merely half hidden by an old brocade curtain. What I love about traditional ownership is that it always includes wonderful fabrics just draped casually about as if organic — faded certainly, threadbare perhaps, but gorgeous stuffs nevertheless. The bedcover was straight out of a Veronese dusty, rich washed-out pink, embossed with silk embroidery, and so heavy that when I lifted a corner and let it fall back against the pillow it made a satisfying flump.

Mine host did not do anything with the gentle demeanour of paid staff. He strode to the curtained door, flung it wide and revealed a large white bath, black and white tiled floor and contrastingly rich tiles on the walls.

'Edwardian,' he said, when I went 'ooh'. 'Bit OTT, but at least they did it out before the local authority chappies slapped a preservation order on it. Rather have plumbing than a Victorian Gothic dressing-room any day. What?'

We nodded. Both of us were, quite undeniably, speechless. He closed the door and gave the curtain a tweak. 'Bath and wotsit's newish. Plenty of hot water. All you need to know, really.' He went to the bedroom door and stood outside in the corridor. I had one of those moments when I went all watery, thinking that Oxford might tip him. It was the sort of thing that Roger might have done.

Mine host stood there, rubbing his hands again. 'We usually have drinks in the drawing-room before dinner.' He looked at his watch. 'About six-thirty? I'll tell you all the stuff then.'

And he had gone.

Any considerations of 'getting it over with' – in my private parlance – vanished. Synchronizing watches, we found we had half an hour to get ourselves into a suitable state for dining. It crossed my mind to fling myself across the sumptuous bed in high abandon and say something seductive in a husky voice, but reality took over. Either we decided to abandon drinks before dinner, in which case we should probably find someone knocking anxiously at our door, or we played the game. I looked at him, he looked at me, and we both flopped down on the bed and guffawed less than seductively into our hands.

'I wonder,' said Oxford, 'if I should ask His Lordship for the nearest place to buy condoms?'

The image of those rubbing hands and that benign aristocratic face being posed such a question was too much. 'He'd either go pink and dissolve, or pretend he hadn't heard,' I said.

'Or take me to one side and say, "Look here, old chap ..."' added Oxford. Then he looked at me more seriously. 'Sorry about this,' he said, 'I had no idea.'

'I really don't mind.' I looked about me. 'It's a fantastical place. Let's look on it as an adventure ...' We couldn't do much else really.

'What a bathroom,' he said, leaping up suddenly and opening the door. He turned on the taps, tried the flush (a chain with china handle) and held the brass shower fitting lovingly. I smiled to myself. If there was one universal thing about *real men*, apart from their not eating quiche, it was their love of the practical. Because it was so alien to me – a tap gives water, a lavatory flushes, a shower sprays – I found it vaguely exciting. Masculine. I watched him poke about at the Edwardian masterpiece and then suddenly realized that we had to *dress*. Grabbing my washbag, I trundled into the bathroom and kissed Oxford on the mouth. The shower piece he still held was squashed rather uncomfortably between us. It began to leak, which had the terrible effect of making us both collapse with laughter again.

'Well, that's that,' he said, looking down at it mournfully, as indeed one might survey a flaccid penis.

'No matter,' I said, ushering him out. 'The night is but young.'

For all the fancy underwear and the delights of the game, there was an unmistakable practicality in us both. Our rose-tinted fantasies were underpinned by cold, hard facts. Those wartime romances must have had a similar flavour – throw yourselves in and live for the moment, because tomorrow he could be posted overseas and die . . .

The place just did not seem to lend itself to Elizabethan coquetries. They, with luck, would come later. So, defeated, I decided to wear the little black frock. You can't go far wrong with plain black, pearls, one inch of knee and a luminous light of lust in the eyes. Especially not at a Brideshead weekend. I looked at him, he looked at me, and I think it crossed both our minds to abandon dinner, strip for action, and do what we came for. But neither of us *quite* knew the other well enough yet.

We were only about five minutes late. 'Don't forget the Ovidian code,' he whispered, as we entered the sitting-room. Just inside the door stood our hosts, George and Roberta Howard, offering their outstretched hands. I took each in turn, and as I shook Roberta's I felt Oxford give my bottom a little pat and squeeze – the rat – so that I gave the aquiline features of mine hostess quite a startled look. I turned, looked at Oxford's innocent face, and pinched my earlobe. 'Just checking,' he whispered, as we moved along towards the drinks.

Afterwards I wished I had kept a diary of that particular

evening. George and Roberta Howard owned Marston Manor and it was the usual story: either do something commercial with it, or lose it. It was not of the right *stuff* – a word much in evidence – to open as a stately home, so a hotel was the next best thing. Oxford refused to tell me how much it cost to stay there, but it must have been very expensive.

The sitting-room contained a Canaletto over the Adam fireplace, clearly the pride of the collection. I cooed over it politely and then moved on to some of the lesser offerings. A good Bellotto – better, I thought, than his Uncle Canaletto – etchings by Chrome and Girtin, and a wonderful anonymous Italian painting rather like a Claude.

'Reminiscent of Giorgione,' I said, with calculated pretension.

'Yes,' said Plantagenet-faced Roberta. 'It is a Giorgione.' She added quite kindly, 'But only a small one.'

Sadly, as is often the case, the collection had begun in earnest and ended in earnest within a very few years. It had never quite got going. A good Reynolds portrait, full length with much Grecian drapery in evidence, hung side by side with an awful Edwardian portrait of a tapering lady who looked like she was halfway to being sucked through a vacuum cleaner, and enjoying the process so much that it had fluffed up her golden hair and brought her cheeks out in an astonishing pair of roses.

Mine host was at my elbow. 'My aunt,' he said. 'Rather fine, eh?' And then, after a suitable pause for reverence, he added. 'Now, may I introduce . . .?'

He guided me away, and I realized that the room contained items of interest besides the works on the walls. Two other couples, to be precise. Daphne and Russell Maddox, who came from Harrogate where, to my inquiry, they did nothing but live. Since they were certainly in their late sixties, this seemed reasonable. Daphne was immense and dressed in something pale lavender and floaty – all she needed was a hat with upturned brim to be the Queen

Mother. Russell was small, sandy-haired and florid, and, it transpired, was a painter nowadays. I politely asked him what he painted. As an amateur he would welcome the question. Real painters would spit in your eye. He waved a vague hand, saying all sorts. If I'd had one more gin inside me, I might have asked which was his favourite, the liquorice in blue hundreds and thousands, or the pink coconut with dark centre. How I do abhor people who take up daubing and then christen themselves painters. He had been an estate agent, so it may be that he took up art as a way of shriving himself for his sins.

Bunny and Wilma Campbell, from Ohio, were on the Scottish ancestry trail. Apparently more Campbells were due but had been delayed at Kennedy. Bunny did something with metals – turned them from something raw into something refined and then sold them on. Wilma raised funds for various causes in that totally American, enthusiastic, unpaid, socially glorious way. Naturally enough, Oxford immediately latched on to the metals as a topic of conversation. He and Bunny leaned against the fireplace, mellowly sipping whisky and discussing things like fatigue. It really was very funny. Here we were on the run-up to our first night of blissful union, but in the company of those to whom it was definitely *de trop* to evince any intimate interest in one's partner. I was almost thankful for my mature years – if I had been one of Colin's floosies I should probably have freaked.

Daphne's similarity to the Queen Mother continued in her approach to gin and tonic. If the tabloids are to be believed, our esteemed royal parent likes to pour her own, and generously, only trusting her own butler to get it right. This is something I fervently hope is true. The notion of getting to ninety and being able to smile for hours at crowds while downing substantial snorters gets my vote for the monarchy any day. Daphne, a mere smiling cipher, was content to slug away and let her eyes roam in a pleasant glaze.

'Why not,' she said when another drink was offered. 'I *am* on holiday.' And as the bottle glugged I admired tremendously how long she took to say when. I was quite sure she would be able to say, 'Why not, it's Thursday,' with equal conviction.

Plantagenet was, understandably, trying to appear to be Lady of the Manor rather than Manageress of the Hotel. A few tentative inquiries from me about breakfast times, how long they had been open et cetera, brought the minimal response that all *those things* would be dealt with later. Wilma, who was five foot nothing and built like a grasshopper, thought everything was wonderful and bore up under Plantagenet's condescension very well. Only later did she hit back, very subtly, when we were asked to admire a very stern portrait of a judge.

'My grandfather,' said mine hostess. And she added loudly and slowly, 'In the law.' Presumably for the benefit of her hard-of-hearing colonial guest.

This latter smiled sweetly, 'Oh really,' she said. 'A soul mate. I was a judge too till I retired.'

Plantagenet looked at her as if she had claimed being crowned in Westminster Abbey as her favourite hobby. 'Really?' she said. 'In law?'

'Yes. My, he does look saturnine, doesn't he? Was he very severe?'

'I expect he hung a few poachers,' I found myself saying.

'A judge, not a magistrate,' said Plantagenet crisply.

Which put me firmly in my place.

Wilma and I exchanged furtive smiles and mine hostess said to everyone, 'Shall we dine?'

The food was splendid and we dined around an oval table of heavy carving and mirror finish. Fish, game, pudding and cheese, served by an authoritative man of middle years who moved his hands around more like a conjuror than a waiter. The serving dishes were silver *and* polished, the plates were Derby. I sat opposite Oxford who was clearly delighted by the theatricality. We had been asked, very quietly as if the question might offend, if we would prefer a table to ourselves – there were four of these, one in each corner of the room – but it would surely have felt like outrageous rudeness to say yes.

Occasionally Oxford would look across at me and raise an eyebrow – 'Pick up my stealthy messages, send replies/I shall speak whole silent volumes with one raised eyebrow.' In reply I pinched my chin, which meant I was fine.

Talk was as a good dinner party, somewhere pre-war, should be. Very general with no stuff and nonsense about politics or religion, though whether this was from consideration of feeling or from the assumption that everyone was basically conservative and Anglican, I was unsure.

'We have some very fine frames here at Marston,' George said to me politely. He lowered his voice. 'Sometimes I think I prefer them to what they contain.'

Well, *quite*.

Waiting for the cheese, I looked around the room – a more vivid experience now that I had two gins, half a bottle of burgundy and a glass of Sauternes inside me. It was elegant, high-ceilinged, with white ornate coving. The walls were papered in a deep, velvety green. The two sets of French doors were behung, again, with rich stuff, of a faded ochreish colour. Beyond these the lawn that had been in sun when we sat down was almost inky. Light came from two wall lamps and candles on the table so that the whole looked even more theatrical. It should have been perfectly romantic, but in reality it was eccentric and funny. I suppose that more accurately reflected what Oxford and I were up to.

I looked at him. He was talking to Wilma, on his right, and laughing. Earlier he had drawn a heart in a little dribble of wine on that lustrous table – 'Words will spring from my fingers, words traced in wine' – and when he had poured some water for me, he picked up the glass and sipped from it first – 'As you hand back the goblet, I'll be the first to seize it/And drink from the place your lips have touched . . .' No wonder Ovid and Corinna stayed so hot for each other. I did as the good book instructed, and licked the place his lips had touched with the tip of my tongue. I got caught in crossfire conversation between Bunny and Russell, but was only half listening – there being a limit to my interest in autumnal French vineyard hopping. Narrowing my eyes, I studied Oxford's mouth and had a sudden desire to kiss it. What would Ovid suggest? 'Whenever there's a chance to touch me, please do!' So, abandoning the desirable but impractical notion of leaning across the crystal and napery and planting one on him, I slid downwards in my chair a little and covertly looked under the table. If I was going to play footsy (it was too wide for kneesy), I wanted to make quite sure I wasn't rubbing up mine host.

The response was most rewarding and pleasurable. I turned back to Bunny and Russell. 'Don't forget the joys of Rouen,' I said, 'on the way down.'

'Your wife,' said Bunny, 'is quite charming.' I suppose he came from an era when it was done to compliment the husband on his ox, home and other chattels.

'My wife,' said Oxford, 'is a genius at tickling all sorts of things out of people.'

'Wife indeed!' I said gaily. 'Why, anyone can see that we are just good friends!'

I think the only one who did not laugh was Plantagenet. She, of them all, knew it was true.

I gazed at Oxford and blinked with innocence. He was pressing his two forefingers together and staring back at me very hard. Wait till we are alone and I will get even with you for that . . .

The meal and games were over. We had turned down the offer of nightcaps, and I suddenly felt as if someone had thumped me in the solar plexus again. 'Could we,' I asked mine host, 'take a stroll around the garden before . . . um . . . we go to . . . um . . .?'

'Bed, I think, is the word, dear,' said Oxford.

George swung the French doors open wide and the two of us went out into the cool night air. It was nice to be alone at last. But it was not for long.

'Good idea,' said another voice, and they all trooped out chattering and exclaiming into the once silent darkness. I had a moment of wild and wondering fantasy that this was going to turn into one of those royal beddings of yore when King, Queen and half the Court piled into the bedchamber to watch the sovereign couple get tucked up for the night.

But down behind the rustling, sinister topiary, illuminating long points of shadow on the lawn, he pulled me into the darkness, where we waited for the others to pass by, holding our breath, holding each other tight, like refugees against an uncertain enemy. It was enough. Even imagined danger breeds a closeness. And, as soon as we could, we dived back through the swinging ochre curtain and ran up the ornate stairs towards the unassailable silence of our tapestried room. Hardly the romantic discretion of Ovid's persuasion, but you have to come up to date sometimes.

Chapter Twenty-three

We are going to a log cabin by a lake in Manitoba for most of the summer, so communications will not be so easy. Not that that will make much difference. We don't seem to be very good at it, do we? Write, anyway! Haven't heard for ages.

••••••••••••••••••••••••••••••

Verity looks at the clock and feels like a mother who has sent her virgin daughter to her bridal bed. She has intermittently looked at the clock from about five o'clock this afternoon. If Margaret isn't having fantasies, thinks Verity, *she* certainly is. She imagines some sumptuous hotel full of noise-absorbing carpets and staff gliding around in uniforms, with blank faces that have seen it all and say nothing. She imagines them arriving at five, ordering tea in the salon and then not having the patience to wait for it to cool; she sees the look that passes between them which says, 'I want you now.' She imagines the privacy and anonymity of their bedroom, the locked door, the champagne on ice, the curtains drawn and the candles lit. She pictures the sweep of sunlit lawn beneath their window and hears peacocks calling from far away as Aunt Margaret's Lover lays her back upon the bed and slowly undresses her. Her friend's eyes glow like coals, her arms are stretched above her head. Fingers stroke the glistening flesh in ecstasy, while the soft pale aurcoles of her breasts gradually stiffen beneath his lingering mouth. Verity, at this point, gets up and moves about a bit. It is now ten minutes past eleven and the two of them must have dined and be getting ready for, if not actually *doing*, round two.

Verity decides that what she needs is a drink. A nightcap, she thinks, and then she bursts into tears. From the back, in her fantasy, Aunt Margaret's lover looked not unlike Mark, and Aunt Margaret's nipples not unlike her own. She will not ring him, she will *not*. He's a gutless incompetent. It will only go sour all over again.

She looks at the clock for the umpteenth time. She unscrews the cap of the bottle and makes a modest nightcap for herself.

'Can't even trust your friends. They always let you down.'

The wall seems to concur.

'She'll probably marry the bugger.' Tears plop from Verity's eyes. 'And I shall be always alone. No more slipping under the duvet in the darkness with a pair of arms around you and a nose breathing into your ear, *ever*. Do you see?'

Plainly the wall does not, since hugs for walls are not generally considered necessary.

'Well, do you?'

The wall may well be making a heroic attempt to understand, but the result is blankness.

'Be glad you are a wall, then,' she says. 'I bloody well wish I were . . .'

Writers should use their sufferings, she reminds herself.

She looks back at her beautiful, bare, clean Italianate and glowing wall. Her kitchen companion. A woman's place is in the kitchen – she feels safe there, unthreatened. Why, even the dishwasher becomes a friend. The scales, the fridge – all her pals, and all keepers of her innermost confessions. Good job Mark *isn't* around any more. With what she has said to the fridge about him, for instance, if he opened it now to take out a beer it would probably savage him to death.

Upstairs she totters into her study. Kitchen – kindly. Food equals love. She switches on her machine and writes.

Your recipe is enclosed.

This particular dish is our most spectacular and popular,

and requires great skill. We suggest you do not attempt it until you are fully confident of success. Once you have mastered it you will find it is requested of you again and again.

WARNING: This will affect your statutory rights.

ESSENTIAL EQUIPMENT
1 ripe man
1 ripe woman
A glass or two of good wine
A little oil
A generous handful of time
A flat surface for rolling out on
A few sweet words for decoration

METHOD
Pour wine into two glasses. Drink a little from time to time. Remove outer garments from the man and woman carefully. Set aside. Check the skin for any remaining undergarments, remove slowly assessing each area uncovered for damage.

Any damage may be removed at this stage with careful application of lips to the area.

Place undergarments with outer garments for use later.

Feel remaining flesh all over for less obvious signs of damage.

If whole and unbruised, rub all over generously with oil, then lay out flat.

Wait for the man to rise fully.

The man and the woman are now ready.

Let them prove themselves, turning occasionally.

Judge when they are done by how they feel. They should be very hot and very damp.

Sprinkle with sweet words.

Leave to rest before returning to original under and outer garments.

Verity is pleased with this. It's funny. It's witty. It shows she can still be on form despite the bitter, bitter pain. It is exactly the sort of thing Mark would like to receive.

She switches off her machine and leaves the study, closing the door with a bang. But he damn well *won't*.

Jill watches David on the Flymo and tries to concentrate on his rather nicely muscular forearms as opposed to his rather round stomach. He is cutting the grass for the advent of Margaret and her new lover. Jill has made their bed and put fresh roses in the room, though the scent of the old rose petals, still in their bowl, lingers beneath their sharper perfume. The odour of love, she thought sadly, closing the door tight to keep it in.

She feels both excited and afraid. Excited because she has looked forward to seeing her friend for so long, afraid because everything has changed now, even to the extent of Margaret's stay. Originally she was going to come up for at least a week. Now it is only the weekend – Friday night to Sunday. When Jill had suggested that Margaret could come up a few days earlier, or even a night earlier, Margaret had made some very convincing excuses for why it was not possible. True, she did say that she would come up again on her own very soon, perhaps in July, but . . . Jill feels she is behaving like a jealous schoolgirl. She looks at David's strong arms and his well-shaped legs in their shorts. Nothing wrong with the way he is made, nothing wrong at all – only somehow, somehow right now he seems to lack the power to engage her. She looks at her watch. They are due to arrive in half an hour. Oh, David is *so* irritating about that bloody Flymo. He had started cutting the grass too late to finish before they arrived. *Of course* he had – because he wanted the new chap to admire its lines and fine engineering. He once had a Porsche, in the good old days of the eighties, and that never got half the admiration and attention. Love me, love my Flymo. Jill smiles. She had better tell Margaret to pass this wisdom on to her lover so that they can all have a really harmonious weekend!

Chapter Twenty-four

'Star bursts,' he said from the window seat.

I sat up, propped against the pillows, burrowed in the bedcover, and smiled at his dark silhouette. He had the base of the tapestried curtain wrapped around him, though his chest and shoulders were bare. He was lit from behind by moonlight and from within the room by a solitary candle's glow – a strange combination of coldness and warmth which created a hybrid image, somewhere between the cool northern painting of Vermeer and the deep warm shadows of Caravaggio.

'Sex is beautiful,' I said drowsily.

If you have no expectations nor responsibilities, I was thinking to myself, and you are turned on by the person you are with, then sex is the simplest and the best of all the rather beautiful pleasures in the world. Of course, I would probably change my mind as soon as hunger loomed around breakfast time. Eating so often supersedes sex as the most pleasurable of indulgences. Yet another example of clever Mother Nature – get 'em eating and fucking and the world goes on turning. But right then, at about three-thirty on a May night in the country, sex seemed a great deal better than bacon and eggs.

I was about to say something along these lines when my kindly *éminence grisette*, the one who perches on my shoulder from time to time and gently suggests that I should put a sock in it, did.

'There's no art to find the mind's construction in the face,' says Duncan, getting it completely wrong and trotting off to Glamis for a quick touch of regicide. But that was politics. After sex the face *does* reflect the feelings. Oxford looked at ease, and I felt at ease. We had pre-ordained ourselves – decisions were out of our hands. It was like being naked on a warm desert island.

'Go on,' he said later, as we lay close and were drifting towards sleep.

'Go on, what?'

'Say it.'

'Say what?'

He turned to me, yawned, and spoke in that tone that denotes the pleasurable slipping from consciousness. 'Say, "I'm glad we've got that bit over . . ."'

'Well, I am . . .' I said, brushing off my *éminence grisette*.

But he was already asleep.

Later, looking suitably ragged, we dressed for breakfast. The morning was sunny, full of birdsong and warm enough for our casement to be open. A smell of lavender and newly cut grass drifted into the room. We could never have designed such perfection, I thought – it could only ever come together like this when the gods decide.

'I don't think . . .' he said, lying back on the gorgeous crumpled stuff of the bed and pulling me towards him, 'I don't think I could face breakfast with that lot again. How about you?'

I shook my head. It could never be fun the second time around. 'Let's have it up here in the room,' I said.

'Good idea.' He began rubbing his cheek with a not altogether roseate thumb. 'And then have breakfast . . .'

As we drove out of the gates, I thought that there was some wonderful material here for Verity. She should book herself in some time and take in the eccentric flavour. That morning, while Oxford paid, I was invited to take a look at the hothouse. It was as if we really were back in Jane Austen's days when any visit to a country seat must, *de rigueur*, include an opportunity to admire the peaches. In fact they were apricots – the precocious fruit – and looked so erotic, like little round and willing bottoms, that I came dangerously close to remarking so. I was about to touch one with a fingertip when my hostess restrained me.

'They are so delicate at this stage,' she said, 'and bruise so easily. When they are a little riper they will toughen up enough to be handled.' She gave me a bright smile.

'Well, isn't that *just* like life?' I murmured, deciding that I would tell Verity all about this place, in every seductive detail, so that she would be forced by curiosity to come here. It would do her good. She needed taking out of herself. I also felt guilty. Perhaps I had rather left her in the lurch. I quickly put the thought from my head. You couldn't go round being responsible for people in that way. Now, could you?

We returned to the lobby.

'Nasty business all over,' said mine host, rubbing his hands. Not a till nor a cash box in sight. How perfect the illusion here is, I thought, and had the uncomfortable feeling that it wasn't the only illusion in proximity.

Chapter Twenty-five

*We were talking about your card from Hexham Abbey. Dad
says he remembers going there as a student and copying the
carvings in the Chantry. I think he misses all that heredity
stuff. Who were you with? You said 'We' on your card. Was it
Jill? Give them my love.*

••••••••••••••••••••••••••••••

We visited Hexham Abbey before driving on to Jill and David.
I found myself wondering whether we had really needed
sex to finish the circle, or whether it was the mythology that
dictated it as necessary for a relationship's completion. Sure,
it's a pleasure, and a free one if you are lucky, but then so is
sitting on a warm beach or having your feet massaged, and
you don't have to wear a condom to do either of those.
Only, I suppose, they don't perpetuate humankind. Maybe
the reason we get in such a muddle about sex is because we
have the primal expectancy of 'mating equals offspring' and
so our encounters mostly leave us feeling we have failed in
our true purpose. Women are upset not because their men
fall asleep straight afterwards, but really because they haven't
been made pregnant. Possibly? Well, whatever, that morning
we agreed to look at the world fearlessly through new eyes,
and, like that, it looked very good.

A small piece of travelogue. Hexham Abbey is a comely
place which still retains many of its Anglo-Saxon origins.
Dating back to 674, it is built in the shape of a cross. The

Anglo-Saxon names connected with it would make a sit-com writer blush. The fair Queen *Etheldreda*, whose husband was godly King *Egfrid*, gave land for the Abbey to Saint *Wilfrid*, who repaid their charity by taking a lawsuit to Rome against the carving up of his see. He won it, but on his return was promptly imprisoned by said godly king. First known example of taking a case to Europe successfully only to come back to find nothing more than a big fat so what ... Current governments, please note. Despite his huff, said Wilfrid left a splendid seventh-century stone cathedra, which had once, if sat in by an innocent sanctuaree, offered immediate and unassailable safety – cause for thought here, all right.

There were more sit-com names in the rood screen – St Cuthbert and St Oswald. The former clutched the latter's head, which produced a kind of saintly sense of sit-com. Apparently some muddle following Oswald's death on the battlefield (hardly a saintly demise) resulted in this part of his anatomy becoming coffin companion to Cuthbert. Rather presumptuous in my opinion – fancy having someone else's head chucked in beside you, not even to be sure of having your coffin to yourself once you have gone to your final rest.

Just like certain trigger words – gusset and truss, for instance – the Anglo-Saxon names rolled off the guide book with increasing absurdity. Cuthbert and Oswald were followed by Walburga and his two brothers St Willibald and St Winebald ... There was also an Ethelberga of Barking. For these names alone it was worth letting William the Conq. overrule us ...

The Abbey's minder, a thin, imperious-looking priest with hair and face like a falcon, looked upon us with growing disapproval. Oxford spent some time with him smoothing the feathers, admiring the misericords, discussing the mixture of styles, commiserating on the decay of the building's fabric. I wandered a little way off and leant against a pillar, watching the two men. I was amused at the thoughts going through my mind, which had little to do with Medieval versus Romanesque. If we had not already been a little late setting off for Jill and David's, I might have suggested a pitstop on the way. But neither of us was sure enough of the other, yet, to suggest leaping under a haystack or bundling up in the back of the car, so we drove in an increasingly high state of unsaid expectancy. *Just* the sort of thing Jill would love, and *exactly* what she would hope and expect to see, I thought, as we rolled through the gates of their drive.

'How do you want to handle this?' he asked after I had switched off the engine.

'As romantically as possible,' I said, 'and say nothing about advertisements.'

He laughed. 'Shame on you,' he said.

I got out. In the distance I could see David on his grass-cutting machine, and the movement of the curtain in a downstairs window indicated that Jill had registered our arrival.

'It might remind David to be a bit more attentive to Jill if we rub his nose in it a bit. Besides' – I took his hand – 'we don't have to pretend anything, do we?'

The front door opened. Jill appeared wearing a very pretty lavender and white dress, and I thought how beautiful she looked with her shimmering eyes and her huge, bright smile.

'Welcome,' she called, arms outstretched to me. We hugged each other.

'He's very nice,' she whispered into my ear.

So how could I tell her the truth?

Chapter Twenty-six

We are packing up. You won't hear much from me for a while. I wish everything was easy between us all and that you could have come over for some of the summer. I think of you and the house and my room often. Well, I guess this is growing up!

••••••••••••••••••••••••••••••

Verity has decided to go swimming in the early evening.

This is part one of plan A, called Cleaning Up Your Act Before It Shows On Your Ageing Face and Body. She feels depressed. It is not relaxing to be constantly wondering what is going on in a northerly direction. She wishes she had had the courage to say to Margaret, 'Please ring me and tell me what it was like *immediately*,' because what it was like and how it is continuing are two questions that dance around in her head all the time. Margaret's taking a lover has left a hole in Verity's needy world and, though she despises the thought, she would feel much better if Margaret rang up to say it was not so hot. Or, even better, if a tear-stained Margaret arrived on her doorstep to say '*Never again.*' There. The deceitful, dreadful thought is out. Swimming will cure such disease, thinks Verity, and she puts on her costume.

The costume says to her, as does her face above, that whatever the 'It' is, it already *does* show on the ageing face and body. 'Thank God I never had children,' Verity says to her reflection. If she had had children, she feels, then the body would have been in an even worse state. Already it is quite bad enough. It is not so much that it is fat, it is not, but it has a saggy quality about it, as do her jaw and her eyes, the whites of which – she peers closely – are definitely looking yellow. That's it, then – she throws the towel into her bag – she has shot her liver too. Such fools love makes of us, she thinks, for she looked quite all right before all this Mark business began. She takes one last look at her bosom, decides it has become sunken treasure, and moves away from the disgracefully cruel mirror. Perhaps she will throw the mirror away and get a very small one – one you can see only bits of yourself in. 'What do you think, Wall?' she yells. But coming back up the stairs is only silence. The wall is an extremely tactful pal to have around.

At least the swimming-pool will be free of threat. At just after six o'clock on a Friday night the children will be going home for their supper, the strapping Adonii of early-morning lanes will be oiling their muscles at home ready for the weekend, the grannies and the disabled will be tucked up with their Barbara Cartlands. She feels she is allowed to make this kind of ageist suggestion since she is nearly in that category herself. So she expects that there will be either no one at the pool or others in a similar plight to herself. 'Nowhere to go, nothing to do, and no one to do it with,' she says mournfully, as she pulls on her jeans. Oh, really! How did she ever get into this state in the first place? And what on earth is Margaret *doing* opening herself up to it? Foolish woman. Verity sticks a bottle of body lotion into the bag and zips it up. 'Body lotion to keep the body all supple and soft,' she intones to herself as she heads down the hallway. And a tear escapes. But supple and soft for why?

She remembers what Margaret is up to. Fucking Aunt Margaret and her pick-up from Oxford. Fucking Aunt Margaret and her *successful* pick-up from Oxford. Last night's recipe seems to have lost its healing quality. When she rang Colin this morning, just to ask him what he thought about it all, he had seemed puzzled.

'Think?' he said. 'I don't think anything. Let them get on

with it. As long as they leave me alone. But I'll tell you what
I do think . . .'

Verity perks up. 'What?'

'I don't think it will last.'

Verity perks up even more. 'You wouldn't like to come
swimming with me now?' she asked. But he politely declined.

Instantly she wished she had not said it and was plunged
into gloom again after he had rung off.

It will last, she thinks, it will. Margaret just has that air of
confidence about her.

Verity sees Mark twice on the way to the swimming-pool.
On each occasion, and once rather dangerously, she reverses
the car only to find it is a figment. One was a man with a
moustache who grinned back at her unedifyingly, and one a
young lad with a shell suit. Verity wonders if such mistakes
may be the result of delirium tremens setting in. She vows, as
she parks at the leisure centre, that she will not draw cork nor
twist cap once tonight. Not *once*. And she is deaf to the inner
voice that mocks and says, 'Ha ha. Heard *that* one before . . .'

Jill is now sitting up in bed at midnight and extremely glad
to be in a room that is on the other side of the house. David
is reading – in that dozy, pre-sleep way – a magazine article
about Japan. He has to go there soon and is irritatingly
unexcited about the prospect. Jill did think about accompany-
ing him at one point – hang the expense – but the prospect
of doing most of her sightseeing alone, and of not having an
iota of Japanese under her belt, made her decide otherwise.
David suggested that they learn some Japanese together. Jill
has long wanted to share an activity with him – perhaps
golf, perhaps orienteering, something they could both enjoy
in a childlike, open way and which would draw them closer
– but learning Japanese for business reasons doesn't appeal.

David turns out his light, rolls on to his side with his back
comfortably pushed up against her, reaches round to squeeze
her thigh once, and instantly begins the breathing that
indicates he is close to untrammelled oblivion.

She nudges him. Hard. 'David,' she says, 'what do you think of him?'

'Who?' says David grudgingly. He knows perfectly well what Jill means but sleep is such a seductive option.

'Her man.'

'He's all right. Very nice chap.' He lets out a deep sigh, full of relish for what is to come. The grass-cutting in the cold, breezy air, the roast duck, the unremitting conversation and an extra glass of port have all had their effect. His eyes have the weight of good conscience upon them. They close in delicious abandonment.

Jill lets him go. She puts her elbows on her knees and her hands under her chin and she says to the lamplit room, 'Well, *I think* he's very suitable and very nice and they've clearly hit it off. First flush, I suppose. Did you see the way they kept touching – toes and later his hand on her back – like they couldn't wait to get to bed? And I've never seen Margaret so smiley and soppy. Disgusting, really – *she'd* have been disgusted by it in someone else. And her eyes looked *luminous* – she was sparkling, the way they say you should in books. And already – *already* – they had that secret shorthand between them. What on earth was all that about Willibalds and coffins? I think it was rude to be so obscure. And he was so damn well interested in everything. And when I asked how they had met, they exploded with laughter – *laughter*. And Margaret put her arm round me – patronizing cow – and said, "In Oxford." And she calls him Oxford. What's wrong with Simon? It's a good enough name. There's something so childish and possessive about nicknames – not like her at all.'

David continues to make the noises of peaceful limbo. Jill automatically reaches out and nudges his ribs – he grunts and moves slightly. The little snores turn into a deep and gentle breathing.

Jill holds her breath. She feels wound up, restless, disturbed. She hears the wind in the trees outside. Or does she? She listens harder. It is a rustling, certainly, but is it the soughing of ash and oak, or the shifting of silk on a bed made for lovers? She turns off the light, closes her eyes and her ears, does not want to hear. But it fills the room, taking over the darkness. There are moans and sighs and the smoothing of limb against limb. It pursues her under the duvet, this noise, and soon it creates images, though she tries to resist them. She does not want such images. She wants to go peacefully off to sleep. Like her husband who is lying there beside her. But still she sees . . .

The faces are disjointed, hard to recognize, though she knows who they are. The faces smile at each other, eyes large and wondering and amused, closing the space between them, kissing so close that lips, eyes, noses become one indistinguishable line. She hears the intake of breath, the throats pulse and make noises of despair, desire, delight. The pool of deep red silk shows the whiteness of their skin to perfection, gives the darkness of their sex an added depth, as they move and slide on its crimson softness. Rustle, rustle, rustle. Their bodies seem impossibly close, impossibly entwined, and the silk has twisted its own seduction between them. A swathe of it rests between the woman's thighs, where the man caresses her, pulling at the silk, touching her dark springing nakedness so that she can no longer resist and her legs move apart from him, slack and willing, yielding and hopeful, so that nothing is hidden.

Jill closes her eyes even tighter but the image grows larger, the sighs and exhalations of intense experience magnify. She watches them, eagerly now, the shame of the watching being part of the pleasure. The woman moves herself languorously, coaxes at his cock, teases it, touches it with light fingertips that dart away as it begins to respond too urgently. Sliding her body down the silk she buries her head in his sex while her hands stroke and caress his belly. What she does with her mouth is hidden by the dark twists of hair that sprawl from her, tendrilling upon his thighs. It is not Margaret's new red mop that she sees, but her own. And it is neither the face of the lover she has brought with her, nor David's, that she sees, but a new face – infinitely tender as it looks down at her and smiles in delighted wonder at it all. She pulls the silk around them, letting it fall and slide at will, so that it becomes as intimate and involved as a third lover, moving sinuously, pulling at them, like another pair of hands. She smells the roses, hears the shush of the silk, and chooses not to resist.

The soughing and the sighing are louder. Jill wonders why the sound does not wake David, who still sleeps peaceful as a child, comfortably pushed up next to her. She moves away a little. She does not want to touch him, he is too real. She can smell the roses that she put in their room, the musky scent of old petals, and mingling with it the unmistakable underscent of sex. Now they kneel and the man runs his fingers down his lover's face, touching her neck, kissing it, moving downwards to trace his fingertips across her breasts so that her voice shudders from deep in her throat and she arches towards him. Very gently he disentangles the red silk from their legs and throws it free of the bed, then, guiding his lover, he moves closer so that she can sit on him as he rocks her softly to and fro, to and fro . . .

Jill turns away, afraid to look, burying her head in her pillow, giving a little sob. To the darkness she says, 'I wish she had never come here.' The silk still rustles, the sighs still hover in the air and the caress of skin on skin still lingers, she can hear it, she can hear it, and David, David lies unmoving beside her. 'I want a lover,' she whispers to the darkness. 'David, I want a lover.'

From the bed comes a soft and comfortable snore.

Chapter Twenty-seven

I was worried about Jill after our visit. She seemed distant –
not just from me but from everything – and was falsely jolly
all the time. I was surprised that she asked very little about
Oxford and made no effort to get time alone with me. It
was, of course, not as easy as it had been in the old days.
You cannot tell a new lover to piss off while you discuss him
with your girlfriend, and our usual jaunt into town for the
Saturday morning market had to include Oxford too. But I
was surprised to find that I wanted to include him, that it
mattered more to me than getting some time alone with her.
Besides, I felt protective of him. David was on the war path
about his grass-cutting and some building work he was
planning, and it would have been unkind, as well as impolite,
to leave Oxford behind to suffer such a fate.

I had thought that Jill and I would be together on our
own at some point, that it would just happen as it always
had in the past. But of course, the opportunities were not the
same. She could hardly do her usual and pop in beside me
under the duvet for early-morning tea and the marriage of
true minds with Oxford nestled there so firmly beside me.

I found our first night especially erotic because it felt so
wicked to be having sex in a double bed at Jill's after the
years spent sleeping alone in my pretty little virginal room
down the corridor. The morning after I peeped into this
familiar haunt. It felt like I was thumbing my nose at it. I
walked over to the window and looked out: apple trees in
blossom, the sheep like dandruff on the unkempt landscape,

a scarecrow or two. All was as it had ever been – only now the focus seemed sharper. It was as if I was only able to see it for the first time having left it. I smiled, twitched the flounced curtain, touched the frilled pillow. I went over to the shelves on the wall opposite the familiar little bed and poked around in a miniature doll's house. It had once been Jill's. Sassy and Amanda used to play with it. Now I moved the figures around, changed the settings of the furniture – and remembered Mrs Mortimer. Kicking up my heels was *exciting*. Yes, yes. I was right. It was about time I gave all this up for the sensuous pleasures of red silk and roses two doors down.

And then Oxford, who had come looking for me, put his head round the door, and his smile quite made my heart lift.

'Whose room is this?' he asked.

'No one's,' I said, and closed the door on it.

David met us on the landing and looked both embarrassed and pleased. 'Sleep all right?' he said. And then went slightly red.

'Yes, thank you,' said Oxford, moving close in collusion. 'Very comfortable bed.'

'Yes,' said David as we all descended the stairs. 'It was ours before we got the new one. I always liked it. Come and have a look at the outbuildings after breakfast. We need some ideas. Jill's expanding.' He chuckled, half proud, half deprecating. 'Quite the businesswoman now the birds have flown the coop.'

'That doesn't sound like Jill,' I said.

He pushed open the door to the dining-room. The table was laid with care – flowers in a jug, napkins with rings, thin white china instead of the usual mugs. Coffee mingled with the smell of bacon, and the bread rolls were warm. Jill had certainly done us proud. I smiled at her, the smile of a contented cat and just the sort of thing she would hope to see.

When I was helping with Sunday lunch and the men were in the sitting-room looking at the papers – a curious ritual, untouched by the flow of liberated waters – I asked Jill what she thought of this new man of mine. She looked up from the carrots she was slicing and, with her eyes full of tears, said he was lovely.

'Do you love him?' she went on.

'Bit soon for that,' I hedged. 'But I am very happy.'

'It shows,' she said, back to being brisk with the vegetable knife.

'It's all right, you know,' I said, going back to the spuds. 'I know what I'm doing. So does he.' It was on the tip of my tongue to tell her that our affair was irredeemably finite, when I stopped myself. She would not like that. Let her have her romancing. I thought of David, who seemed even more pudding-like than her description. She could do with something to tickle up her sense of romance.

'David seems . . . um . . . busy,' I ventured.

'David's all right,' she said shortly, and changed the subject to Saskia, Giles and the perils of her daughter's camper van. 'Do you ever envy me this life?' she asked. 'I mean children, husband. All that?'

But David came in and opened a bottle of wine, part of the next stage of the ritual, and the conversation changed to more general things.

Chapter Twenty-eight

If Jill had felt a little distant and restrained, Verity was exactly the opposite. The day after we got back, while I was still lying in my bed sipping tea, alone again and therefore able to assimilate the last seventy-two hours, she came knocking on my door, ringing my bell, rapping on the window with a persistence and firmness that no amount of ignoring her would allay. I picked up my tray reluctantly and tottered off downstairs with it, letting in my visitor on the way. My commitment to Tintoretto's *tendresse* for Elisabeth and Mary was wearing a little thin and I began to feel it was more like picking over the bones of a dead still-life.

'Well?' she said dramatically, pushing the front door closed with her bottom. 'Well?'

I marched off towards the kitchen with the tray held like a libation.

'Well? *Well?*' She came scampering along behind.

Over my shoulder I said, as if it were a little nursery rhyme, 'By the simpering of my gums/Someone well fucked this way comes . . .'

'Ooh,' said Verity. '*Oooh*. It was good, then?'

Elisabeth and Mary reasserted themselves.

'Brilliant,' I said.

'The great love of your life, then?'

'Early days.' I shrugged.

'But you are going to see each other again?'

'You bet.'

She sighed and flopped down. Relieved, I thought.

'Next week.'

She gave a little rubbery exhalation through her lips. 'That's a long time,' she said, half to herself. 'When I met Mark, we couldn't bear to be apart for a second – we were on the phone, sending notes, turning up on each other's doorstep, having sex like rabbits . . .'

'Yes, well,' I said, forbearing to add, 'And then look what happened . . .'

She put up her hand and said, 'I really don't want to know the details.' But of course, she did. So I told her all about it while I made the coffee.

'So,' she said over her mug, 'what about commitment?'

'No other partners.'

Silence.

'And?'

'Nothing. That's it. Then we don't have to worry about condoms.'

'Is that all you can say? What about the future?'

'Oh, *Verity*! The future will simply take care of itself.'

Verity did not look convinced. Nor very happy. I decided to cheer her up.

'Verity, let me tell you about the crazy hotel we stayed in. It was an absolute *hoot*.'

Her wet sunken eyes were not those of a woman much concerned with hoots, but I persisted.

She looked at her watch, it was nearly eleven. 'Do you think I could have a brandy?' she asked, interrupting my flow. 'I don't feel very well.'

I gave her the brandy. Even had one with her, though the shock to the morning system was acute. And when she had gone, with that glow of goodness that comes from truly being selfless once in a while, and therefore comes not often, I proceeded to run a bath.

Verity sits there thinking that this is where she went wrong. Here is a shining example of how to get a relationship right from the beginning. She failed miserably at that. He wasn't really so bad, was he? All right, he did flirt with other women, all right he did forget to call her sometimes, and stayed away longer than she wanted when she needed him, but it was all her fault. She sees that now. All and entirely her fault. Margaret is so relaxed about everything, so confident. Verity feels humbled. She could beat herself over the head with a brick. Margaret observes that she needs cheering up. And begins.

The shop was transformed. In the couple of weeks since my previous visit the layout had been much improved. At last all the framing samples were properly displayed, hanging on the wall behind the counter, with price ranges labelled above them. The counter was at least a foot wider in both directions, something I had always promised to deal with but never did, and a full-size poster could now lie on it lengthwise without draping over the edge. It looked much more professional. Behind the counter, where Joan and I used to perch with our coffee like a pair of broody hens, the slotted open cupboards were now finished. I had begun them three years ago in a burst of modernization fever. I felt both pleased and piqued. Joan's available eye shone with pride.

'You've transformed the place,' I said.

'Well, Reg and I have been working after hours. He did most of the carpentry and stuff. I worked it out. Looks good, doesn't it? It's been more fun than trying to keep a boyfriend happy.' She embraced *le flick* and looked around, now with two proud eyes. 'At least this was successful. Spiteri Junior has definitely gone,' she said, pleased. 'So now we really are on our own.'

Reg popped out. Took one look at my hair colour, and popped back into his den again.

'Bless him,' said Joan comfortably.

Was this the girl who had once whispered from behind her grubby hand her suspicion that he was a nocturnal flasher?

'Busy, are you?' she asked. 'Enjoying the freedom?'

Was there an edge to the question? I struggled with my conscience. On the one hand Oxford and I had planned all kind of trips and treats for the next few months. On the other – well, I still had responsibilities here. Conscience pricked, and won. 'Would you like me to come back sometimes? Just to help out?'

If I had expected gratitude, I was disappointed.

'Oh no. We're fine. Really we are.'

I should like to think she was being brave.

So I took my redundant self home and gave her a grape-peeling lesson. That's to say I watched daytime television. Than which, arguably, there is no more decadent nor opulent waste of time in the world. Especially when you awake some hours later to the firm conviction that you have arrived in hell because two brightly clad young humans with smiling sickness are leaping about in that little square screen exhorting you to sing, 'If you're happy and you know it clap your hands . . .'

Part Two

Chapter One

After Margaret went home with what Jill found herself describing in her head as Lover Boy, Jill found herself suffering from what she – also in her head – referred to as PMT: Post Margaret Trauma. God, they had been so drippy. It took several days to overcome and several more days before she could bring herself to enter the spare room and remove the offending sheets. Margaret had left the room in a state befitting an exiting guest. The offending sheets and pillow cases were properly folded at the end of the bed, the four naked pillows were neatly arranged on the mattress, no more than barren contours beneath the spread-out blankets and immaculately smoothed crimson silk bedcover. The air in the room was musky with dried petals, and the fresh roses set there had become full blown. As Jill opened the door, sending in a draught, they finally released their blooms to fall in a soft scattering of faded colour on the dressing chest. It was a tableau to love, Jill thought, and she crossed to the window and threw it wide open to release the pungency of what she knew, heart and head, had taken place there. The wisteria tap-tapped away in the late afternoon light and Jill lay down on the bed and wept and wept and wept.

Later she gathered up the used bedding. She had left the door locked after the lovers had departed, but as her daily woman was now beginning to act as if she had Grace Poole shut away in there, she could no longer avoid dealing with the practicalities and did so with a certain painful tenderness. She carried the used linen as a vestal virgin might carry the robe of some deity, her arms out rigidly before her, her back straight, and she was aware that she looked slightly mad. Going down the stairs, she paused to press her nose into the soft bulk of the fabric and she thought she could smell the scent of desire and joy in its folds.

When Margaret rang a day or two after the visit, Jill responded as best she could to the 'Well, what did you think?' and the 'Thank you for having us'. But with an excuse she put the telephone down as soon as she could, with relief. She had a creeping, depressing feeling that nothing would ever be the same again – not with Margaret, not with David, not with hearth and home, and not – most certainly not – with her long-term love affair with the production of vegetables. She straightened her back, told Sidney that she wished him to take on more help in the busy growing season, and loafed nervously around the house reading magazines and having long scented baths to while away the time. This strange behaviour lasted for a few days, though it felt as if it were much longer, and was terminated one afternoon when David returned early with a toothache that had dramatically begun to turn into an abscess. His ravaged, swollen face appeared round the bathroom door and his eyes, puffy as they were with pain, extended themselves in uninhibited wonder at the sight of his wife up to her neck in bubbles of lavender oil and listening to Cole Porter love songs.

Guilty to see her husband suffering and harrowed to have her secret discovered, Jill could not forgive him in her heart. Something died in her affections for him as she climbed soapily out of her delicious, watery cocoon to hunt down the oil of cloves and the aspirins.

'What on earth were you *doing* in there?' he asked peevishly as he hovered behind her while she sought the necessary medicaments.

'Riding a bloody bicycle, David!' she said, peering into the cabinet. The resultant irritation made her spitefully put more oil on the cotton-wool swab than was proper, so that his mouth stung for hours.

'Some men,' she said, having dressed herself and made him tea, which he could not drink because it tasted of cloves, 'might have found it exciting to come home unexpectedly and find their wives naked at four in the afternoon.'

'Some men,' he said in a muffled, grumpy tone, 'might find it *suspicious*.'

Jill felt cheered. 'Oh,' she said. 'Do you?'

'Not at all,' he said with confidence, smiling bravely through the pain.

Later, when the aspirin and the antibiotics he had collected on the way home had begun to have an effect, Jill poured him a very large whisky. He declined because of the drugs and so she drank it instead.

'Women in the country do have affairs, you know. They get bored and they – well, look elsewhere.'

'Yes,' said David, not looking up from the crossword, his free hand pressed to his cheek. 'But not you.'

'And why not me?' She had another whisky.

'Because you are *not* bored. The reverse, thank God.'

'How do you know?'

'You always say how busy you are – rushed off your feet, busy, busy, busy . . .' He filled in some squares.

Jill wanted to pour her whisky over the newspaper, but sipped it instead. 'Busy may not be the same as not being bored.'

'Hellespont!' he said, throwing down the paper in triumph. 'Cracked it, tooth or no tooth.' He smiled at her, looking quite horrible with his misshapen face.

'There's no need to be so smug,' she said defiantly, 'I'm not exactly past it. Look at Margaret . . .'

He patted the space next to him on the settee and extended his arm. A familiar gesture that both wrenched her heart and made her want to throw up. 'Come and sit here,' he said.

'Now you've finished the crossword?'

'Exactly.'

She did as he said. Maybe any touching would be a

comfort. He tried to take the whisky glass from her, but she held on to it like a child with a sweet.

'Nobody's past anything in this house,' he said comfortably. 'And despite my aching tooth I did pause to notice how you looked as you stepped out of the bath. Not bad at all.'

Jill had the nauseating feeling she was being addressed as a carrot. That was the kind of thing David used to say when she inspected the crops and pulled one from the earth to show him. 'Not bad at all . . .' Yes, it was exactly as if she were being held up for inspection, with a careless hand grasped around her young green shoots.

'I thought Aunt Margaret looked well,' she said, tracing circles round his knee. 'Didn't you?'

He pulled her towards him, arm round her shoulder, so that her head came to rest on his chest. 'You can always tell a woman in love,' he said. 'It just shines out of them. She'd dropped about ten years. Amazing the way she was showing her legs.'

Jill snapped bolt upright, banging her head against David's swollen cheek as she went.

'Shit, Christ, *fuck*!' he yelled, pushing her away and holding the place tenderly with his hand. He moaned softly and rocked himself for comfort.

'Oh God, I'm so sorry!' she said. But secretly she was pleased.

She stood up, draining the rest of the whisky. 'Do you want dinner?' she asked, looking at her watch. It was nearly six. She didn't feel like cooking for herself and was glad when he mumbled that he certainly did not *now*, and instead stumped off to bed to watch television and let the pills do what they could.

Bad cess to you then, she thought, wandering off to her office for no particular reason, aware that she was slightly drunk. Showing her legs, was she? Yes, she *was* . . . *And* stretching out a bare toe as she sat on the carpet near her Lover Boy, so

208

that she could touch his leg with it. Provocative, really outrageously provocative, just like a teenager. *And* quoting Roman poets all over the place, with him chiming in the odd word here and there as if they were Romeo and bloody Juliet. Eyes across the dinner table and touching all the time. Private jokes! She swiped at a seed catalogue, which went tumbling to the ground along with a cascade of assorted paperwork. She would have left the mess by way of personal revolt were it not for the card that caught her eye. She bent and picked it up. Did the hungry, she wondered, still get sent signs like manna? For the card invited her to the opening party of the organic farm shop over the hill and far away. It was tonight, six-thirty onwards, and it was only just past six now. She could just get in the sodding car and go. Leave David to his bulging cheeks and bed-bound TV and be social somewhere. *Anywhere*, even if it was only an organic farm shop.

She skipped upstairs and plugged in her curling tongs. David, propped up on pillows, already in his pyjamas, said, 'Curling tongs?'

And she said, 'Pyjamas?'

She chose a long white pleated dress from the wardrobe, the one that David said made her look like a refugee from an E.M. Forster film. Why not? she thought, rubbing scent beneath her armpits. With her hair in random curls and a rose-pink scarf round her hips, she thought she looked – well, if not like Helena Bonham-Carter *yet*, then the way she might become over the years.

The drive felt like a liberation. Empty roads, a short cut she knew past fields of young corn and the dying yellow of going-over rape fields. Poppies made their blood spots in the hedgerows and among the waving sunlit fields. The air was surprisingly warm. Or perhaps it was the whisky? Her bare arms were, she noticed, brown and healthy-looking up to the elbows, but white as milk above. It was the mark of a field worker. She turned on Radio Three but the undulations in the landscape caused interference – anyway, it was only

some old medieval dirge being played. What she wanted was
Elgar's *Enigma*. Corny but perfect, like all good clichés. But
there was only a tape of *Gerontius* in the car. Well, that would
do. She fast-forwarded it to the Good Angel's sweet farewell
as Gerontius prepares to step into purgatory. She would
have wept for the pleasure of it, only she did not want to
mess up her mascara. She felt alive, whole again, like a
young girl. Even the white dress seemed part of the sensation.
She looked down and smiled as the Angel's voice soared –
she had never tied a scarf round her hips in her life before.
Well, well. And why not?

And that was how it began.

When she arrived, the first person she saw was Sidney
Burney. He was standing his ground in a large, contrivedly
rustic room that had once been an immense barn. Swags of
herbs hung from the rafters next to sides of bacon and
impossibly decorative strings of white onions and pink garlic.
Clean, white refrigerated displays of live yoghurts and butter
and cheeses were chastely admonished for their modernity
by renovated farm carts containing assorted, old-fashioned,
nobbly vegetables. The nobblier the better for purveyors of
the organic, she thought, smiling to herself. She picked out a
dried apricot from a handsome wooden box and chewed on
it as she wove her way towards her employee. As she ap-
proached, his eyes went shifty, lighting momentarily on the
rose-pink scarf before looking away. She sashayed her hips
dangerously, pretending it was necessary to pass by the
various obstacles en route. In fact she was trying herself out,
like a teenage girl who has suddenly discovered her attractions, and, like a teenage girl who has just discovered alcohol,
she also wanted another drink. If Sidney Burney was hardly
Mellors, he was a start.

'What's that?' she asked, suspiciously sniffing the glass of
murky liquid in his hand.

'Proper cider,' he said shortly. 'They say.'

'Who says?'

'Them . . .' Sidney pointed vaguely with the stub of his

pipe in the direction of a cluster of people standing by one of the huge-wheeled carts. Above the backs of heads Jill could just make out two pretty smiling milkmaids dispensing the stuff from large pitchers. People were drinking it with relish, while at the end of the cart another apple-cheeked girl cut wedges of yellow English cheese. Everyone looked so happy, and there was the added sense of well-being that comes from getting food and drink free. She was glad to be here, a part of it all. Better than being stuck indoors with someone who currently looked like a potato.

'What's it like?' she asked, cider never having been her tipple.

'Very good,' Sidney said, taking a swig as if to prove it.

'I'll get some,' she said. 'What do you think of the place?'

He stared slowly around at the rafters and the carts and the decorative drapings of horticultural produce. 'Very pretty.' He nodded and sucked at his pipe. 'They'll make a deal, I shouldn't wonder.'

'Where are they?'

'Who?'

'The owners?'

'Oh – around,' he said vaguely. And then pointed. 'There's the missus. In the blue . . .'

Jill followed his pointing pipe and saw a plump, round-faced, smiling woman in Laura Ashley cornflower print. Her arms beneath the short puffed sleeves were solid and brown all the way down, and her bright, scrubbed face looked healthy and kind. Jill avoided her. Jill did not wish to associate with wholesome women like that tonight. Jill felt she had associated with wholesome women like that for quite long enough. She looked around as she made her way towards the drink cart to see if she could spot somebody louche, but she couldn't. Only Peter Piper from the local paper. She avoided him – he was already very red in the face and she did not want to get stuck with him. She could talk to him anytime – tonight she was hoping for adventure. It was a bloody silly name, anyway. She smiled to herself and promised that if he came over, she would tell him so at last.

She reached out a hand and a smiling milkmaid put a glass into it. She reached out another and a hunk of cheese was placed in it. 'Bread's over yonder,' said the cheese-giver, whose smile looked tired. Not surprising. Up here if there was anything going free the locals were wise enough to grab every ounce of it. Part of the legacy of having been milked dry by successive centuries of Southern government.

Jill moved away and towards the bread table because she had to eat something and didn't fancy the cheese. It stung her throat, it was so strong. It was the kind David liked. She placed the nibbled chunk discreetly on the edge of the cheese cart as she moved on, hoping no one would notice, and she took a drink of the cider to wash away the sensation.

If anything the cider was worse. Being somewhat uninhibited, she pulled a face and went 'Urrgh!' She looked at the glass in childlike disbelief, and was about to set it down when a voice near by said, 'You don't like our cheese and now you don't like our cider. What *do* you like?' This had to be the owner. There was something quite commandingly proprietorial about the possessive 'our' . . .

She looked up.

A man gave her a slightly sardonic smile. He had sandy grey hair and looked rather military, very straight-backed. He was wearing a countryman's check shirt and lovat tie. He had a small scar on his cheek just under the left eye, a slight ruddiness to his pale freckled skin, and navy-blue eyes with sandy lashes. *Not* her physical type. As he smiled, she noticed that the little scar crinkled up. She felt herself begin to blush slightly – both for the cheese with its little teeth marks which she could see resting accusingly where she had placed it behind him, and for the loudness of her cider critique. She looked down, then up. She had forgotten the question.

'What?' she said, going for bluntness.

His smile widened. 'I said, what do you like if you don't like the cider?'

'Champagne,' she said airily, thinking he didn't know her from Adam and she could soon slip away.

'That doesn't surprise me,' he said rather softly.

She moved away a fraction. 'Doesn't everyone?' she asked, her voice sounding like some tinny actress. She plunged the glass to her lips and took a second draught of the horrible stuff. 'I suppose it gets better,' she said as graciously as she could. She was about to generalize about the place when instead she found herself saying quite spiritedly, 'Why didn't you come and look at our produce?'

'Who are you?' he said quickly.

She told him.

He removed the glass from her hand, put it down and took her elbow. 'Will you come into the office for a moment?' he said.

No fear, she thought. She removed her elbow as delicately as she could. 'I have to be getting back.'

'The reason why,' he persisted, lounging against the edge of the cart now, ankles crossed, arms crossed on his chest, very relaxed despite the throng of people all around him, 'is that we drew a line on the map above which we decided not to venture.'

'That seems a bit of a Rupert Bear decision,' she said, regretting the personal short-form immediately.

He laughed and the scar disappeared completely. 'Rupert Bear?'

'Oh, nothing. Just a family joke – for being a grown-up and behaving like a child.'

'Considering the face you pulled and the noise you made over my cider was worthy of an eight-year-old, that's cheek.'

'Nevertheless' – she stubbed her finger against the side of the cart for emphasis – 'to draw an arbitrary line is not good business sense.'

'Otherwise we would have been looking for potatoes in Doonray. You have to stop somewhere.'

She giggled in spite of herself. 'Glowing potatoes.'

He raised an eyebrow. 'Hmm?'

'Doonray – it's a nuclear power station.'

'Figure of speech,' he said, and she noticed that he un-crossed his ankles and was a little less affably poised.

'Well, anyway,' she said, 'I have to go. My husband is ill.'

He looked about him. 'Is he here?'

She laughed. The idea of David with his puffy face and pyjamas roaming the rustic displays was absurdly funny.

'No,' she said, 'he isn't really interested in my business. He's got toothache.' She giggled again. And put a hand to her mouth instantly.

'It's *your* business, is it?'

'Yes,' she said, fixing him with what she hoped was a quelling look. 'Mine. All mine.' Damn, that sounded more like a petulant three-year-old. 'I must go.'

'We should come and . . . um . . . look over what you've got, then?'

She looked over towards the cornflower-blue Laura Ashley and back at him. Their eyes connived.

Sidney Burney, amazingly, was suddenly standing at her side. He wanted more cider.

He nodded and made some kind of gruff noise in his throat at her, which she took to be a greeting and apology for pushing past.

'One of my helpers,' she said grandly. 'Aren't you, Sidney?'

Sidney looked hunted.

The sandy eyebrows raised and lowered themselves. 'Well, you seem to think the cider is OK. Have some more.' He turned, gestured. 'Jane, more cider for the gentleman.'

Jill thought this was so patronizing she nearly threw up. This man was as bad as David for making her want to do that. She moved away, willing her rose-pink scarf not to sway. He followed her.

'Will you introduce me to your wife before I go?' she said, challenging.

He stopped. He, too, looked towards the cornflower blue. 'Not now,' he said easily, 'she seems rather busy.'

'Jill?' said a voice. It was Peter Piper. 'Jill, where's David? Come and talk to a lonely old reporter. Have you got some stuff here?'

'Not yet,' said the smiling man at her side. 'But we may rectify that if the goods are worth having.' There was a very slight pressure to her forearm. 'Goodbye then,' he said, and Jill's heart went a resounding thump.

When she looked back from Peter's face, the man in the check shirt had gone, weaving his way through the crowd, turning to look at her for a moment with a smile. Jill thought how unprepossessing sandy hair just turning grey was. She also wondered, driving home, how much erotic Roman poetry he knew, and would he crack up over Anglo-Saxon names? She looked at the beautiful gold-tipped hills. She felt depressed. Some adventure. She was going to have a dreadful hangover in the morning.

Verity is not being kind to her wall. It was all right throughout the summer months when the door was open and the stocks, roses and sweet peas floated in their scent. Right up to the beginning of the autumn it was all right – she had a script to finish and some commissioned articles on 'The Wonderful World of the Media' and 'What Has Happened to All The New Writers?' But now, with script and articles done, money in the bank and time on her hands, she feels the chill of lonely nights descending with the early-evening darkness. And with the darkness also descends the twinkling aurora borealis of the gin bottle. And with that twinkling luminescence come the long monologues to the Tuscan blankness. 'Well, then,' she had asked it as the dreary damp days of August gave way to an Indian September, 'where shall we betake ourselves, my Italian lover?' And though she pressed her cheek against him and ran her hands longingly over his smooth skin, he offered her no solution. This was at half past one in the morning when the twinkling luminescence had done its work. Verity was lonely. *Fucking* lonely as she told her confidant. And where was Margaret? What use had she been as a single entity living down the road? *None*. Absobloodylutely *none*! –

'You'd have thought, Wall, wouldn't you, that she could have spared a few days – a week even – to come away with me somewhere? But no. Oh no. *She's* got a bloody lover, hasn't she, Wall, and that takes care of that. Out here and there, away at weekends, pulsing with activity all the time. Or in bed – I've seen the curtains drawn late into the morning and I know . . . She certainly wasn't lying there on her own, because his car was parked outside. And I met that Harry at the Channel Four party and he *seemed* to be all right, except he threw up after the brandy and confessed, too late, that he was a lapsing alcoholic . . . Just what I needed. *What* I needed was someone fresh and alive in my life to clean *me* out – not the other way around. And when I casually suggested that we might go away together, Margaret – the old bag – says, all prissy like, that she'd love to, maybe later, only she's a bit tied up with going off to Nîmes with fartface to look at the new Norman Foster building. Well, Wall, she could have come here and looked at *you*. Now, couldn't she? You being so perfect and all . . . And when I say to her "But there's plenty of time to fit something with me in as well as him," – stinkfeatures – she goes all funny around the eyes – shifty – and says, "Well, maybe, perhaps . . ."' So much for making a pact. Verity feels seriously betrayed nowadays.

Verity leaves off cuddling the wall and pours out some fizzy water. She is aware that this kind of drinking can seriously damage your looks and therefore your chances. But chances for what? 'I don't want chances. All I want is a little bit of friendship at a difficult time in my life. And not her looking at her watch every five minutes . . .' Verity mimics her friend to the wall – she quite often entertains the wall in this way nowadays. '"Must fly – I'm meeting Oxford at seven." "Must dash – we're getting the three o'clock flight." "Can't stop – Oxford's coming over."'

Ah well, Verity thinks with satisfaction, it'll end in tears.

She just wishes it would end in tears a bit sooner ... She kicks the base of the dishwasher at the memory, the dishwasher now being her discarded companion since it refused to follow her drunken advice on the subject of doing a quick rinse, and wept copiously all over the floor instead. The kick hurt, making Verity feel better.

'She's even been bowling, Wall. I ask you. At her age! And did I want to come and make up a threesome? No, I bloody well did *not*. Gooseberrying all night. Bowlabloody-rama, Wall. I ask you. Second childhood. It'll be *raves* next, and coming home reeking of Ecstasy.'

Half an hour later, when it is clear that the wall has had enough, Verity retires to bed, only to sit up suddenly, remembering that she has had nothing to eat. Down she pads into the kitchen to make herself a sandwich out of two old Ryvitas and what there is left in the fridge: a half lemon and a past-sell-by packet of Primula Lite. In the back of her brain Verity finds this funny. She also thinks that were one to carry on like this, one might invent a new kind of sandwich filling – through the mere serendipity of it. As she chews on the piquant combination, she thinks that it might make a fun article. 'What secret sandwich fillings do the stars of stage and screen prefer?' Aspects of Verity are, she considers, still working very perfectly. Ah well, roll on Christmas – at least she has been invited down the road for that. Only another six weeks or so away. And a lot could happen in that time. Seven weeks and it will be the New Year. Verity sucks at the pithy rind – and bursts into tears at the thought.

Chapter Two

We must make sure that we speak to each other on Christmas Day. What are you doing? We are spending it here on our own. And then we're going skiing. Why don't you come over?

•••••••••••••••••••••••••••••

You can cram an awful lot into quite a short space of time if you are determined and if you have few responsibilities. And I began to understand why by far the most keenly sought requirement among lonely hearts advertisers is someone to go travelling with. Enjoying the reflected experience of a close companion's eye is a charming way to spend time. And if you fetch up in bed together and get on well there too, you've almost hit the jackpot. Of course, we were blessed by total harmony because neither of us had to make ground, establish lasting rules or feel insecure about saying what we wanted. Madrid and the Prado, Nîmes and the Norman Foster building, were fine. My Murder Mystery Weekend, his suggested few days under canvas, were not.

The other thing about all this dashing about and hedonistic activity was that it afforded very little time for serious soul-searching conversation – not that there was any need. Once I did ask him if he would ever want to talk about his wife to me, but he only shrugged and said maybe, so I left it alone after that. Wait for the Zen, I counselled my curiosity, and maybe one day it will rise. And if it didn't? Well, after all, I didn't want him to dig into my skeletons. It seemed a fair compromise.

Because of the transient nature of our relationship, I neither expected nor sought to meet his friends and family. What we did as a couple we did alone – apart from the eternal Verity. Most of our time together was spent at my house – his flat being in the uncomfortable state of packing up required for a complete life change – and that seemed to suit us both. We would meet a couple of times during the week and at weekends, though we took nothing for granted. We never quite got back the extra dimension of fun and theatre that Marston Manor, Hexham and Jill and David had provided, but it was still pretty good.

By the time Christmas hove into view, I was ready for some peace and staying put. Our last trip of the year was a silly couple of days at the Metropole in Brighton, that place so apocryphally renowned for adultery and illicit weekending. Here quite the reverse of Marston Manor was true: if you didn't sign in under different names and rush off to your room immediately, you were definitely suspect. By now we were less inclined to pulverize the bed linen at every opportunity, and more inclined towards companionship. It did not seem too remote a possibility that one day we would simply be friends even if oceans and continents separated us, so it was somehow even more amusing and bizarre to be staying in such a hotbed of scandal. Brighton is the perfect place for rude rompings. Not only do you have the Metropole with all its salacious history, but the newly tarted-up Royal Pavilion as well. With its exquisite bad taste and oriental sham, it made the perfect companion to our hotel.

Oxford was very informative about buildings and style, and pointed out small things that I would not have noticed if he hadn't been there – aspects of structure, why certain fittings worked, what the function of something that I took as purely decorative might be. He was also very good on furniture. At the Pavilion, as we were going through the rooms, both aghast and fascinated at so much hideous junk, I pointed to an interesting and rather nice plain wooden recliner. It had a sloping back and a long, narrow seat and was a little lower than normal chair height. 'That's a nice sort of daybed,' I said, and he laughed. 'It's nothing of the kind. It's a rogering stool for when you want to take your mistress from behind.' The woman to *our* rear gave a small squeak but, notwithstanding, lingered a while staring at the object fixedly and holding on to the hand of her escort very tightly. When we first met, I thought, we would have been dashing back to the hotel after something like that to practise the suggestion for ourselves. We seemed to be moving towards a conclusion quite nicely, despite Colin, prophet of doom.

Afterwards, by way of relief from the tinsel and trash, we went to look at the sea, grey and churning in the cold December light, and I saw that Oxford's eyes were far away as he looked out to the horizon. There had been a barely perceptible change in him over the last couple of weeks – a kind of flexing up to the future. We were going skiing for New Year and had made no plans after that. From then on we would be winding down. Saskia would be home before I knew it, and he would be gone. To everything there is a season, as they say, and an allotted span.

The big fly in the ointment concerning the End of the Affair was Verity. But when I said to Colin at one of our lunches that she would most likely crow and crow, he came out with one of those amazing shards of enlightenment that men occasionally manage. 'Why not let her?' he said. 'It might do her good . . .'

Perhaps I will, I thought. It *might* do her good. But I compromised: if she was to crow, then I wasn't going to let her begin until he had actually gone. Otherwise I should have weeks and weeks, if not months of it. I would just tell her, very quietly, once he was safely away. By then her crowing would be a welcome diversion before Saskia came back. Verity might be good at real-life jigsaws, but I rather fancied I was better at the metaphysical ones.

Then Fisher rang and arranged for me to come to his office with my Picasso portfolio, which quite took any other thoughts from my head. He had sounded *so* wicked and mysterious.

'Linda and Julius will be there. Eleven sharp. And I'll take you out to lunch afterwards.'

'What on earth do you think it might be?' I asked Verity over coffee the next morning.

'*I* don't know,' she said, 'and I can't think because I've got a hangover.'

'Don't drink, then,' I said, with my mind still busy on Fisher.

It was only afterwards that I thought perhaps I had been a shade too sharp. The trouble was that I had just sat through another of those tedious *stichomythia* sessions, where she'd say something like, 'What's the part of you he likes best, do you think?' And I'd say something flippant back, like, 'My toes.' And then she'd sigh, and take on her Mark look – far away, sad and dewy – and say, 'He used to massage my feet. It was lovely.' And then I'd say, 'Yes, sex is wonderful.' And she'd say, calling her eyes back from the dewy wastes, 'I'm talking about *love*, Margaret.' And I'd say, 'And I'm talking about *sex*, Verity.' And then she'd say, 'You are such a hard case sometimes.' And I'd get worse and say, 'Better than melting away. Oxford and I have an understanding.' And she'd say, 'You can't have an understanding about love, it happens.' And I'd say, 'Not to me, I hope.' And she'd say, 'Mark and I were just meant to fall in love. Couldn't stop ourselves.' And with great self-denial I'd *not* say, 'Yes, and look at you now . . .' but make coffee or something and change the subject. But it would inevitably come back again. 'Tell me about that first hotel. It's so romantic.' And I would. And she would say, 'Mark and I did it in Green Park up against a tree at night. It was wonderful . . .' And back would come the dewy mistiness.

I had to keep thinking of the Tintoretto very hard to overcome such mordant sentiment and not say, 'Well, why not go back with him, then?' Which really would have been letting the side down. Quite clearly he was as good for her as a drink of arsenic.

Chapter Three

Happy, happy Christmas, dear Aunt M. I wish we were together, and I send you lots and lots and lots of love. Missing you like crazy. PS. I've written to Fisher about the show. Isn't it exciting? Love you.

•••••••••••••••••••••••••••••••

When you are feeling very secure in yourself – that one-millionth part of your life if you are lucky – any coldness from someone you care for can unsettle you. On the other hand, any coldness from someone you don't care for at all can be quite refreshing. And that is how I felt about meeting up with Linda and Julius again at Fisher's.

They were sitting side by side in a pair of art nouveau rosewood chairs, the kind with arms and elaborately inlaid backs which are generally held to be very comfortable. But from their posture you might have been forgiven for assuming they were perching on a Fakir's bed. Rigid was the first word that came to mind, followed by angry. Much of this latter was, I suspected, between themselves, though they were maintaining a stout effort to transfer some of it to me. This only made me feel all the sunnier, although it was a sharp and frosty December day. I absolutely beamed at them as Fisher gave me a glass of sherry and gently guided me into a third chair, which was set to one side of them. Julius stared at me over his sherry glass in silent displeasure. True to my estimation of his character, desire had changed to opprobrium. I crossed my legs, let my skirt move up fractionally without rearranging it, and gave him a bright, open smile.

'How nice to see you again, Julius,' I said, recalling the answerphone velvet voice.

'Mmm,' was all he said, a little uncomfortably.

'Linda!' Transference of gummy smile. 'How well you look.' People, I find, usually take this to mean that they've put on weight.

She returned the compliment with such a rictus that it was hard not to laugh. As a matter of fact she *did* look rather well, for anger had added some colour and vitality to her usually pale complexion.

Fisher stood at his huge desk opening the portfolio, touching it with surprising reverence. Then he said, even more to my surprise, 'Ah, the work of the Grand Master. A rare and lovely thing . . .' I caught his eye. It had an innocence about it that looked wholly unnatural. 'Come and look, you two,' he said, gesturing at the spread before him. 'A feast indeed.'

I downed my sherry in one. Now this really was a piece of theatre.

Linda and Julius stood next to Fisher as he began to expound on the treasure before him. 'See,' he said grandly, with unpardonable creepiness, 'the flow of the masterly line. This is the work of perhaps the greatest modern artist of all time – at the very end of his life and yet showing no hint of faltering . . .'

Fisher! I wanted to cry. How can you *say* that?

Julius was nodding in that way people do when they wish to ape the cognoscenti, and Linda's eyes were snapping over the pages as Fisher turned them, and she was clearly uneasy with the rudeness of the images but determined not to flinch. My evil imp overtook the Good Angel of Reason and I sauntered over, popping my head casually between theirs. Fisher gave me a quick look of warning. I smiled at him as if to say it was all right.

'Hmm,' I said. 'Priapic art – perhaps the finest interpreter of the style. Why, I think he could even teach those old Greeks a thing or two . . . And just look how reverential he is towards the joy of sex '– sex, that is, as the procreative principle. I should say that, if anything, these etchings display the wider theme of Essential Progenitive Ardour. What do you say, Fisher?'

'Absolutely.' I could see he was now thoroughly enjoying himself. 'You should have been an art historian,' he said wryly.

'Oh no. Me? I just like to look . . .' I leaned further towards the open portfolio and began pointing at things that especially took my fancy. 'See,' I said, 'how delicately those buttocks melt down on to the Bull-man's glorious phallus – wonderful – I can almost feel it myself.'

Julius had gone completely rigid. Forced to stare at the image which I was pointing at, he could only do so with the pop-eyed glaze of a regimental sergeant-major who has just discovered his wife *in flagrante* with the colonel.

'Just look at the marvellous strength of the image, the tenderness of the drawing, the way he has thickened the line at the base and around the balls, and then thinned it again as he takes it up towards the –'

Linda looked at her watch. 'I have a lunch date,' she said. 'Do you think we could move on? In fact' – she looked at Julius – 'I think we've probably seen enough.'

'Oh no,' I said. 'Fisher, may I?' And I turned the pages gently until I came to the one that I remembered from the exhibition. 'Your mother liked this one, particularly,' I said to Julius. If Mrs Mortimer was listening up there, she would have laughed at my impudence. It was true that she had whizzed her wheelchair up to it and made a long and defiant speech about why it was such a ripping image, but it was more an exercise in her telling me off than in art appreciation. The picture represented a group of leering goat-men, hiding Bathsheba-style, huge penises in their hands, peering through some rushes as a group of nubile girls frolicked in the water or washed each other on the bank. In short, it was the absolute male fantasy of voycurism and one hell of a masturbation party. Some of it was very badly drawn (perhaps the Grand Master did it one-handed?), but some of it was very beautiful indeed. The girls were expressive – not *quite* innocent angels, and their gestures as they touched each other were palpably tender.

'Hmm,' said Fisher, noncommittally.

'It gets to the heart of the matter, do you see, Linda? You have to destroy to recreate, sully to make pure again. This image' – and here I fixed Fisher with a very hard look – 'is the essence of innocence corrupted.'

'Yes, yes, I do see,' said Julius, unlocking his jaw for a moment. Now that it had been explained, he could gaze with a connoisseur's licence on those swollen naughty bits cavorting so girlishly.

Fisher closed the box. 'And you see that it is all in perfect condition. Quite untouched, I should say, from the day it was bought. It's a handsome set, a *very* handsome set. I shall ask Margaret to let me keep it here until you have made your decision.'

He took out his card and wrote a number on the back of it. 'This is my number in the country. I should be grateful if you could keep it discreet, but if you need to talk to me during the next couple of months and I'm out of town, do ring.' He ushered them towards the door, a hand on each of their elbows. Lowering his voice, he said, 'I do so hope this can be made to happen. Let us keep in touch.'

In return Linda gave him a smile that would have done credit to a patient about to undergo surgery. If she had said, 'Oh, thank you, Doctor,' I would not have been surprised.

'What on earth is going on?' I said in the restaurant.

'Keep your voice low, please,' said Fisher, graciously accepting the menu from the waiter. 'This is one of my regular haunts. The duck is very good.'

'Bugger the duck. I'm speechless . . .'

'You are clearly not. And you never *are*. I hoped you would leave it all to me.'

225

'All what?'

'The sales pitch.' He looked over the top of the menu. His eyes were sparkling with wicked good humour. 'Now, just be quiet and leave the *rest* to me and concentrate on food. Then you can tell me all about this new lover of yours. He seems very nice – if a little . . .'

'A little what?' I leapt in, feeling stung for some reason.

Fisher raised an eyebrow. 'I was merely going to say, a little different from what I expected.'

'What did you expect?'

'Someone altogether safer, I suppose.'

'*Safer?*'

'Mmm,' said Fisher, studying the menu, 'someone quite dull who wouldn't threaten the status quo. This one is . . . well . . . quite pretty and I should have thought the kind you might well fall in love with. Have you?'

'Nope,' I said, also studying the menu. 'And I don't intend to, either.'

We ordered and sat back sipping mineral water, Fisher having sent back the wine to be cooled properly.

'Tell me what all this is with Linda and Julius. You were talking complete rubbish.'

'So were you, my dear. And very convincing it was too.'

'But you're a respected art dealer. It's your profession. People rely on your honesty.'

Fisher smiled. 'I am now extremely old and extremely tired of the way things are devalued nowadays. And so I play a bit of a game that will hurt no one and may do some good. After all, remember the sainted art historian Berenson. Half the world thought he was God. And after he died, half the world discovered they had bogus Titians. But no one really minded.' He touched the wine bottle that was held out to him and nodded. 'None of it matters to those who care about art. Only the more money-minded need be concerned.'

'But it's nice to know that the canvas you own was once touched by the master's hand – that's the inner link.'

'Quite. And those who understood that refuted the post-Berensonites and went on believing that what they had was genuine Titian. It came to the same thing. Belief. People believe what they want to believe. Otherwise, I imagine we would all shoot ourselves.' He leaned forward and looked positively fierce for a moment. 'Remember this. Art is the bridge with the realm of the spirit – the necromancy of humanity. That is something you should know, or remember if you had forgotten.'

I blinked. He was being more than usually profound. 'Talking of which,' I said, 'Saskia said she was going to write to you. Has she?'

He looked surprised. 'Saskia? How nice. No. Not yet.'

'When she does' – I fingered the tablecloth – 'will you . . . um . . . be a little circumspect?'

'I always am,' he said. But he looked a little too intrigued.

He asked me to leave the portfolio with him and to trust him. If I could have raised an eyebrow, I would have. 'After that performance?' I chided. He shrugged, amused. 'But the duck was good . . .?' He said, 'In some areas I am utterly trustworthy.'

Chapter Four

Dad said that if he did get a show in London, why didn't I show with him? What a compliment. Skiing was great. Sorry you missed your trip. Never mind, Paris will be nice instead. Gather ye rosebuds, I'll be home soon!

••••••••••••••••••••••••••••••

Elizabeth was a canny lass and an even cannier ageing Queen. Marriage she had flouted, virginity (and thus the status of available sweetheart) she espoused. Her dearest Leicester had married illicitly, disposed of his wife and then upped and died, leaving her bereft. And her new favourite, the handsome, dashing, desirable Essex, had overreached himself to end his days on a traitor's block. Personally, I think that when she finally signed his execution order, Elizabeth was remembering his comment to a friend about her 'bent old carcase' rather than the fact he had tried a spot of political usurpation. In love, which would be the worse betrayal?

Men. You can't live with 'em, and you can't live with 'em.

So must Elizabeth have said to her mirror each night thereafter before blowing out the candle on her ageing face. I doubt she was always a virgin, but she sure as hell became one again once the looks started to go. However, with her red wigs, her toilette that could take a day, her essential femininity, which was quite literally allowed full reign, she turned herself into the greatest actress of what was probably the most theatrical period of our history. And proved herself to possess such consummate skill in the role of Virgin Regnant that long after her teeth had fallen out and her skin had wrinkled to a walnut, she still got wooed nightly by a band of courtiers unable to do other than suspend reality and become a willing, participatory audience.

From beginning to end she never failed to appeal to the gallery, as conscious of playing a part as she was of the part she played. She gave out only what she chose, and very sensibly always took control. She did not give a furbelow for what people might think, which is why it all worked. If *you* don't care, then nobody else will. So nightly, and sometimes in matinée, she would strut her stage. Masques and dancing were part of the ritual. What it must have been like in the last few years for an Elizabeth who was nearly seventy, toothless and bald, as well as tired out from the excesses of successful stateswomanship, to step a light pavane scarcely bears thinking about. Yet Mary Fitton, maid of honour, would lead in the time-honoured masque and afterwards Her Majesty would be wooed to dance. Once the sovereign asked Mary what she represented in the fancy dress, and the maid replied, 'Affection.'

The Queen puckered her lip scornfully. 'Affection!' she croaked. 'Affection is false.' Yet still she rose to dance. It would not do to crumble. Let the ritual and the romance flourish to the end.

And if her Shakespeare, and mine, was the honey-voiced descendant of Ovid, past master of the rituals of love, then it was well for us both – ageing virgin and temporary lover – that whilst enjoying the honey and the melting, sweet phrases, we should also remember that, 'Honeydew comes from the backsides of aphids.'

It does not do to let too much pink light in without being conscious that beyond this is always darkness. I am quite sure that had Bacon given up physics for entomology and passed on this great aphid fact to his Queen, she would have added to her little personal homily in front of the candlelit mirror, 'Ah, verily, verily, Mr Bacon, one would do right well to remember that,' and danced on, nightly, in the masque with the merest hint of wryness in her smile.

So Oxford and I had enjoyed our ritual, *our* masque. Alas, alack, as Elizabeth might have said, to make progress in the world it helps to be one of a pair. I cannot say that I approve, but it is so. Not surprising, really, when you consider how close we are to the animals. A bachelor badger or a single stoat gets the bum's rush wherever they may try to park themselves within the tribe. All right, we humans have come a long way. We don't leap on the necks of single women and bite them in case they are out to steal our mates, or clash with our antlers if we see a man getting too close to our female counterparts, but try going to a dinner party as a single gel and chatting to an attractive partnered man and just *see* . . .

It seemed perfectly fitting that we should spend Christmas apart, he with his family in Suffolk, whom I had never met and did not choose to. Falsity can go only so far before it becomes unpalatable, and we could both imagine the eager eye of a caring mother on this new companion in her widower son's life. When I suggested to Verity that we spend the festive occasion together, she raised her eyebrows and said, 'Festive? Huh!' But I knew she was relieved. Me too. Without Saskia it would have been hard to spend Christmas alone.

Oxford went off to Suffolk about a week before Christmas, and now that I had time to think, suddenly I felt bad about Jill. I had not seen her since my visit with Oxford, and we had scarcely talked on the telephone. Communication between us had trailed away. My fault probably. Deciding to make amends, I rang up to invite myself. I realized at once there were creases to smooth because she sounded far from her exuberant old self, but she cheered up a little when I said I would be coming alone. Perhaps she was ready for some serious one-to-one attention, I thought to myself – long mornings of sitting up in bed together putting the world to rights. It occurred to me that she must, in any case, be feeling pretty glum as Giles was spending Christmas in Holland. '*Cherchez la femme!*' I said cheerily, but she didn't laugh.

David must be feeling lost, too – especially as Jill had decided not to visit Amanda. That meant the two of them would be spending the holiday alone – unheard of. Maybe, I speculated, they planned to have a romantic few days *à deux*. But when he briefly came to the phone, he didn't exactly sound like a man who had a romantic yuletide tryst with his wife to look forward to. 'I hope we'll get a chance to talk,' he said *sotto voce*, which was unlike him.

I set off on a bright, clear December morning. As I drove, I thought of the last few months with pleasure. It had been a great big treat and nobody's fingers had got burned. I had just about got it through to Oxford that it was all perfectly fine. He harboured the male view of the thing, which was that 'men must work while women must mourn', and several times showed his anxiety about how I would feel once he had gone. It wasn't arrogance, but the automatic masculine assumption that when they are off and doing they leave behind a bereft, passive female. I wasn't having any of that. As I passed through Stamford, I remembered the time we had set out on this journey together, and how we had stopped at the George for tea. How pleased with myself I had been. That feeling had never left me, not really, apart from the occasional fear that I might be going in too deep. I still felt that the arrangement was successful and honourable and had worked. But what my friends would say about him when he suddenly upped and left for South America was curious to contemplate. No doubt when I defended him, they would call me brave. Ah well. Maybe I could tell them one day.

I got to Jill's about an hour or two earlier than I had expected, after deciding not to do a detour at Hexham after all. Jill rushed out of the house to greet me with sparkling eyes and pink cheeks, which she attributed to my arrival. As I followed her through into the kitchen I was about to say,

'You look like I feel after a night of lust,' when I saw there was someone seated at the table. At first I thought it was David, but my eyes re-registered to make out a man older than him, a man with a refined but slightly weathered face, a green shooting sweater, and brown hands that clutched a mug of tea. He had a charmer's smile and gave me the creeps.

'This is Charles Landseer. Charles, my friend Aunt Margaret from London.'

'Sounds like a title,' he said easily. He stood up and shook my hand.

'Any relation to *the* Landseer?' I asked.

'Yes. Somewhere dim and distant,' he said, smiling into my eyes. Maybe that explained why I did not take to him. I did not take to Landseer's work, either.

'I'm just off, actually,' he said. 'Jill, let's talk some more about the matter. I'm sure it will be fine.' And he left.

I raised an eyebrow at Jill.

'Business,' she said shortly. 'He runs an organic shop not far from here. He's opening another further south shortly.'

'Ah,' I said. 'Good for you.'

'What did you think of him?' she asked, which seemed a funny question.

'Can't say I took to him much, not that that matters. Seemed just a bit too oily – I can't explain. Anyway, it's lovely to see you.' I went over and gave her a kiss. I sensed that she was not her usual friendly self.

'Jill,' I said, worried, 'are you all right?' The sparkle had left her eyes and her cheeks were no longer blooming.

'Oh yes,' she said, passing a hand across her forehead. 'Just a bit tired, that's all.'

'Simon sends his love,' I said. 'I'm glad he's not here. Gives us a chance to talk.'

But if I was expecting anything but the most superficial conversation, I was disappointed. Jill seemed distracted and ill at ease. Occasionally I saw a look of such misery on her face that I was reminded of the woman sitting in the car

232

outside the tube at Holland Park the night I walked back with Saskia. Later, when we were sitting with our gin and tonics, lamps lit, fire burning, David yet to arrive, I asked her what was the matter. But she only muttered something about the business. My attempts at sympathy won only a dismissive shrug. 'I don't much care, to be honest,' she said, and put another log on the fire. She moved like an old woman – the pink-cheeked sparkler who had greeted me earlier had vanished. I watched her go back to her chair and sink into it gracelessly. Even her drink was scarcely touched.

'Jill?' I said, leaning forward. 'What is it?'

She managed a smile and squeezed my knee. 'Oh, I'm *sorry*,' she said. 'Just a bit out of sorts. Put it down to hormones.' She laughed ruefully. 'Or lack of them.'

'Is that truly all?'

She waved her arm dismissively. 'Oh yes, I'm sure it is. And the fact that Sidney Burney is leaving for pastures new.'

'*Sidney*? Surely he's Mellors and will stand by you for ever?'

She shook her head.

'I always thought he loved you.' I laughed and sipped my drink. 'I always entertained great hopes of a tryst among the forget-me-nots for you two.' But if I had hoped to make her laugh like she used to, I was impressively wrong.

'Don't joke about it, Margaret,' she said tersely.

I looked at my glass, puzzled and a little hurt. But not half as hurt, I was aware, as she. Could she really care that much about one employee – even of such long standing – leaving for another job?

'I suppose he was something of a mainstay here. Why's he going? Can't you give him more money or something?'

'You're damn right he was the mainstay,' she said viciously. 'Everyone knew that. It's all just one big fucking betrayal.'

Jill? Swearing? Jill with tears running down her cheeks? It had to be hormones. I mean, Sidney Burney was a good worker but he wasn't indispensable – especially not with the unemployment situation. This reaction had to be due to something else, and hormones seemed as likely a cause as any. What a shame hormones are. Nasty little things – they cause nothing but trouble while you've got them and then suddenly, like careless children, they leave home and never come back.

'Have you thought about HRT?' I said.

She laughed bitterly. 'Head Replacement Therapy, you mean?' She got up and pushed at the log with her toe. It rolled into the grate and she swore again. I picked up the tongs and chucked the log back on the fire.

'There,' I said. I squatted beside her and gave her the untouched drink. 'Have a swig. It might soothe the savage breast.'

She took it but her eyes were far away, staring into the fire, miserable again.

'How could he do it?' she said.

'Well, presumably he'll work out his notice.'

'What?' she said, clearly not understanding.

'Sidney. He'll have to work out his notice before he goes.'

'Oh, him,' she said. She rubbed her hand across her face. 'Oh, I'm not bothered about *him*.' Which left me in a curiously confused state. Usually David's presence inhibited our conversation, but that day I was glad when he came home.

At last Jill seemed to rally a little. We ate supper by the fire on trays and the three of us chatted about this and that. Strangely it was David, not Jill, who asked how I was getting on in my 'love life', as he put it and so I rattled away about all the things we had done. I hoped the tale would take Jill's mind off her own troubles and I tried to make it as funny and romantic as I could, but she went to bed early saying she had a headache. Only as she got up to go did she give me a real hug; it felt as if we were bidding each other adieu for the last time rather than just saying goodnight.

'I've put you back in the little room,' she said. 'After all, you won't be needing a double on this trip, will you?'

I wondered if Oxford and I had transgressed in some way. There was a definite edge to her tone which made me feel uneasy. I too went to my room shortly afterwards. In the kitchen, while we cleared up the supper things, David asked me how I had found Jill.

'Hormonal,' I said. 'Or that's what she seems to think.'

He breathed a sigh and looked, I thought, relieved. 'Ah,' he said. 'Is *that* what it is?'

Somehow I felt I was letting my sex down. Hormones were so easy to impugn, but I really didn't know what else to say. David was clearly relieved by the suggestion, and maybe it was so. I couldn't think of anything else that would make my usually readable friend so upset over something like Sidney Burney.

As I lay in bed, I tried to read but could not stop my mind wandering. I wanted to talk to Oxford about it all, a foolish wish under the circumstances. *Jill* was the one I always talked to. I was sure it would be fine again in the morning. I snuggled down, pleased to be on my own again in my familiar little bed. It belonged to my real self, part of my private history, and was nothing to do with this tempo-rary coupledom I had created.

I awoke to find my room bathed in bright sunlight – a cheering sensation in dark winter days – and I got up immediately to make tea and take it back to bed. I knew the ritual well enough. I would lie in bed sipping my tea and at some point Jill would appear in her old white towelling robe and squeeze in beside me with her coffee. She would say, 'Ugh! How can you drink that stuff?' and then we would put our worlds to rights – or somebody else's – talking in low voices until David called out that it was time for breakfast. The day would then unfold with nothing planned except, perhaps, a dinner party in the evening. With the children away the house was much more silent – something I had not noticed last time, I suppose, because Oxford and I filled up the space. Of course, Jill must be missing the old routine like crazy – the large teenagers sitting around in the kitchen, some new girlfriend on the telephone for Giles, the frantic 'Will you be in for supper tonight?' and 'Are you coming home?' All that change, and hormones too? Oh, come on, Margaret, I said to myself, it's no *wonder* she's feeling the strain.

So I waited. Eventually I heard someone padding down the stairs and into the kitchen. Soon I expected to smell the aroma of good coffee and to greet my morning visitor. I lay back, closed my eyes and let my mind drift pleasantly. I was glad, again, that I was up here on my own, glad that I had not turned myself into part of a couple permanently. Times such as this were infinitely precious. This is what you lose, I told myself, when you yield up to a partnership that engulfs.

I waited until my little yellow pot of tea was empty and cold. No Jill. Eventually I went down to the kitchen with my tray and found a note on the table to both David and me. 'Had to go out,' it said. 'Will be back at lunchtime. Business. See you one-ish. Jill.'

So much for the sisterly confessional.

David asked me politely if I would like to do anything in particular, but I could tell he hoped I would say that I was fine. So I did. I went for a walk but only a short one. The fields were depressingly empty and the air was too cold. Back indoors I relit the fire. As the kindling began to crackle and the small logs settled themselves into the blaze, I sat back on my haunches and felt pleased with myself. Building a good fire contains a primal satisfaction, I suppose. I watched to make sure it had caught properly and then stretched out on the settee and began to read Ovid. It was no hardship to me to be on my own for a while – it only becomes hard when you are lonely inside, and that I never would be. I was reading the *Cures for Love* – the vicious antidote he produced after the *Amores*.

Aim for a glut of passion: glutted hearts break off liaisons;
When you feel you can do without it, still hold on.
Till you are fed up to the back teeth, till love chokes on abundance.
Till you're sick at the very sight of her house . . .

Poor Ovid. How very hurt he must also have been by that

unsatisfactory four-lettered phenomenon. His words betrayed a bitterness that made me shiver as I reread it, despite the crackling warmth from the fire and the snuggle of cushions.

> We hope to be loved, so postpone the final break off
> Too long: while our self-conceit still holds
> We're a credulous lot. Don't believe all they tell you (what's
>   more deceptive
> Than women's words?)

'Why not *men's*, perhaps?' I crowed, and shut the book firmly. Same old story. Ovid began so well with all that lovely stuff about seduction, fun, love, sex, affection, and ended in a welter of bitterness and pain and regret. 'I am right, I am right,' I found myself saying as I went into the kitchen to start making lunch.

There was bread, cheese and soup. I called up to David, who was in his study, that I would start without him if he preferred and he came thumping down the stairs looking embarrassed. 'Really,' I said, 'I don't mind at all if you've got work to do. I'm perfectly happy and content pottering.' He looked relieved. Never ask a chap to sit around the kitchen making idle conversation while you get on with something domesticated – it just makes them squirm. It didn't bother Oxford because we were just playing at domesticity, so it was fun. For real, it becomes too intimate an occupation for most.

Jill got back late – nearer two than one – and she looked pink-cheeked and sparkling-eyed again. Her old self plus another ten degrees. She hugged me. 'Have I been completely horrible to you?' she said. She hugged me some more. 'Sorry.' And she bit into a spring onion with a relishing crunch.

I asked if she had dealt with the problem of Sidney satisfactorily.

'What?' she said abstractedly. 'Oh, *yes*. It was nothing, really. I don't know why I let it get to me. I've just been over to see – ' She swallowed. 'Well, anyway, I've just sorted the whole thing out.'

'So he's staying?'

'Oh, no. He'll go. Charles really needs him.' She stopped, anxiously. 'You remember Charles?'

I nodded.

'And there'll be another bus behind – like we used to say in the old days.'

That was about the sum total of old days' talk that weekend. Jill's mood went up and down several times and I couldn't get close. On Sunday morning I found her singing in the kitchen at about eight, already dressed and making a demented mess and noise with two mixers going. She said she was experimenting in making cheesecakes for the new organic shop and would take them over there later. They had apparently supplied her with the cheese and if it was successful she would produce them on a regular basis. David, who peevishly appeared shortly after me, told her in no uncertain terms what unsound business it was, and how foolish it was to take on new commitments when she had so much else to do. She tapped him playfully on the nose with a spoon – to his fury and my amused amazement – and said that he was only jealous because she was able to diversify. He went off shaking his head. I made my tea, took it back to bed, and afterwards had a long bath. When I returned to the kitchen the cheesecakes were all laid out on trays ready to be dispatched. They looked excellent and I congratulated her. 'I never even knew you could bake,' I said.

'You never know *what* you can do until you try,' she replied happily. 'And now I'm going to take them over there. They're open today.'

'I'll get my jacket,' I said.

She stopped on her way through the door and turned with an expression so strange that it was hard to fathom – somewhere between irritation and fear, I thought, before it shifted to a tight smile. 'Oh,' she said. 'You don't want to come. It'll be boring for you. I won't be long.'

'No . . . really . . . I'd like the ride. And if they're open, I can take something fresh and countrified back for Verity.

Something healthy – she's drinking too much on account of the blessed Mark.'

Jill turned away from me. 'Get her some cider,' she said, 'if you really want to come.'

In the car Jill put on Delius quite loud. 'Do you mind?' she said before I had the chance to ask if we could turn it down and talk. 'I just love it at the moment.'

Truly, I decided, whatever Oxford and I had done, we had done seriously. Jill was now so brittle that if I had bent her arm it would have snapped. Ah well, I thought, what is friendship for but to suffer all these vagaries, and I settled back to listen to the music and enjoy the scenery. At one point I looked at Jill. Her eyes were on the road ahead, but also very far away. It was a similar look to one Oxford had begun to wear sometimes recently.

'Here we are. There it is,' she said suddenly, as excited as a child. A large barn came into view. A few cars were parked on the gravel outside.

We carried in the three large cheesecakes. They were decorated with flower petals and looked magnificent, I thought. I carried the one Jill had entrusted to me with extra care. I had a feeling that if I damaged it in any way Jill would never forgive me. Whatever the reason for this sudden rush of baking, it was bigger, infinitely, than the sum of its parts.

The shop was fairly full – the usual crowd of people picking over things – those who were bored on Sunday, those who were travelling and had just stopped by, those who wanted something to do with the children. It had a nice earthy smell, and whoever had organized the displays of vegetables and cheese and strange rustic drinks needed a medal.

Jill marched past the curious on-lookers to a small office at the back. 'Oh,' she said, 'it's empty.' She began looking around the shop, scanning with a desperate eye.

'Why, Jill,' said a woman's voice behind us, 'how nice to see you.'

I turned, so did Jill, and we stood there making quite an odd picture with our great rounds of cheesecake.

'What are these?' the woman said, smiling in puzzlement. She was small and plump with a bright face.

'Cheesecakes,' said Jill. 'I told Charles I would have a go with that Stainforth cream cheese. I think they are good. And I could make more – for you to sell here, I mean. I told Charles.' She spoke as if persuading someone that her life depended on it.

The woman frowned. 'Did you?' she said a little crossly. 'He said nothing to me about it. They look wonderful. What should I do with them?'

'Is Charles here?' Jill asked, scanning again.

'No. He's gone down south for a day or two – the new shop. Here, let me take one of those.'

I thought for a moment Jill would decline, for she pulled away a little, but the woman was insistent and took one into her sturdy brown hands.

She shook her head. 'I don't quite know what he had in mind – I mean, how do we keep them fresh? And what about portioning?' She looked up at Jill for an answer.

'That's not my problem,' Jill snapped, so that I was embarrassed. 'When exactly will he be back?'

'A couple of days – maybe three. My husband seems to be a law unto himself at the moment. Well, well. I suppose I could put them in the freezer, though I don't think the flowers' – she touched them lightly with her fingertip – 'would survive well. Oh dear.'

Jill's eyes had begun to fill with tears. She looked like a disappointed child.

'Look,' I said, knowing someone had to rescue the situation, 'why don't you have them as freebies? Give people tasters and see what the response is over the next couple of days? Then, when Charles comes back, he can sort it all out.'

It was agreed and we left the three offending orphans with their somewhat harassed new owner. I wanted to look around and get something for Verity and Oxford, but Jill was already walking towards the great barn doors. Dammit, I thought. I called after her that I would be out in five minutes and began to rummage around. I bought elderflower cordial for Verity, and some cheese. The fruit looked wonderfully ecological with their strange specks and irregular shapes, so I bought apples too. For Oxford I bought a flagon of cider that looked as if someone had washed their socks in it. It had a warning skull-and-crossbones label which I thought would amuse him. Maybe in the Nicaraguan jungle he could use it to disinfect his gut.

Back in the car, Jill sat looking forlorn and puffy-eyed. She had clearly been weeping.

'Tell me what's up,' I asked.

She blew her nose. 'Nothing – except disappointment.' She smiled wanly. 'And hormones, I expect.' She turned on the engine and revved with angry vigour. She turned to me with a slight smile. 'And I've just realized that I forgot to put the meat in the Aga.'

'It's all right,' I said, feeling a heel, 'I did it.' I shrugged. 'Well, it was just sitting there in its baking tray, all ready, so I just popped it in.'

'Which oven?'

'Top.'

Jill laughed. 'Aunt Margaret to the rescue. Well, in that case' – she punched my knee lightly – 'we can take the scenic route home, and listen to lovely Delius all the way.'

'Bloody men!' she said as the music crescendoed. 'They always let you down, don't they?'

'Nice woman, the wife,' I said conversationally.

'Yes,' said Jill, almost spitting out the words, '*isn't* she?'

I assumed she was still angry about Sidney.

For the rest of the afternoon I talked about general things. About Saskia and her father and my hopes that the exhibition over here would never happen. Neither David nor Jill understood this.

'Time marches on,' said David.

'Not for my sister,' I reminded them none too gently. 'She never had the chance to march on anywhere. Remember?' They both looked uncomfortable. So what? It wasn't their sister. 'Well, he'll get short shrift from me if he comes over here poking about in the ashes again.'

'Oh, I doubt he'll do that,' said Jill.

'No? I'm not so sure. It's what Sassy wants, more than anything. I can tell. She has a way of sending in a big gun when she wants something badly, and then letting it lie. But she's a tenacious little bugger – always was. I'd give her the moon – but I won't give her this.' A surprising anger rose in me.

'So love hasn't softened that inner bit, then,' said Jill.

'Love?'

'You and . . . that man . . . Simon. It's been too long for it just to be ships that pass in the night.'

That summed it up quite well, I thought, but I didn't have the urge to say so. 'It's not love,' I said. 'It's pleasant, friendly, sexy convenience. Never let them penetrate beyond that, then you won't get hurt.'

I waited for Jill to make her usual response to this – cries of 'Shame!' and 'How can you say that?' But she didn't. Surprisingly she nodded. 'I know what you mean,' she said, getting up to bring in the ice-cream.

I read the label. Everything sound, additive-free and organic. 'Did this come from the new place?'

Jill nodded as she doled it out.

'Everything we get comes from there nowadays,' said David. 'Costs us a fortune in petrol.'

He was smiling, but Jill banged down the spoon and glared at him. 'Oh, David,' she said angrily, 'you are such a mean bastard!'

He looked at me in embarrassment. I looked at him in wonder, and decided to leave immediately after lunch. Whatever was happening up here, there was nothing I could do about it for the time being. It disturbed me to feel so helpless.

*

On the drive home I considered asking the two of them down for Christmas, but realized that if I did, and they came, Amanda would never forgive either them or me. Funny, I thought, how once you have a family you are never truly free to think for yourself. Love being the other side of possession as well as a good many other things, I felt lucky to have come through with Saskia more or less unscathed. True, I was dreading some kind of confrontation over Dickie – *Richard* – but I could handle that. Indeed, as I drove back, I began to think I could handle anything. That suggestion about the stupid sodding cheesecakes had been a mistress-stroke.

One should not congratulate oneself – I knew this – yet at the same time I could not refrain. For was I not, really and truly, remarkably happy? Looking around me, I had only to see that I was. And Simon – *Oxford* – was too, at least so far as we were concerned. Do self-congratulations go before a fall, I mumbled to myself as I arrived home, or what . . .?

Verity was delighted with the elderflower cordial and made us up a concoction with gin (of course), vermouth and a lacing of the rustic liquor. It was, I had to say, very good. Just as well, for she bent my ear for some two hours or more. It became obvious why women turn to drink: it's not the ones with the problems, but the ones who have to listen to them. No wonder so many doctors commit suicide. Imagine that kind of thing week in week out. It was on the tip of my tongue to give up and suggest she take some valium when at last she decided to go. She wove her way precariously down my path. Her last words, said somewhat forlornly from the gate, were 'I'm so looking forward to Christmas.'

I began to wonder if I was.

I had given Oxford a leather travelling bag, which seemed about the most sensible thing to buy him. I put into it some lavender sachets because I thought that when he was far away somewhere so alien the smell would be peculiarly English. More than anything, smells seem to be evocative of association, drawing those involuntary responses that remind us what a mystery we humans are. Patchouli always brought my sister back to me, boiling cabbage was school, baby powder was Saskia, and, of course, the smell of face powder and Yardley Black Rose was my mother. I wondered if Oxford would leave behind an olfactory memento. . . . Time would tell.

He gave me some CDs, things we had listened to in the car or at concerts. He had also made up a tape of various things he thought I would like: a bit of African music brought back from one of his student trips, some jazz, Tallis, whom he called the architect of the musical sublime. I found the effort touching. There is something very special about having a gift made for you. I never believed it when I was a child and my parents said, '*Make* us something, we'd really like that . . .' I yearned to be able to buy them smart things, properly over the counter. My years with Sassy, being given all those struggled-over embroidered coasters, pictures, bits of haphazard pottery, which I now cleaved to so fondly, made me appreciate the value of the hand-made. It is about someone liking you enough to spend some of their precious time to create a pleasure for you. An aspect of love, I suppose, of the broadly based kind.

Now I had to cope with love of the Tintoretto kind. The prospect of the whole of Christmas Day with Verity, me, the gin bottle and Mark-in-the-ether was a little daunting. Colin would not come. 'Leave me out of it,' he said. He was going away somewhere hot.

I worked a day or two in the shop to help out with the Christmas rush. I was a little relieved to find the two of them were not entirely self-sufficient. They had hired a girl who looked something like the pinched little marchioness of Nickleby Legend – she scarcely came up to the counter and looked badly in need of a meal. But it was a good omen. It meant I wasn't entirely redundant and I was pleased to get my hand in again, even if Joan did tend to boss me about in the same way she bossed Reg. Since I was only a halfway house, I didn't object. When I went back there permanently,

I would reassert my authority. Reg was taking Joan to his mother's for Christmas. I thought that was very nice. For one giddy minute I thought about inviting them all over to me, for my heart was plunging hourly. Verity was having deep dips over Christmas, but I realized that the advent of Reg, Reg's mother and Joan would not alleviate this. However, I made up my mind. Verity was *not* going to sit in a puddle of morose remembrance over the guinea fowl. I bought a Christmas television guide and marked up the day. When in doubt, stick on the box.

There were plenty of absurd things to keep us going. Someone famous having his house party opened up to the goggling viewership (filmed in September, I imagine), someone else famous going around perching on children's hospital beds, and old films by the handful. I remembered how Jill had effectively blotted out any chance of talk by turning up the Delius. Well, maybe *Mary Poppins* wasn't in the same league, but what Verity needed was a bucket of sugar to make the medicine go down, and telly was the next best thing. I also bought a video of one of the oldest and worst of the *Carry On* films. Ho hum, I thought, just let her try to get maudlin over *that*.

Jill wrote a short note in my Christmas card apologizing for her silly behaviour. She added, much more in the old style, that David had relented and invited Amanda and Co up after all. 'They both think I am completely potty,' she wrote. 'So I might as well act it. I've got the rosemary and rue, but would be obliged if you could send up a suitable frock for Ophelia, whom I suddenly understand rather well.'

'Just avoid sitting on your arras,' I wrote back. My reward was a fairly normal phone call. She was rushed, she was harassed, she was half looking forward to, and half dreading, the descent of her daughter, but it sounded as if Christmas had got her in its usual grip – hormones or no. She was very surprised that I was spending Christmas apart from Oxford. 'You can't be in love, then,' she said sadly, adding with astonishing ferocity, 'If you were, you would be *miserable* without him.' Ever the romantic, I thought, as I went back to decorating the tree.

Now, that *was* sad. No Saskia to help me, after all these years. I rang her on the spur of the moment, but she was out Christmas shopping. Dickie sounded as if he would like to talk. 'You must miss her,' he said. I had never yet exchanged more words than 'Can I speak to Sassy, please' or the like, and although it was the Season of Goodwill, I did not choose to do so now.

'Of course,' I said, and I asked him to tell her I had called. He wished me Happy Christmas. 'And you,' I mumbled – for wishing him anything happy was pretty phoney.

'You talked to Dad?' Saskia said later, when she rang. I could tell by her voice she was hopeful of something.

'Oh yes,' I said evenly. 'I was just decorating the tree and it reminded me of you.'

'I'm doing one here,' she said happily. 'We just went out on Sunday and cut one. Dad's never had a tree before and –'

'Mine doesn't look anything like as good as usual,' I interrupted. 'Not got your touch . . .'

And I steered her right away from the topic of what Dickie was and was not used to. She was drawing me a picture of a lonely, one-dimensional life and also trying to draw me into the pathos of it. But I would not be drawn, I would not. I felt lonely for Lorna, didn't I? Time never closes the gap left by a loved one. Why should I make cooing noises over the man who was responsible for that lonely space?

Chapter Five

I worry sometimes at the thought of leaving him alone again. But he says he's used to it. Sad thought.

•••••••••••••••••••••••••••••

Well, we got through the guinea fowl and the Queen, and Verity seemed to be on good form for a change. The only difficult bit was when she asked me what gift I had bought my absent lover. Her eyes widened, her mouth gaped, she sat back on her heels – we were playing Monopoly – and said, 'You bought him *what?*'

'A travelling bag. A very nice leather travelling bag.'

'Christ!' she said, abandoning her bid for a hotel on Vine Street – nasty in-between place of no account anyway. 'How could you possibly do that?' And we were off again.

'What do you mean, how could I do that? I just went out with my cheque book, walked into a shop, and bought it. You know – like you do when you go shopping, Verity.'

'But a travelling bag? I mean, *fuck it.*'

'Don't swear like that.'

'But Margaret –' She ran a despairing hand down her face, impossibly dramatic. 'No wonder the tag "Aunt" stuck. That's a ridiculous thing to buy a lover. Think of the message . . .'

'Message? I wrote a card that said "From me with love".'

'No, the message contained in the gift itself. That is . . .' She gave me one of her overweening patronizing looks. 'Well, I mean . . .'

'*What?*'

'Lovers exchange gifts that contain portents, or expressions of something. You buy Simon a travelling bag and he'll think you want him to go away.'

'Well, I do.' Mistake. Her eyes widened.

'What?'

'I mean I don't want him to feel tied.'

'Well, you bloody well should. What is the point of having a man if you don't want to tie him down?' She folded her arms. 'He'll go. He will. And *then* you'll know what it's like . . .'

The crowing had begun. Sometimes women are their own worst enemy. And sometimes a cliché is the only thing that will do.

I looked at my watch. Five-thirty. Time for drinking? We'd had tea and cake in front of the fire and I had protected Verity from her Sarah Gamp impersonation for quite a long time – and, anyway, *I* needed one.

'Right,' I said, reappearing with gin, tonic, ice and lemon on a tray. 'Drinks time.'

Verity stared mournfully into the fire, which was gas coal and therefore, thankfully, spared us the poignancy of dying embers. 'Mark's Christmas card came from Australia,' she said.

'Well, that's a relief.'

'God, you're a hard woman,' she said. 'I don't understand you. Here you are on Christmas Day with me – an old and miserable boot – when you have somebody lovely to love you.' She pointed a finger. 'You . . . are crazy. Whatever the justification you give it, *you are crazy*.'

'Better,' I said, handing her a glass, 'than feeling lonely, Verity, when they go.'

'*Touché,*' she said, raising her glass. 'I'll drink to that.' And, by George, I'll say she did.

It was when she said, 'Buddhists believe it is insulting to mourn at the funeral of one who has had a long and fulfilled life,' that I knew it was time to see her home. Walking back in the sharp air, I thought that when all this lover stuff was over in my life, I would emulate Betty Ford and take Verity in hand a little.

And that was Christmas.

We were walking along the river's edge, waiting for the pubs to open for Sunday lunch, with those great, aggressive wads of rain forest, commonly known as the Sunday papers, wedged under our arms. One of the pleasures about opening these things away from home is that you can leave all the advertising that spills out of them – 'Is Your Home Fully Insured?', 'The Historical Book Club, Six Books for a Penny', 'Join the AA and get a free digital tooth pick' – for someone else to throw away. These Sunday lunchtimes had become an occasional ritual which we spent mostly in companionable silence. I suspected that this was what I would miss more than anything when he had gone. After all, it was one thing to cavort around in bed with someone – which can, with a little adjustment of the fantasy button, occur with many men – but quite another to sit for three hours reading the papers, eating toad-in-the-hole, and still to feel quite content and happy.

'I'm really sorry about the skiing,' he said. 'But when your mother breaks her arm and you're buggering off round the world in a few months, skiing seems a bit trivial. She can be quite volatile, my mother.'

'Do you know, I honestly didn't mind.'

He laughed. 'If things were different, I'd marry you for your amenability.'

'It's not entirely altruistic. I'm not sure I could cope with a volatile mother-in-law. My own mother was bad enough.'

'Did you never want children?' he asked, standing for a moment to watch the blue-nosed baby scullers with their fragile purple knees.

'Nope,' I said. 'Sassy was enough for me. And you?'

He shook his head. 'My wife did. But I didn't. I may have done in time, but . . .' He began walking again. 'As it happened, we didn't have a lot of that.'

'Do you want to talk about it?'

He smiled and shook his head. 'Nope. Let's just go and eat.'

Chapter Six

We have been doing so many things in these last weeks that I haven't had much time to write. I'll call you soon. Besides, I've got something very exciting to tell you. I got your card from Paris. Dad said maybe he and I would go there together one day. I should love to see the Cézannes with him.

....

Verity roams her house on a dull late winter's evening. Bloody February, miserable month. She is searching for an answer from her several domestic confidantes. Will the telephone tell her? She stands beside it. 'Speak, you bugger,' she says to it. '*Speak*.' The telephone does not. Frankly, it is exhausted and confused, for she has been picking it up and dialling all but the last digit of a number before flinging it down on to its rest for most of the day. Any pal would feel bruised by such an experience so it remains silent, mute and impervious. Verity shakes her fist at it, thereby spattering it with drops of gin and tonic. No telephone enjoys a cold shower after a day of abuse. So it will not speak, it will *not*.

Neither the hairbrush nor the mirror has fared any better. A hairbrush feels that its purpose is to give a healthy shine to a head of hair while the mirror sits there to compliment the end result. It does *not* feel that its owner is entitled to give herself a cursory run through the crowning glory and then hurl the servant bristles across the room. And this happened not once but several times, in one instance shattering a piece of Spode which said servant hairbrush always enjoyed looking at in its rest periods. And the mirror, which would like to reflect love of self, the private assessment between human and mineral, does not appreciate being called a stinking traitor. These two objects can't find a good word to say for Verity at the moment. So far as her abuse of them goes, she has had her chips.

The bath? This has scum around it. It used to be a good friend – always accommodating, putting warm arms around her, providing scented calm to ease the bitter wrath. Not any more. If she cannot be bothered to be civil, then it will not be bothered to give comfort. From now on, the bath has vowed, when she gets in it will be gritty and greasy to her naked flesh and remind her of her sanitary betrayal. It politely ignored her perching bottom as she ran through a litany of happier times. Sure, it thinks, you did get up to all kinds of juicy things in me with that Mark, and I was quite happy to let you – despite being designed for only one. But to say you will never clean me again in hating memory is to break contract.

Already the wash basin is flinching from a build-up of old soap, spatterings of toothpaste and worse. The lavatory could be next. It has had to put up with her bringing in the odd male, swaying as they pee, forgetting to put the seat down, leaving old condoms floating around after producing howling noises from down the corridor. It has gone too far. Spring is nearly here, and well-brought-up Crichton-ware expects a thorough clean around this time – not to be treated like the kind of facilities found in a squat on the Edgware Road. Uh-uh, Verity. Your bathroom suite stays united in this. No more kind accommodations to be had here.

Downstairs stands the cold, white German dishwasher. It is deeply offended for it was designed to rid the world of smells and bacteria, not to sit in other people's muck and create them. If the German were any less controlled, it would break down. It may well do so anyway because its owner has forgotten to give it salt for quite a while. Life without salt for a dishwasher is pure cruelty. Besides, it gets bored looking after so many gin glasses, and, though mindful of a particular need, bearing in mind its own origins, for a liberal attitude to ethnic minorities, it finds that sitting in take-away curry and residual Chinese for over a week does not incline it to unbend towards Verity one little bit. So when she crouches down and holds its sides and weeps into its melamine reflection asking for an answer, it abandons the notion of Zeitgeist and embraces Gestalt, because in Gestalt each individual part affects the other, which is what is happening among the half-scraped biriani and sweet-and-sour.

The fridge is fed up. Nothing in it for ages except ice cubes, tonic bottles and left-over smells from rotting vegetation. Verity promised it two weeks ago that she would fill it with good, fresh things – tomatoes, cucumbers, lettuces, olives, carrots, potatoes . . . and, of course, those offending onions. She would, she said, eat healthily. She would, she said, abandon the chink of the glass for the clink of the spoon as it mixed up a good dressing. She would make soup, she would eat wholemeal bread and good-quality butter. And the fridge had believed it all, sat back, almost pouting with pleasure at the dishwasher (the fridge being Italian and inclined to be female), thinking, Here we go at last, back to doing the job I was made for. Then . . . Zilch. A lentil and coriander soup slowly going off, and the salad weeping into itself, getting soggier and soggier. If Verity thinks she can come here now and ask it to open up for her on anything good, she is mistaken. It is full of reproach and means to make that plain.

Even the wall, dear Tuscan friend, has had enough. It is one thing to have a hot cheek, sticky with tears, pressed up against you, and quite bearable to be shouted at from time to time – these things happen – but when it gets a glass flung full in its face, followed by a stream of scatological invective and several kicks from its owner's DMs, that would try the patience of a saint. The wall may have been beatific in some ways, but it is no Francis of Assisi and never said it was. Verity can go boil herself from now on. The wall has started to crumble and will never be the smooth, silent strength it once was to her. One kick dislodged a small piece of terracotta, and more will follow. It is a wound too savage to forgive. Verity may well crawl around on all-fours picking up the shards of glass and biscuity plaster, but the wall will never forgive her. Never. Its wound it will bear as silent testimony to her disgusting displays. *Minestra riscaldare*, soup reheated, as it has tried to point out, never works. No, no. Marco is yesterday, *Marco ieri*. Verity must in future bear what she has to bear alone.

Only the gin bottle, sitting on the bench opposite, feels jaunty. It has been crooned over, stroked with love, poured regularly and feels on top of the world. Its ancestors always said it was designed to create chaos and brought it up on the tale of a famous artist called Hogarth who actually made an icon to its power and called it 'Gin Lane', but it never truly believed that one so small could show such muscle. Now it knows its strength. Wink, wink, it goes at the other malcontents in the kitchen, king of the castle now. That nasty female friend down the road may have sent its brother to a trash heap and brought in the artillery of fresh orange juice and fizzy mineral water, but *she* hasn't been around for long enough. 'Busy, busy, busy,' says Verity to the gin bottle from time to time, 'busy, busy, busy with her lovely, lovely, lover.' Good, thinks the gin bottle, for I feed on loneliness best of all.

'Answer me, answer me,' cries Verity to this atmosphere of alienation. Doing her Sarah Bernhardt again, think the appliances. Better than Callas, mocks the wall. Upstairs the mirror and hairbrush draw closer together, remembering that once she was Snow White, and knowing that now she is the Wicked Stepmother, the Bad Queen, the Harridan. They wonder if they will be able to survive, being such puny, fragile objects.

But the telephone is not autonomous and it is suddenly

wrenched from a soothing, long sleep by one of its companions up in Hampstead. Damn fool time to ring, ten o'clock at night, it thinks, but it has to oblige. If it doesn't, there will be gynaecological explorations the next day and British Telecom is renowned for employing engineers with hands like shovels, fingers like Cumberland sausages. It is rumoured that they do this on purpose to keep the equipment on its toes. So it beeps for the upstairs and rings for the downstairs and Verity, who is on the point of giving the gin bottle another thrill, puts it down in wonder. Margaret, she thinks, Auntie Margaret, she hiccoughs, Auntie Margaret back early from Paris.

Verity is muddled but clear on one point. Her friend is a very brave woman, a very brave and *wronged* woman. For Mr Perfect, Mr Simon Oxford Bloody Perfect is abandoning her brave, wronged friend and leaving her. Leaving her *for ever*. Oh, they may be in Paris now having a last fling, but Margaret must be weeping inside, *weeping*. Verity hiccoughs again and weeps herself. The question she wants answered is, if Mr SOBP can do such a thing when he seemed so nice, then what the fuck is Verity doing resisting Mark? He may have been an oppressive wally, he may have messed about from time to time, he may have been a bit cruel here and there, but he never went off to *Nicaragua* suddenly, did he? Tenerife once, using her money and not telling her – but *Nicaragua*? It was a bit bloody final. Cruel? Cruel? Mark was only on the baby slopes compared to that. In fact – Verity begins the long, slow crawl up the hallway – in fact, compared with all that, Mark is a gem. Which is why she sent him that funny recipe she once wrote.

Verity finds nothing strange about approaching the hall telephone on her knees. She quite often goes about the house like this at night, and early in the morning too. During the day she can become *homo sapiens*, can do her work sitting up even if the screen is a bit fuzzy, but at these other times it just feels better and safer to behave like most other mammals.

She answers the phone brightly, aware that cunning is required when you have been consorting with the spirit of the bottle. It is a man's voice, a familiar man's voice, a *very* familiar man's voice.

'Verity,' it says, 'I need you.'

'Good,' she says, 'come back. All is forgiven,' and she puts down the receiver with the slow care it prefers.

That is the answer, then.

She is thinking now, thinking fast, but not on her feet – she is thinking on her knees as she ascends the stairs. A slow process, but with something positive to be gained now, unlike sometimes when she gets up to the top and forgets why she attempted the climb in the first place. Leaning over the side of the unwelcoming bath, she turns on the taps and pours in shampoo which produces peaks of white pearliness that make her sit back in wonder for a moment. Where did it all come from? She negotiates a more upright position and reaches for the bath oil, which she rubs into her head under the gushing water. Something is not quite right, for the foam is below her nose, instead of above it, but she works on at herself, bubbling inside with happiness. Old times, she says into the echoing tub, just like old times, as she rinses, and rinses, and rinses her hair. She gropes for a towel, is about to wrap it around her head when she smells it. Not a good smell. Not at all a good smell. Crawling along the passageway, dripping wet, laughing to herself, pulling the smelly old item behind her, she arrives in the bedroom. Made it, she thinks, and she hurls the towel at the linen basket, where it drapes itself grimly over the wickerwork. Not my fault, it says to the mirror and the brush. Too bloody right, they agree. All watch with concern as their owner teeters around, pulling open drawers for fresh underwear, rifling through the wardrobe for something exotic to put over the top of her unsteady body. She makes a game attempt at walking down towards the bathroom, but seems to be going backwards. She turns around and takes it backwards, which sort of works – although there are a few unexpected encounters with walls and bannisters on the way. Once in the bath she feels on top of the world. Water, she thinks, I must drink plenty of water. Bloody old Aunt Margaret keeps urging her to do this, so she will, she giggles, but she won't tell her that she is right – oh no. Smuggins with her bloke – well, now Verity has *hers* back . . . Ha, ha. Ha *bloody* ha . . . She slips her head under the water and guzzles. As she rises, grimacing and amused at the nasty taste, she thinks she is very obedient and that is why something good has happened to her at last. 'Good girl, Verity,' she says, staring at her toes, which wiggle of their own pleasurable volition.

Her legs! She stares at them as, by some strange Lazaran miracle, they rise up, one after the other, out of the sudsy water. They look like a gorilla's. Depilate. She tries the word out – finds it is jolly difficult – and reaches for the razor. Mark's beloved razor, left behind when he went, something she was not able to throw out. She begins the slow and careful task of removing unwanted hair – a sharp razor, this, very sharp, and her hands, although she tries to hold the razor down with both of them, are not very adept. The water begins to go red. Verity wonders why. More water, she thinks, and turns on the tap, guzzling again as it slooshes out. She leans back, warm and contented. Just for a moment she will rest – and then onward with the task of making herself beautiful for him again.

The bath will never recover from the trauma. If a bath can have a Nightmare on Elm Street, this is it.

Half an hour later, Mark discovers what he takes to be his ex-lover's suicide. When his ring at the door went unanswered, he took the key from the flower pot and let himself in. He had lost his job and felt desperate. He needed looking after. He hunted her down, to find her here in a bright pool of gore. If the bath feels in need of therapy, it is nothing to what Mark feels he will need. Fucking women, he thinks, as he hauls her out. She comes to as he gives her mouth to mouth, and she responds in the only way a woman being made love to can. She closes her eyes as she kisses him back, for Mark's expression, in her opinion, is not all that it should be under the circumstances.

Jill props the letter next to the card from Paris on the mantelpiece. Both are from Margaret. The card says, 'Our consolation prize for missing skiing – this is *much* better.' She touches it, then the letter. No, she does not find the tale of Verity very funny, despite Margaret thinking she would. It comes too close to moments she has experienced herself recently. April nearly here and she's the fool. Amanda is still not speaking to her properly, observing only the niceties, imparting information dutifully but full of reproach. Giles will be home for good soon, but although last year she looked forward to his return desperately, now it means nothing to her, as the days mean nothing, for there seems to be no happiness left in her world. She crosses to the window seat. This is where she has taken to sitting most days, half hidden in the curtains, knees drawn up, chin in hands, watching the gradual changes taking place outside, unable to participate on any but the most detached level. Every part of her feels bruised, the taking in of breath too real, too painful, asking too much of her. As she asked too much.

Why she did not just burn the card, she does not know. Perhaps there is some kind spirit somewhere who knows that its continuing existence has a purpose – that one day she will be able to look at the boulevard with its cafés and couples, see the little red arrow Margaret drew to denote their hotel room, and not feel bruised any more. So it stays, a reminder only of the darkest moment in her life. She is sure of that – there was never anything darker before and she would plead with any god that there should never be such a darkness again. She has not been in the room since. No doubt the red silk is still twisted and crumpled, hanging down from the bed in its coil of mockery. That was where it all began, and where it all ended. They should have gone to a hotel. Then at least she would have been left with a room that had blessed two real and open lovers, and not her and her ersatz attempt. Not attempt. Failure. Margaret and her man were the last real lovers in that room. She knows that now. She should never have tried to compete. Never.

Why she did not listen on that first occasion, she will never know. She was not quite hooked then: she could have rejected the prognosis, said 'Jolly good sex' and all that, and gone on her way. But no. She heard but did not listen. She did not listen because she did not want to hear.

'This is an affair,' he said. Why then did he stroke her cheek, caress her breast, as he said the words? 'This is a delightful, delicious bonus in our little humdrum lives, just for a time. You are married. I am married. And we will both stay that way. We understand that. Do we?'

She had let him kiss her as she nodded and replied that she did, of course. Two grown-up people, just a bit of fun and excitement among these here hills ... But it had never been that for her and she thought she had managed to hide it quite well – the pain, the dreams, the terrible, terrible loneliness that being apart from him gave her. This is Love, she knows, and she must bear it alone. But everything is diminished in its light.

David, her dear, loyal, unsuspecting husband, became no more than a nuisance, something to be got round, but a compliant cuckold. His long trip to Japan made the meetings wonderfully often, completely abandoned, once or twice lasting for whole nights so that she could imagine what living with him would be like. Even when he said there had been others before her, she paid no attention. For was she not real, there, now, determined to stay? So there would be no room for future women. She was Future Woman. She would never give him up.

Giles and Amanda slipped into near meaninglessness. *Amanda*! Poor, poor daughter of hers. Poor, poor grandchildren, having a grandmother who was demented and sick with grief when her lover did not see or speak to her for a day. They came into the kitchen, the children, on New Year's Eve. She had made an excuse. She had made cheesecakes that had to be delivered – she had forgotten. She must do it, but she would be back for dinner. The shop was open late that night – a lie, but no one would check, everyone trusted her, and how *that* made the hurting twice as bad. The cheesecakes were on the bench, four of them, and she asked the children to help her carry them to the car. They were eight and ten – *eight and ten*. When the littlest stumbled in the yard, dropping his burden, she had screamed and screamed and screamed with rage – all the rage pent up for so long – hitting him across the head with her free hand, until Amanda ran out into the cold, only half dressed because she had been changing. She stood there shivering, with protective arms around her children, protecting them against their own grandmother who had saliva on her mouth and raw rage in her throat. But she had not abandoned the exercise. No, not she. She had *still* gone because the drug was too strong. In the car she had settled herself back, smoothed her hair, dabbed at her mouth and reapplied her lipstick. She arrived at his house looking as if she had not a care in the world, and had been let in by his surprised but always friendly wife.

'We are going away tomorrow,' she lied, 'and I forgot to bring you these. I am sorry to intrude on your – '

Then she noticed. They were not having a family party as he had said. There were no others there. He was sitting on the floor by the fire playing a card game. Plates and cutlery and the detritus of a meal were pushed to one side on a trolley. A meal for two. Early dinner. Brandy glasses by the cards. He was wearing little maroon leather slippers with his initials woven on the fronts in gold. Horrible things. She wanted to kiss them.

His nice wife suggested that she have a drink. She declined. His nice wife asked where they were off to tomorrow. She said Morocco – the first thing that came into her head, because of the leather slippers probably.

'Ah,' said the nice wife. 'While the children are away, it is very nice to play.' She gave a coy little smile with her plump and healthy cheeks. 'We, too,' she continued, gesturing at the cards and his smile – no one could possibly know, he did it so well, the smile of a polite new friend. 'This is our first New Year's Eve without them. We thought we'd just be the two of us and enjoy it.' And the smile went on. She was wearing some kind of kaftan – in silky black and red. Seductive gear. She'd get a poke tonight. Poke, poke, poke.

Poor Amanda. 'You need a doctor,' she had said. Her daughter was already packing up the camper van when she got back. She was setting off for home, a long drive, late at night, but she would not hear of waiting until the morning. How much she wanted to fall into her daughter's arms and tell all, seek forgiveness, understanding. But she could not. She blamed her for this inability and was less abject than she might have been. To be angry with the world is an infection – you want everyone else around you to be angry with it, too. Amanda left angry, very angry. It would take a long time, if ever, for Jill to make amends, a long time for the children, already tucked up and asleep in their mobile bunks, to come near her again. Only David, who had not witnessed the scene, but knew it was bad, could put his arm around her as the lights of the van drew distant. She put her head on his shoulder as they walked back into the house and she let him run her a bath, give her a brandy and tuck her up in bed. The next day, when the doctor came, she asked for Hormone Replacement Therapy. Which seemed to satisfy everybody.

Giles is coming home soon, but she scarcely cares. And the little market garden which she had loved so much is gradually sliding away from her. These are critical growing times, but she has no Sidney (*he* had even taken him away, market forces *he* had said – she had let *him* even do that) and now she had no heart for it. Spring cabbage, that is all she is now, spring cabbage.

The last bit of her heart had deserted her for that room upstairs when she had knelt, naked, weeping, clutching his knees, pushing the bones of them into her breasts. Why could they not go to Paris? Her friend was there. Look, look – see the card. She had flown down the stairs, brought it back to him.

'I think we are getting in too deep,' he said, dressing. 'I think this should finish.'

'Just a few days? A couple of nights in a lovely, wicked French hotel? Why not?' She knew if he would do that, she could capture him. Even, maybe, cause it to be discovered, so that he would have to abandon that pudding wife with her bucolic smile, and come to her for ever.

He shook his head, kissed her lightly on the forehead as she crouched on the bed, clutching the red silk to her for comfort, and left.

No, Verity's story was not funny. Not funny at all. Margaret, secure in her cocoon of love, her legitimate happiness, could get things very wrong.

Chapter Seven

We got a bit drunk on our last night. Well, I suppose we would, wouldn't we? We sat in my kitchen, across the table from each other, and shared a bottle of champagne. He had already gone, really, and the talk was almost all about the journey: what he would find when he arrived, whether he would ever be able to get letters back to England, how our meal this evening would probably be his last decent food for days, if he knew anything about inflight catering. We had already said most of the important things over the last few weeks – that it had to be, that we always knew it had to be. The panicky question 'What have we done?' was calmly answered by our reminding ourselves that what we had done was what we had set out to do. We had enjoyed so much in that very brief time, but it was a tiny piece of make-believe – and now the lights would come on again. It had been a little bit of theatre, jointly directed, our audience kept in the dark.

There was a sentimental flurry across the champagne glasses when he pushed the book of Inigo Jones's sketches towards me and asked me to write something. For a moment I couldn't think what. Absurdities such as 'Have a nice trip' or 'Best wishes' were hardly appropriate. Nor lines from Ovid's *Cures for Love* – too bitter. I stared around the kitchen looking for inspiration among the bits of paper stuck here and there. Perhaps a recipe for wood restoring? Or an article on why yoga is bad for you? Or a clipping on rose blight (why did I keep *that*?). And then I saw the much yellowed, slightly grease-spattered, years-old Baltimore Desiderata which Saskia brought back from a trip to Canterbury. Better than rose blight, anyway. Privately I thought that if you followed all its advice, you would never do anything except sit indoors with a blissed-out smile on your face, much less 'go placidly amid the noise and haste . . .' but there were some appropriate lines.

The world is full of trickery
But let this not blind you to what virtue there is –
Many persons strive for high ideals and everywhere life is full of
    heroism.
Be Yourself.

'I know this,' he said. 'I used to have a copy of it in my office at home.'

'Most people have a copy at some point in their lives. They stick it up, sigh over it, and then do the opposite of all it recommends.'

'That's rather cynical,' he said. 'Not like you to be so withering about the spiritual struggle.'

'No? Perhaps you never really knew me.'

'No,' he agreed, touching my hand. 'I don't suppose I did. Not the inner you. Nor you me. Certainly not the darker side.'

'I don't believe you've got one.'

'And I don't believe you've got one.'

'Perhaps we should leave the illusion that way?'

The truth was that I was feeling jumbled up and uneasy, which was less to do with his imminent departure than with facing up to Saskia's imminent arrival. Raw. I was very definitely feeling raw, an emotion which champagne and a farewell to someone I knew I could trust only encouraged.

Verity hadn't helped earlier in the day. 'I *told* you he would go away if you bought him a travelling bag,' she said triumphantly, before switching into her condescending mode. With Verity it always helps to remember Elizabeth's favourite maxim, quoted by her every time her ministers told her to wallop France or pile into Scotland: 'It is folly to punish your neighbour by fire when you live next door . . .' So I kept my peace.

As she had achieved the Grand Order of Foolishness by reconstituting Mark, I did not doubt that she would all too soon be suffering once again. But I had to admire the professional in her: she was already in the process of turning it into a script. I did say, hesitantly, that perhaps Mark would find it a bit . . . well, embarrassing to be the focus of such public scrutiny, but she gave me a pitying look. What, after all, did a small-time picture-framer – one who has lost her man to the fucking *jungle* – know about true creativity? Conjuring up Tintoretto was particularly hard after that; if Verity had stumbled at that point I would, quite easily, have kicked her. 'You are so brave,' was her parting shot and, as she turned on the path, she gave me a little moue of pity.

Too much to swallow whole. 'How's the legs?' I called, for the entire street to hear.

'Mark treats them with lavender oil for me every night. He is so sweet to me now . . .'

Jeezus, I thought, the illusions and delusions we can create for ourselves. It made me and Oxford look like a small-time conjuring trick.

But that little exchange was the first scratch on a bite which had been received a little earlier, when Saskia called. It had begun easily enough with her saying how much she was looking forward to getting home, how amazing that this time next week . . . etc. All the right stuff. But then the change of emphasis – I knew her so well – which set my heart beating uneasily.

She was looking forward to getting back and would look for a proper studio – just to work in – so that when her father came over he could stay in it. For the really exciting news was that Fisher had come up trumps, done his bit, and found a venue for the exhibition in the autumn. Time for healing now, was the message. So Dickie would be back – if only for the opening of the show – and it would take me back to other private views in the past, other back-slapping art events, where he had been fussed and fawned over and made drunk, while my sister cruised around with that wide, hurt smile on her face – making the best of it, always making the best of it. This time it would be worse, for it would be a hero's return.

Raw, then.

We took another bottle up to bed and sat up close to each other. 'Are you up to hearing a confessional?' I asked. I knew then that we would not make love again. It was a swap. If I was to unburden myself about the past, it would leave me too open. He was no longer my lover, this Oxford man, he had passed over to the other side. If he was to be anything at all, this Oxford man, he would now be my friend.

So I told him. And suddenly it was as if the sky had been rolled back. 'So he's got away with it,' I ended. 'His daughter loves him without asking him to account for anything. Just like her mother did.'

'You don't blame Saskia?'

'No.'

'Then why not give her this happiness too?'

'Because I can't bear the thought that he should be so perfectly free.'

'You're never free,' said Oxford. 'Believe me.'

'Are you all right?' I said eventually.

'I'm thinking,' he said. 'And drinking.'

I flopped back on the pillow and raised my glass. 'Here's to success. You deserve it.'

'Hmm,' he said, noncommittally. He put his arm round me and we chinked glasses. Then he pulled my head to his chest. 'I'm going to tell you something.'

'Something you need to get drunk to say?' I quipped.

'Yup. My confession now. You wanted to know about my past, and why Nicaragua. Pin back your ears.'

This was the last thing I expected, the moment when both of us removed our masks and stepped in front of the closing curtain. I duly pinned back my ears and sat still and quiet, hardly daring to breathe.

'I was still at architectural school when I met my wife. She was doing secretarial work, as a temporary, though she wanted to be a model. She was extremely beautiful and extremely young. She, her mother and her aunt came with her when they fled the Somosa regime and they lived in a scrubby little house in Hounslow. I was twenty-four. She was nineteen, and all the students fancied her like crazy. We were a randy lot – no one dared go into morning lectures without a hangover and tales of deflowered virgins. I thought it was great. She worked there and suddenly we all found reasons to visit the office. She had a pair of eyes that knocked us out, and she was just beautifully made. Tiny. Too tiny for modelling. No flirt, but friendly. We all tried to take her out but she wouldn't. We almost ran a book on who'd succeed. Salad days.

'It went on for about a year like that and we were all due to leave. I got a bee in my bonnet about her. I had a way with women and it peeved me that she wouldn't even come out with me. It got to me. I began to court her in earnest. Flowers, walking her to the tube, giving her poetry – stuff like that. By now I was in a small practice so I bought her things. And I turned up at her house. Met the mother and the aunt, all that. Gradually Jani succumbed. But not in bed. It became such an obsession that I ended up marrying her. Everybody happy. I had something exotic to flash about with, and I messed about elsewhere. It was a great life. We were married for eight years. I didn't want children and I suppose I thought it would go on like that for ever – best of both worlds. And then she died. Brain tumour. Pop. Gone. It was only then that I realized what I'd lost.

'At the funeral her mother told me all the things that Jani had kept to herself. Horrific truths. And I began to understand that thing Lorca calls *duende*, "the blade of pain". It was a fairly standard story for Nicaragua, probably for most places that are permanently at war. Raped at twelve; father shot in front of her; brothers missing; still some family left out there. Nobody ever spoke of it. I think she might have tried once or twice but I wasn't a good listener. I became one at her funeral, though. I knew that I, too, had betrayed her, and I began to grow up. Not at first but slowly. I had no idea what losing her would mean. Then a solution came – not a cure, but a solution.'

'Why *did* you advertise?'

He shrugged again. 'The old me surfacing? Or maybe I just wanted to let a little affection in – and out – without harming anyone in the process. I wanted to do it honestly.' He smiled suddenly, slightly wickedly, and was much more like the old Oxford. 'Once I'd made my mind up to go away, I got a huge burst of positive energy – brain and body. It's a strong force.'

He began to dress. 'Well,' I said, watching him for the last time. 'It doesn't seem to have done anybody any harm.'

A dip in a pillow, two used glasses and two nearly empty bottles of champagne. The residue. 'Bye,' I whispered, as his cab turned the corner.

It was about midnight. I sat on my bed, mopped at the tears, and wondered what to do. Sassy was coming home in a week. If I was going to make any reparations, it was better that I did so while she was still there. But not yet, I thought, not before I'd had a good stiff drink. Despite the solemn and dreadful warning of Verity, I needed a good stiff shot of something and went downstairs to get it.

Chapter Eight

Fisher was holding a large catalogue up to his face and above it his very blue eyes creased in mock fear. He backed away as I came into the room, feigning supplication. 'Are you going to hit me?' he said.

'You might like it.'

'Tut, tut.' He laughed and put the catalogue down on his desk. 'People have a strange view of my sexual orientation. I don't like to be hurt, not at all.'

'Neither do I.'

'Neither does anybody, Margaret.' He sat down opposite me, gesturing to one of the chairs.

'It's all right,' I said. 'I've spoken to Saskia. So long as I don't have to put him up when he's over I can tolerate it.' I sat down, crossed my legs, and gave him what I fancied was a penetrating look. 'It'll be quite a coup for you, won't it? Bringing Dickie back to London for his first show in however many years?'

Fisher looked at his nails. 'It will,' he agreed, with great satisfaction.

'And a father and daughter show will pull in the press and the punters.'

'Most certainly. But Saskia is a good painter. Early days, but she is undoubtedly worthy of an exhibition with her father. His work is very fine. She sent me some slides.'

'Did she, now?'

'She's been very professional in her approach. And determined. Especially determined that he should come back here to show again. If it hadn't been me, it would have been someone else. The bait was too strong. London is stagnant, longing for revivals, look at the sixties show. It will be good to put on something that looks back as well as forward.'

He got up, went to a chest at the side of the room, and took out a file. 'Do you want to look at them?'

'No,' I said.

He removed a sheet of slides and held them up to the window. 'They are very good. Figures, quite monumental. They have something of Nash and Moore about them – but not derivative. The torso as hero – or heroine.' He gazed a bit longer. 'Quite, quite exceptional.' He held up another sheet. 'And these are landscapes – or rather snowscapes, done very recently, and some heads – Saskia, I think. Beautiful. Beautiful form, real feeling. The earlier ones, a series of heads . . . female . . . were not so good.' I could tell that he was genuinely caught up by them, no longer playing around. 'And these' – he held up another series – 'are Saskia's. She's begun by working from photographs, I think. Deadish. But then she's thrown out the snapshots and worked more freely – mostly drawings and gouache. Quite simple but very effective. Talented.'

'We knew that before she went.'

'Have a look?' he said.

I crossed to the window and held them up. They were from photographs I knew very well – me, Lorna, Dickie, Sassy as a baby. Fisher was right: the initial ones were woodenly graphic, but most were very fine. I had to smile. 'Chip off the old block,' I said grudgingly. 'He was precocious, too.'

Fisher drew his watch out of his waistcoat pocket. 'Julius will be here soon. And this time' – he raised a finger at me – 'I want you to say nothing whatsoever. Especially nothing about the beauties of the masterly phallus. I don't think Linda will ever recover from that.' He chuckled. 'I'm not sure I will either. Just look cool. Unimpressed even.'

'I always am unimpressed with Julius.'

Fisher was an acute man. 'Did he make a pass? Tut, tut.'

'His wife didn't understand him.'

Fisher laughed. He was pouring sherry and stopped to give me a look. 'She'll get her swimming-pool – and without touching a hair on the Mortimer collection's head. Well, not so's you'd notice.'

I wandered around the room, sipping my sherry, leafing through old catalogues – Derain, Frink, Medieval Ivories, the Barron Collection. Even Fisher's catalogues were a collectable item nowadays. Part of me was still angry about Dickie, but part of me was curious.

'Where will the show be?'

'Ah!' he said, pulling something out of his antique plan chest. A real poseur in some respects, Fisher. 'West End. Cork Street, as a matter of fact. Oddly enough – and this was pure coincidence – we got the old Blake Gallery. Which is where, of course, this was shown.' And he heaved my Picasso portfolio on to his desk.

'I remember it well,' I said wryly. 'Mrs M. gave her own private view there, with her electric wheelchair. It was chaos.'

'Quite a girl,' he said. 'And quite an eye. Remember that Matisse head?'

'Of course. The tender line.'

He nodded. 'Indeed. The tender line. The girl was one of the Stein grand-daughters – patrons of his from the early years. Some say he was a dirty old man with her. Sherry?'

Julius arrived, pink and flustered, having been – he said – caught in traffic. Since he had a smear of lipstick on his chin, and since it didn't seem to be his colour, I had a feeling he had been caught in something more than that. 'Oh, isn't Linda with you?' I said brightly. He said no, she was away with the boys. 'Ah,' I said, 'I expect that makes you feel lonely. You've got jam' – I peered – 'or is it lipstick on your face?'

He looked at me shiftily as he rubbed the mark away. My hearty kiss on both cheeks made him look only more uncomfortable. He gave Fisher a flat, square package done up in brown paper. Fisher took it and unwrapped it carefully. Inside, beneath two stout pieces of cardboard, was the framed drawing I had coveted, the Matisse *Head of a Girl*. I waited for him to expostulate, to sigh, to make one of his genuinely rapturous remarks, but bore in mind that I must not follow suit. In the event there was just a calm nodding and an offer to Julius of sherry and a chair. I longed to look at the head more closely, to see it the right way up, but stayed put.

'Nice day for April,' I said to Julius. He grunted. 'Give your wife my love, won't you?' He crossed his legs and flicked some imaginary fluff from his knee. I wondered why he was here and why he had brought the Matisse. Art lives beyond the tawdry human ways from which it springs? Fisher and I agreed *that* often enough over a glass or two when the braying interior designers had gone home. Otherwise we could never walk through a cathedral, nor wonder at the Colosseum or St Mark's, for being conscious of where the loot to build it came from and how many died in producing the dream.

Some papers were signed, first by Julius, then by Fisher, and then by me. At last I realized what was happening – and he had asked me to remain *impassive*? From the moment the blotting paper descended and the ink was dry I became the owner of the Matisse, and Julius and Linda Mortimer became the owners of the Picasso portfolio. Like swapping tinsel for gold – you can't eat either but you know which you prefer.

'Hmm,' I said, looking at my new possession impassively, critically even. 'It'll go very well in the hall by the pot-pourri.'

Fisher had the grace to turn away for a moment and affect a cough. Julius noticed nothing. He left the portfolio where it was and turned to leave.

'Aren't you going to take it with you?' I asked.

He shook his head. Why did he look so smug when the smugness belonged to me? 'It will be safe here,' he said, 'until the right time to sell.'

'What about Linda's swimming-pool? Be simply awful for her if we get a good summer again.'

'Work has already begun,' he said shortly, and escorted by Fisher, still in his Grand Consultant mode, he left.

I ran my finger around the glass of the frame, following the line. Whatever else Matisse had done, this was pure enough to be holy.

Fisher was not the man for kisses and hugs, so lunch seemed the best alternative. With champagne, of course, and with the drawing propped up on the chair next to us – the third guest, the most honourable. I wondered how he had persuaded them to part with it, for I knew very well that it was worth much more. He would not discuss the matter. Everything was perfectly in order, he assured me, the paper-work was quite legal, and neither the Mortimers nor Aunt Margaret had been dishonoured. It was only then that I realized he had made up the difference himself – which was why the swimming-pool was being built.

He continued to refuse an explanation despite my question-ing, so I vowed to ask Julius, at which point he got quite huffy and made to leave the table. I had to back down to keep his company. We looked at the girl, who looked back at us in innocence, with her infinitely tender, tender line.

'Worth it,' said Fisher suddenly. 'Wouldn't you say? De-spite any possible iniquity surrounding it?'

I nodded. 'Worth it.' We chinked our glasses. I could not resist trying again. 'How much did you pay on top, Fisher?'

He looked at me, sipping from his glass, the periwinkle eyes all impish again above its rim. 'Have you any idea,' he said, 'how much commission I stand to make when the sale of everything goes through eventually? And have you any idea how much I *intend* to make out of Dickie and Saskia's exhibition?'

'I thought you had retired.'

He winked. 'No, not quite. But I will after that lot. And handsomely. Now I suggest we change the subject. How is that chap of yours?'

I told him.

He was not very impressed. 'You don't seem at all good at keeping your men. Dickie was your lover once, I think? Before Lorna swiped him.'

A direct hit. I don't think anyone else would have dared. I just stared at him as if he had smacked me.

He tapped the picture. 'Life goes on, Margaret,' he said. 'As does great art.'

As if that wasn't enough, the next day I received a card posted from Heathrow – a picture of Concorde – which said:

These are the lines that follow on from yours:

Be yourself.
Especially do not feign affection
Neither be cynical about love
In the face of all aridity and disenchantment, it is perennial as
    the grass . . .

Unnecessary. I had already spoken to Saskia. And, though briefly, to Dickie.

Perhaps for Elizabeth also the masque, the games, the glory were unsatisfactory? Yes, she might strut out bejewelled to applause, but the pearls she wore were once the famed possessions of her cousin Mary. Avaricious disregard, or the tender link, *memento mori*? She signed the paper, certainly, but she also wept copiously when the news came from Fotheringay. Did she weep for the loss of a queen or for the death of a woman? Both, probably. And her mother was a third. Did she understand *then* why her father had also signed such a piece of paper? Or if not understand, did she forgive, if only a little? She did not keep Mary's crucifixes, although they too were beautiful and precious. Those she emphatically did not want; only the pearls. Poor Elizabeth, vain virgin of the baroque: the masque had to continue for she could not afford it to stop.

Epilogue

Rivers move on.

Mark ditched Verity as soon as she had sold her script. No man, not even one so down on his luck, could sustain his honour under such punishing limelight. Verity said that my meeting Oxford had given her hope, which was crushed when he left me. Mark seemed an angel by comparison. What could I say?

Jill came to stay and Verity said afterwards that she was undoubtedly having a very unhappy affair. Verity, I thought, you drink too much, but Jill confirmed that it was true. She said Oxford and I had just looked so romantic and she had wanted a little piece of heaven too. What could I say?

Joan and Reg married. When I asked Joan how she dared risk something for ever when she used to reckon a year was too long, she merely said that he was where she could keep an eye on him. 'Only one?' I nearly said, but forbore and handed her a rubber band instead.

Oxford wrote a few times and I replied. But my heart wasn't in it. And neither, it seems, was his. We'll exchange Christmas cards, and then one day those will cease. He will be free of the reeds, and that will be the last of Aunt Margaret's Lover. At least, the last of *that* one.

'*Si latet ars, prodest*,' says Ovid. 'Art is a lie that makes us see the truth,' says Picasso, two thousand years on. 'Look at me,' says the Matisse, as it hangs in its constancy on my wall.